Advance Praise for *The Moonlight Healers*

"*The Moonlight Healers* is a profound tale of love, family legacy, secrets, and the extraordinary power within us all. A deeply felt debut, brimming with impossible choices."

—**Patti Callahan Henry,** *New York Times* **bestselling author of** *The Secret Book of Flora Lea*

"*The Moonlight Healers* is a bravura turn. Elizabeth Becker's novel is a lustrous and nuanced exploration set over generations of women that shows the magic we are capable of bestowing on others, and ourselves."

—**Jeffrey Dale Lofton, award-winning author of** *Red Clay Suzie*

"Gorgeously written with impeccably drawn characters, *The Moonlight Healers* is a dazzling debut. I absolutely loved this richly imagined, magical story spanning generations of mothers and daughters with a beautiful and impossible gift."

—**Jillian Cantor,** *USA TODAY* **bestselling author of** *Beautiful Little Fools*

"Weaving two storylines that span one family, *The Moonlight Healers* is a page-turning drama that masterfully transports readers to war-torn France and modern-day Crozet, an idyllic small town. I savored every word."

—**A.H. Kim, author of** *Relative Strangers*

"Tender, wise, and moving. I loved the way Becker wove together the story of generations and the incredible power of one heart to touch another. I wish I could live inside the Winstons' family orchard, and I know readers will love visiting it too!"

—**Polly Stewart, author of** *The Good Ones*

"*The Moonlight Healers* weaves a lyrical, magical love story about mothers, daughters, and the ties that bind us across generations. Elizabeth Becker is a dazzling writer, and her unforgettable characters will always have a place on my bookshelf."

—**Katharine Schellman, author of** *Last Call at the Nightingale*

"An emotionally heartfelt debut that explores the moral dilemmas of life and death through the hands of a folk healer. Becker beautifully connects the characters in a magical, deeply moving story that will stick with you long after the book is closed."

—**Dana Elmendorf, author of** *In the Hour of Crows*

The Moonlight Healers

A Novel

Elizabeth Becker

GRAYDON HOUSE

Recycling programs
for this product may
not exist in your area.

ISBN-13: 978-1-525-83042-6

The Moonlight Healers

Copyright © 2025 by Elizabeth Becker

All rights reserved. No part of this book may be used or reproduced in any manner whatsoever without written permission.

Without limiting the author's and publisher's exclusive rights, any unauthorized use of this publication to train generative artificial intelligence (AI) technologies is expressly prohibited.

This is a work of fiction. Names, characters, places and incidents are either the product of the author's imagination or are used fictitiously. Any resemblance to actual persons, living or dead, businesses, companies, events or locales is entirely coincidental.

® is a trademark of Harlequin Enterprises ULC.

Graydon House
22 Adelaide St. West, 41st Floor
Toronto, Ontario M5H 4E3, Canada
www.GraydonHouseBooks.com

Printed in U.S.A.

For my parents, Jon and Betsy Jewett,
who knew I was a writer before I did.

And for the nurses, the healers, the unsung heroes who stand in the light and in the darkness, who carry life and death in their hands. This book is for you.

Richmond, Virginia
2019

1

LOUISE

Louise stood in the quiet of the orchard where she'd been born. Around her, the mountains rose against the pink skies. The tree branches were ripe with fruit, the light of a thousand fireflies glowing beyond them. She knew there was someone up ahead, out of sight, just on the other side of the tree line. She had caught a glimpse of a woman in a long, white nightgown, her hands trailing the branches.

She tried to follow but her body wouldn't obey. She was stuck, anchored in place, her legs heavy. From somewhere behind, she heard the distant sound of sirens, muffled, as though she were under water. She squeezed her eyes shut as the noise grew louder, clearer.

When she opened them again, the orchard was gone. She was alone, in the passenger seat of Peter's car, blinking into the bright June sun that streamed through the windshield. Only it wasn't a windshield anymore. The center was gone. All that was left were shards of glass along the edges.

Her head throbbed, her thoughts jumbled. She tried to sort

through the confusion and find something real. Peter had been in the car. He was driving. She knew that. She clung to the solidity of that fact like a lifeboat.

But he hadn't been wearing a seat belt, despite her chiding. She remembered the van swerving into their lane, Peter's voice shouting her name, a white flash as the airbag exploded, and then only silence.

Louise continued to search her memory, moving up from the depths that surrounded her toward the light of the surface, and her stomach twisted as the previous night crashed back on her. The reason she hadn't wanted to open the door for Peter this morning. A bright, moon-drenched sky, the blue-green glow of the pool lights in the backyard of Kyle Tan's house, hundreds of voices, laughter, lukewarm beer in sweaty cans.

And Peter.

Peter at the end of the night, standing in front of her, saying the three words she used to want to hear more than anything, but years too late for her to be able to believe him.

Louise didn't want to open her eyes again. She didn't want to see the empty driver's seat, or the broken windshield.

She pushed her mind back to the night before.

She had been awkward at first at the party, unsure of which circles to join. But then she and Peter took a shot of coconut rum, followed by another. Louise recalled the blooming affection, the rush of nostalgia for people she had barely spoken to over the years propelling her into conversations and games of flip cup, into one more beer, then another, her desire to leave early receding as the night went on.

They had been there for hours when Peter asked her to take a walk, pulling her to the edge of Kyle's backyard, his hand firm around hers. She wasn't sure if he had ever held her hand. If he had, it had been years, since the days of pretend play and tree houses.

They were both drunk by then, and they laughed as they

stumbled over enormous old magnolia roots that raced across the ground like primordial snakes. The branches were dotted with soft, white flowers, their sweet scent hanging in the air as Peter stopped abruptly and gazed down at her.

A preemptive sadness cut through the haze of alcohol. She knew what he was doing. She was leaving in five days for New York to attend Summer Start, a six-week program for incoming freshmen at NYU. This would be their first summer apart, the first summer in years they wouldn't be counselors together at Camp Staunton Meadows, where they had cemented their friendship as kids, sitting on warm grass under a glittering sky, drinking flat Cokes from the camp store.

Louise knew he was going to tell her goodbye, or good luck, or some other horribly meaningless phrase that would signify the end of the world they had shared since childhood.

But when he looked at her, there was no sadness, only a question. "I think, maybe... I love you," Peter said.

Louise's mouth curved up into a smile even as it hit her that he wasn't joking. After all these years she knew what his voice sounded like when he was being real.

The pause lasted for hours. Music from the party shook the ground beneath them. There were loud splashes from the pool, the distant sounds of glass breaking inside. She wanted to turn away, but he held her eyes in a way that made it impossible.

"Oh right," she finally said, widening her smile. She felt frozen, trapped between two worlds. One was the safe, dependable life she knew, where Peter was her best friend. And the other was a future she had long convinced herself she didn't need, where Peter loved her the way she loved him, an unbearably wonderful but fragile idea.

She grasped for words that could defuse the tension, though she knew how false they would sound. "Isn't that how it always goes in the movies? Graduation-party declaration of love."

Peter watched her, his expression still hopeful. But then his entire body seemed to fold inward. He looked down at the ground and cleared his throat. "Right."

When he looked back up at her, he was smiling, but even in the dark she could tell it wasn't genuine. "You're too smart to fall for it, though." He glanced back toward the house, the boisterous noise of their classmates. "I need another drink. You want one?"

She nodded blankly, and he turned and walked back to the party.

In the car, Louise opened her eyes. With a shaking hand, she groped for her seat belt. It was her fault. All of it. But she could fix it. If she could only find him, she could put everything back together, make it whole again.

Louise leaned against the dented car door, but it wouldn't shove open. The guardrail was in front of them. They must have hit it. She slammed into the door harder a second time, with all her weight, and this time it gave. She pulled herself out with a wince at a soreness in her shoulder.

There was a person lying on the road, a few yards away. She felt herself sway and grabbed for the car frame, her whole body trembling as comprehension roared toward her like a freight train.

She took a few careening steps, her legs numb, until she reached him.

"Peter," she said hoarsely.

His eyes were open, and for a second, she wanted to laugh. Of course, he was okay. He was right there, awake.

But then she noticed the trickle of red from his bottom lip, the way his mouth hung, the horrible angle of his neck. His eyes weren't bright anymore, just dull, empty spheres.

Louise crouched beside him, recalling her CPR training from her babysitting certification course two years earlier.

She pressed hard into Peter's chest. "One...two...three...four...five..."

She took a ragged breath as her vision swam.

"Six...seven...eight..."

His skin was still warm. It couldn't be too late. She had read stories of trauma victims brought to the hospital in full cardiac arrest, kids who had drowned, or heart attack victims. Sometimes they were down for nearly an hour. But they came back.

"Come back."

She wasn't sure if she had said the words out loud or in her head. She continued to press into Peter's chest. There was something about the depth of compression, the degree and number of inches. She had known that in the class, gotten a hundred percent on the quiz. But it was so much harder on a real person. She couldn't even tell if Peter's chest was moving.

She reached "thirty" and started the cycle again. With the blood coming from his mouth, she couldn't bring herself to do rescue breaths.

She heard voices behind her, people approaching, but Louise ignored them. She could do this. She felt the wetness on her cheeks, the scream inside her lungs, but she didn't stop.

"Please come back," she said, her words choked. She didn't care who heard it. She didn't care about the people on the road watching her with pity. She didn't care that she looked ridiculous. She only knew that he had to come back.

"Twenty-two...twenty-three...twenty-four..."

This time she pushed down onto Peter's body so hard she thought she might break his ribs, but instead a jolt of heat shot out from her own chest, sparking down her arms and into her hands.

She jerked away as though she had been electrocuted. She didn't know what she expected, burns maybe, a wound, some sign of the current that had just exploded at every nerve ending. But she was uninjured, the skin of her arms intact.

From the sirens she could tell the ambulance was right beside her now. Several car doors slammed behind her, followed by loud footsteps.

Two people in navy blue uniforms set down a stretcher and equipment and knelt next to her. There was a C-collar and oxygen tanks, medical kits. It all fell to the ground around her.

The paramedic across from her pumped up and down into Peter's chest, and the other jammed a needle into the crook of his arm.

There was a hand on Louise's shoulder. "Let's get you taken care of. They've got him now."

Louise looked up to find a very tall firefighter in full gear above her. He was wrinkled around the eyes, gray at the temples. She gazed past him farther up the street. The entire road was lit up with flashing lights, blue-and-red pulses all wrong against the pale sky. She felt the strange desire to laugh. It was absurd. A few minutes ago, a blink of an eye ago, Peter was beside her in the car, on the way to the pool.

"Let's get you checked out," the firefighter repeated, his voice kind but firm, his hand tighter on her shoulder.

Louise let herself be pulled to her feet. But she couldn't move away. If she left, they would stop. If she was still there, if they worked to save him, he wasn't fully gone.

"Come on now." The firefighter tried to steer her, but Louise continued to watch the paramedics.

"Switch," the male paramedic said, and seamlessly, as though they had done it a thousand times, they switched roles.

"Rhythm check," the female paramedic said as she took her place beside the monitor. They both checked the little screen.

Louise's knees buckled, her legs no longer willing to hold her up. Without a word, the firefighter slipped his arms under her shoulders and half carried her toward another ambulance. Already the crowd was dissipating, bystanders back in their cars. No one wanted to be there for the end.

"Mike?" The female paramedic's surprised voice lifted over the group of emergency workers, loud and clear.

Louise stopped.

"Holding compressions," Mike said.

Louise ignored the firefighter's murmur of protest. She felt her legs steady beneath her as she pushed away from him and walked back toward the emergency workers. No one spoke. The only noise was the distant street traffic, the rustle of the tree branches along the road.

Louise brushed past police officers, her body propelled forward by that new urgency in their voices. She could feel the plea form inside of her. She would do anything to hear his voice again, give up every carefully plotted plan, trade New York and college and her perfect future for one continued second of his existence.

"Showing sinus rhythm," the female paramedic said, her focus on the monitor. The male paramedic put his fingers on Peter's neck.

Louise was right beside them now, Peter's face barely visible over the oxygen mask. Her breath caught in her throat at the look in the male paramedic's eyes as they found hers.

For a long second, the longest of her life, the entire world balanced between the two of them. The streets were empty. The cars and flashing lights gone. There was nothing but the words that would follow, that she heard before they even reached her, before they formed on his lips, finally, out loud, the most beautiful and impossible words she had ever known.

"He has a pulse."

HONFLEUR, FRANCE
July 1942

2

HELENE

Helene woke before dawn as she always did, when the narrow old house was quiet and deep with sleep. She lay very still on her small wooden bed, and stared out the dormer window, trying to suppress the panic that gripped her.

Normally, she would rush out of bed the moment her eyes opened, dress in clothes that had been patched or hemmed a dozen times, and tiptoe down the long staircase from her room in the attic in the dark of the blackout curtains. It was the only useful thing she could do, trudge out to the bakery or butcher or market each morning before the long line had formed, and so she did it with total devotion, made it a ritual, even throughout the long cold winter days, with snow on the ground and a white sheen of frost coating the handful of fishing ships left in the harbor.

But today, she sat upright in bed and hugged her knees to her chest. She still couldn't fathom that in only a few short hours, she would leave her home and family to train as a nurse at the Hôtel-Dieu, a Catholic convent and hospital in Rouen.

"You will be safer there," Agnes had explained to her weeks ago. It was midmorning, and her mother had just returned from spending the night at a delivery on the outskirts of town. The baby arrived past midnight, but because of the curfew her mother had to wait until daylight to make the trek home. She was pale and red-eyed as she stood at the sink. "A cousin of mine is there. I haven't seen her since we were little girls, the handful of times she visited from the south with her mother. But I wrote to her, told her of your work with me, that you would be a valuable nurse at the hospital. And she agreed."

Helene's shock almost immediately gave way to fear. She didn't want to leave her mother, her grandfather, be cast out alone in a strange city in the midst of a war.

"No," Helene had said, startling herself. She never said no to her mother. Everything was *Yes, Maman*. Each time she woke Helene up in the middle of the night because a woman was in labor or someone was in the last hours of life. Every time she asked Helene to miss school to gather wild weeds in the countryside that had been overlooked by the farmers but treasured by Agnes for their medicinal properties. Helene always followed her mother, even when the boys at school called Agnes a witch, even when she sometimes longed to be like one of the other girls in town, whose lives were light and easy and unburdened by the intimate knowledge of life and death.

"It's not a question," Agnes said.

Helene looked down at her hands, blistered from the previous day of helping clean their family seafood shop downstairs. Once full of the rough voices of fishermen and the briny smell of ocean, the store now stood empty, but cleaning it had become an important part of their day, a tiny act that felt like resistance.

Without a word Agnes reached over and placed her hand on top of Helene's. Familiar warmth spread over her skin. She knew the sensation well, from her earliest memories, scraped knees or burns from the stove, the way the pain receded the moment her mother touched her.

Agnes removed her hand, and the blister was gone. If Helene weren't her mother's daughter, if that same ability didn't live in her own body, she might have marveled at it. An outsider would be sure it was an illusion. Or witchcraft.

But to Helene it was simply her mother's very being, a magic that was ingrained in their blood, as real and dependable as the tides.

Agnes took a step back from the table. "You can be useful there," she said. "They need nurses."

"But I'm not a nurse, Maman." Helene studied the spot where the blister had been. "And if they knew about this, what we can do, they would hate me for it."

She heard the smallness in her voice, the little girl's plea. She didn't understand how her cousin could function in a place that would condemn her if they knew the truth of her abilities. The church had persecuted their ancestors for centuries, accusing them of witchcraft and demonism. It was the entire reason they now practiced their gift in secret.

"They will not know," she said. "I couldn't ask Cecelia in the letter. It's not safe these days with the mail searched. But she must have found a way to work as a nurse and a healer. To hide what she needs to hide. It's not so different from how I work here, Helene. Why I prefer to see patients at night, when the world is asleep."

"But I can't even..." Helene's voice faltered. She felt the familiar shame, that what came so easily to her mother was still such a struggle for her.

"Maybe you'll find it there, Helene," Agnes said gently. "What you've been missing. Cecelia might be able to help you, more than I can."

"You're my mother," Helene replied. "What could she teach me that you cannot?"

Agnes smiled sadly. "Sometimes, I fear I make it all worse for you. Maybe being away from here, away from all these memories—" She glanced toward the parlor, and Helene knew immediately what she saw there. It was what Helene saw every time she was in that room, the bed her uncles had set up for her father in his last weeks, the curtains drawn, the air heavy with a sweet, sickly smell she could still conjure even four years later. "Maybe you just need a fresh start."

There was a sorrow in Agnes's pale green eyes Helene had never seen, but her mouth was set, her jawline firm. There would be no more argument.

And so, two weeks later in her attic bedroom, the rain now pounding the eaves above her, Helene had no choice but to wait for dawn.

When the edges of the blackout shade were framed in light, Helene got out of bed and put on the dress her mother had brought to her room the night before. It was a simple cotton, its blue color slightly faded, with one mismatched button on the back to replace a lost one. But the dress had been new once, a gift presented in tissue paper. Helene remembered her mother in it, leaving for the train station with her father, off to meet vendors in Paris for their family seafood company, her father skinny as he always was in her memory, but handsome in a suit and tie.

The dress was slightly short on Helene, who had several inches on her mother, but otherwise it fit, and as she tied it at the waist, she inhaled the fabric's smell—cedar, mostly, from storage—but also the faintest, lingering notes of her mother's old perfume.

Helene brushed her hair, clipped it back, and splashed cold water on her face from the washbasin. Then she opened the blackout shade and carefully made her bed as she did every morning, tucking the sheets into tidy, sharp corners.

When she finished, she let her fingers run along the blanket, frayed in places but warm enough on cold nights, then her late grandmother's quilt folded at the end of the bed, and when she couldn't bear it anymore, she left the room.

One floor below, Helene stopped on the landing outside her grandfather's bedroom and stared at his closed door. Today, for the first time since the rationing started, he would take her place in line instead. *I'll see him again soon*, she told herself as she continued down the back stairs.

When she entered the kitchen, she found it was already bright, the shades lifted to allow the sun rising behind their house to fill the space with light. Her mother stood at the stove, boiling a pot of water, and at the table, to Helene's surprise, sat her grandfather, already fully dressed in a gray wool suit, the day's paper open in front of him.

"Ah, there she is. My little duck. Up so late this morning." He took a sip from his mug and grimaced only a tiny bit at the bitter chicory mixture. Then he motioned to the chair beside him. "Sit, sit. Your mother is making us breakfast."

Helene took a seat across from him at the table. "You're up early, Grandpapa."

He folded his newspaper. "I have been given my instructions, haven't I? March to the store at sunrise. Any later and there will be only—" he smoothed his scruffy white beard "—I believe the phrase was 'mealworms and moldy bread.'"

Helene knew what it cost him, to perform this role, wake up early and dress to stand in line for scraps. He was no stranger to the early-dawn hours. For nearly all of Helene's life, except on Sundays, her grandfather left the house before anyone else was awake, off to the little boat docked in the harbor, where he would spend the morning dredging for scallops or oysters. Before the war he fished with his surviving sons, Helene's two uncles, Marc and Jean Luc, who were now prisoners of war in Germany, captured during the brief, failed Battle of France. In Helene's older memories, before he got sick, her father was there too, off at dawn, back for the midday meal, all of them crowded around the table in their work clothes that smelled of the ocean, briny and fishy and wonderful.

The Germans had taken her grandfather's boat almost immediately after the occupation, "repurposed" it, they had told him. But even if they hadn't, it would have been far too dangerous to continue. There were already stories of fishing boats from towns nearby that had run into underwater mines or submarine attacks in the channel.

"Grandpapa, I'm sorry." Helene couldn't look at her grandfather. "You shouldn't have to…"

"Little duck," he said gently.

Reluctantly, Helene met her grandfather's eyes. Away from his boat, his rough, freckled skin was softer, the bright redness of his nose and forehead fading with each passing week. Every day there was less of the sea in his appearance, less of him entirely, his wide, round stomach dwindling, his once-full cheeks sunken beneath his beard.

"No apologies. We will get on," he said as he laid his palm on hers. The skin was comfortingly the same as it always was, callused by decades of ropes and the work of hauling heavy pots of pink clams and gray oysters.

She nodded, even though there was so much she needed to hear him say. She needed to know he would stand in line every day, even in winter when the edges of the harbor froze and there was snow on the ground. She wanted him to promise that he would be deferential to the soldiers, answer their questions but avoid their eyes.

But mostly, she needed him to promise her there would be something left of him when she returned, that he wouldn't fade away completely.

"Breakfast," Agnes said as she set a plate down in front of Helene.

Helene swallowed, her mouth dry and her appetite gone. Her mother had spread a precious bit of butter on a small rectangle of dense, stale bread, as well as all that remained of the apple preserves stored in the basement from last autumn. She also placed a boiled egg on the plate, along with tinned herring.

"Maman, this is too much."

"You will eat your breakfast, Helene," Agnes said, her back already turned.

"Be a good girl," Helene's grandfather said as he winced through another sip of chicory. "And do as your mother says."

Agnes returned to the table with her own smaller plate and the three of them ate in silence. Every so often Helene stole a glance at her mother, who absently thumbed the pages of her journal, a now-worn book started by Helene's grandmother, filled with remedies and notes from her work as a healer in Cordon, the mountain town where Agnes grew up. Helene's grandmother died before she was born, but Helene sometimes felt like she knew her through the journal, by the small flourishes of her handwriting, the delicate drawings of native plants and wildflowers from her home in the Alps.

Agnes looked up from the journal. She hadn't worked the night before, a brief respite from the births and illnesses that constantly demanded her presence, but she still appeared as though she hadn't slept, the blue shadows under her eyes as deep as bruises. Agnes too was less substantial lately, her muscles carved away by the effects of rationing, her once-indomitable strength from growing up in the mountains receding little by little like the tide.

"If we wait any longer, we will miss your train," she said, her voice light, as though she was simply hurrying Helene off to school. She addressed her father-in-law. "And for you, the lines will be down the block already."

Her grandfather cleared his throat. "Of course," he said. He patted Helene's arm, and rose to his feet. "I must be off." He tapped his coat pocket. "Just need…"

Helene got up and walked to the small chest by the door.

From the top drawer she pulled out a blue piece of paper with the word *Viande* printed on top, half of its small squares for the month already stamped. "The butcher today," she said as she handed it to her grandfather. "Ask for the ham hock. No one ever wants it, but there's enough meat on it for a stock."

He nodded.

"And tomorrow, I usually bring a can of tinned sardines to Monsieur Paul. He expects it now. He puts aside the rutabagas that haven't been bruised." Helene looked around the kitchen. There was too much, a thousand intricacies of the system she had created for them. He would never be able to do it on his own, lower himself to barter and negotiate for extra skimmed milk or carrots, find salt or sugar the rare times they were available.

"We will get on, my dear." He stepped toward her, and before she could say anything else, how much she was needed there, he wrapped her in his arms. "I will take care of her. And you will be good and useful, until we are together again."

Helene buried her face in his coat, and even though the smells were all wrong, wool and soap instead of salt and fish, even though his arms around her were thinner, his back slightly stooped, she felt solid ground return beneath her.

He kissed her on the cheek, once, and without another word he left the room, the blue ration card clutched in his hand.

Helene listened to the sound of his steps on the handful of loose treads, the slight rustle of fabric as he reached for his hat.

"We must be going too," Agnes said quietly from the table.

Helene knew the time for argument or protest had come and gone. There was nothing to do now but follow her mother.

Agnes and Helene walked down the alley toward the street that ran to and from the waterfront. They turned inland, away from the harbor, its normally lively banks gray and empty, the colorful old wooden fishing boats replaced by the hulking white metal of several German E-boats.

"You have all your documents?"

"Yes, Maman."

"And your ticket."

"Yes, Maman."

Agnes quickened her pace as they turned down another street. At the sharp staccato of boots on cobblestone, they both looked up.

A young officer strode toward them, his dark green uniform crisp and pressed, the gold buttons gleaming. They were always so clean, their clothes spotless, not a single hair out of place, their cheeks round, and it only put into sharper relief how dull and threadbare the townspeople had become.

Agnes and Helene waited as the officer approached. Though they were accustomed to the sight after nearly two years, Helene could sense her mother tense up.

"Madame, mademoiselle," he said as he stopped beside them, his French accent earnest but stilted.

"Bonjour, monsieur," Agnes said, her tone courteous. They had no choice but to be small, to take up as little space as possible.

He addressed Helene. "And you, *mademoiselle*, you are going to school?"

The soldiers often went out of their way to talk to her, and when they were kind and well-mannered, when they fumbled, as this soldier did, for the correct French words, she often wanted to talk back, exist for a moment as simply a seventeen-year-old girl talking to a boy.

She shook her head, ashamed as always for allowing room in her mind for them to be anything other than the sum of their parts.

"To catch a train," her mother said, a steadying arm around Helene's waist. "To Rouen to see family. We have our papers and documents, if you would like to see them?"

"No," he said, his posture straighter. "That won't be necessary. Off you are then. Good day."

They moved away up the street. "Come now," Agnes said when they were out of earshot. "We'll be there soon."

A few minutes later, they stood across from the small train station. It had been years since Helene was there, and the modest timbered building was now draped, like so many places in town, with an enormous banner featuring the Nazi flag, its white-and-black center offset by a red so bright and garish her grandfather described it as *"la parodie."* There were several vehicles parked outside, black sedans and military trucks, as well as a carriage with two handsome black horses tied up beside it, their shiny tails swishing away flies.

Helene's hands were clammy. She searched her mother for any sign that she might bend, change her mind. "Maman," she said.

Agnes reached into her own bag and withdrew her red journal. She placed it in Helene's hands. "It's yours now. For when you need to be reminded of who you are."

Helene couldn't believe her mother would part from her most precious possession, the closest physical tie to her own mother.

"Keep it somewhere safe."

Before Helene could argue, Agnes took Helene's face in her hands. She was only inches away, so close Helene could see the pores on her nose, the lines at the creases of her eyes. "Do as I taught you," Agnes said. "Nothing more. Nothing else. Do you understand?"

A memory hung between them at her mother's words, a lifeless cat bounding back to its feet, Helene's squeal of delight, her mother's horrified expression.

Agnes held Helene's gaze. "Promise me."

Helene forced the memory away and nodded as her mother released her. "Yes, Maman."

Agnes looked toward the enormous round clock on the station facade. "Go on then." She handed Helene her valise. "You'll need to find your train. A seat by the window."

"Yes, Maman," Helene repeated, but her legs wouldn't move.

"Go on," Agnes said again, with a light push on the small of her back. "We will see each other again soon, very soon."

Helene gripped the journal as she studied her mother's face. She knew its landscape better than any other, could trace its peaks and valleys in her mind. Her mother wasn't soft, or delicate. Her jawline was sharp, her nose angular, her cheekbones prominent and almost masculine. But when Agnes was in her element, doing the work she believed in, or simply drying herbs with Helene in the kitchen, her hardness became its own kind of beauty, as formidable as the cliffs that ran along the coast, gleaming with the moonlight that reflected off the sea. Helene had never felt that kind of purpose, never seen in her reflection the grace and determination her mother exuded. All she ever saw was her own uncertainty.

"Of course, Maman," she said.

And then, before Helene could say anything else, before she could even say goodbye, Agnes pivoted and walked away, her steps leaving pale imprints on the dirt road.

Helene watched her mother's form fade into the old streets, the sidewalks growing busier. She stood with her valise in one hand and her ticket in the other until Agnes was gone, until there was nothing left but the town and its hazy sky, the glint of sea beyond it, still and deep and waiting.

RICHMOND, VIRGINIA
2019

3

LOUISE

The streets were dark and empty as Louise's mother, Bobbie, drove her home from the hospital. By the time the doctors agreed to release her, after what seemed like every possible test and scan and evaluation, it was nearly midnight.

Louise watched numbly as the familiar sights of her neighborhood flashed past, the quiet storefronts, restaurant patios with chairs stacked neatly, 1920s bungalows lined up in rows.

It all kept playing on a loop in her mind. The ambulance ride, the hours in the emergency room, her mother's shocked, horrified face. And the minutes right before the crash, the fight she'd had with Peter. They rarely argued, and yet he had been distant when he picked her up to go to the pool that morning, his features strained as he stood at her door, holding a grease-stained bag of fast food.

She thought it was because of what happened at Kyle's party, even though he'd told her he remembered nothing from the night. But as they drove away from their neighborhood, he looked at her and asked the one question she wasn't expecting.

"Do you really want to go to NYU?"

Louise hadn't known what to say at first, was relieved that it wasn't about Peter's confession the night before. But she also didn't understand the question. NYU had been her plan for years, an idea sparked in a tiny hotel room on Louise's sixteenth birthday, after a tour in which Louise's mother had gushed loudly over every library and dorm and class building. She and her mother had sat up in their hotel bed that night poring over the course catalog on her mother's phone.

"Look at all these econ classes, economics of media. Economics of innovation. Microfinance and calculus. Your big nerdy math brain would be in heaven," her mother said, half teasing. But her eyes were so bright and alive that Louise could feel the excitement take root inside of her own body.

"Yes, come on, you know that," she said to Peter. "I leave on Friday."

"And then what? Major in economics? Go off to conquer the world of finance?"

The bite in his voice surprised her. Peter had been uncharacteristically quiet about her plans for college ever since she told him she had chosen NYU, but she had tried not to take it personally. He hadn't gotten into a single college, not even his "safety" school, and even though he tried to laugh it off, she knew he was deeply embarrassed about it.

"What is your sudden problem with NYU? It's a great school."

He chewed on the nails on his left hand, a nervous tic. "It is a great school. For some people."

Louise's head pounded from her hangover. She didn't want a fight. She only wanted to enjoy their last few days together in Richmond. "What is your point, Peter?"

Peter continued to chew on his nails, even though they were already worn down to the skin. "It just doesn't…it doesn't seem like you." He checked the mirror as he merged onto the traffic going over the James River, which churned beneath them, high from the previous months' rains.

Louise rubbed her temple. She didn't know what he was talking about, who exactly he thought she was. Every single moment of the last two years, every class, every extracurricular, had been mapped out to lead her to NYU. "We're not six years old anymore. Playing dress-up in your basement. From what I remember, you wanted to be an astronaut. How's that going for you?"

Peter's mouth twitched at the memory, but he kept his eyes on the road. "Point taken—it's just..." He took a small breath, as though steeling himself. "Tell me this isn't just for your mom," he said. "Say it once, and mean it, and I will never bring this up again."

"Why would you say that?" she asked. Her mom loved NYU, but *Louise* had chosen to apply. *She* had chosen to enroll. And yet Peter was acting like she was some kind of puppet? "Of course it's not for my mom."

"She'll be okay, Louise," Peter said lightly. "She's been okay now for a long time. You don't have to base every decision off of what you think will make her happy."

Louise's stomach twisted. Peter knew, more than anyone, how that worry had shaped her life, how her mother's unyielding sadness, her bouts of depression in the years after they moved from her family's orchard to Richmond, had carved its way through her childhood like a river, creating vast gorges and valleys. Now he was acting as though she could simply pretend it never existed, as though that experience didn't still live in every cell in her body.

"So be like you then? Tell everyone I'm taking a year off because I didn't get into college? Still get celebrated with my parents buying me a car? It doesn't work that way for me, Peter. No one pats me on the head for being a screwup—"

Louise stopped, immediately flooded with regret. "I didn't

mean that," she said quickly, but Peter didn't look at her, his jaw clenched.

Louise went on, rambling. "I think it's great you're going to take some time off. You get to travel. And go anywhere. And... and do anything." She watched him anxiously, waiting for a sign he heard her.

"I'm not a screwup," Peter said quietly.

And then in a flash of brightness, a screech of tires, the memory ended, replaced by another image: Peter, sprawled on the ground.

Every time she closed her eyes now, she saw him on the ground, broken and vacant, and then in the course of both milliseconds and an entire lifetime, alive, wide-eyed and awake and talking to the paramedics.

Her mother parked the car in front of their house, and for a few seconds neither spoke. She had been quiet since the hospital, tense in a way Louise didn't understand, even as test after test came back normal, even after they spoke to Peter's mom, Marion, and found out his tests were also normal, that they couldn't find anything broken or damaged other than a handful of minor scrapes and bruises.

Louise looked back at Peter's dark, white Cape Cod–style house across the street and touched her bruised shoulder.

"Let's get you inside," her mother said. "You must be starving. I can make you something if you'd like."

"Mom," Louise said, her voice cracking. She felt the words rise inside of her, the words she had wanted to scream all day, at everyone she saw in the hospital, at all the doctors and nurses who shook their heads and said they were both so lucky, to have survived, to come away without any real injuries. She had wanted to scream at Peter when she finally saw him, on her way out of the emergency room. He was being kept longer, for observation, and he had been asleep when her mother steered her into his room, and even then, Louise wanted to yell the words, wake Peter up and tell him what she knew beyond any doubt, what she saw on the street.

"Mom, Peter was dead," Louise said.

There was a silence so deep that Louise wasn't sure Bobbie had heard her.

"You just went through something very traumatic," she finally said. "It's normal to be...to be confused. You need to sleep. It will all feel better in the morning."

With a wince, Louise unbuckled her seat belt and followed her mother up the brick walkway toward the house. "You're not listening. He was dead. He went through the windshield and his neck was broken. I know it was. I saw it."

Bobbie stopped and turned toward her. Even in the dark, Louise could make out the paleness of her skin, the way her hands trembled slightly.

"All that matters is he's alive. You did CPR. You saved his life, and he's going to be just fine."

"I told you his neck was broken. It was bent. It was all wrong."

Her mother shook her head, as though trying to force away the truth of Louise's words. "You were in shock. Your eyes played tricks on you. You didn't see what you thought you saw."

Louise felt a surge of anger. "I wasn't in shock. It was real. I saw him. He flew out the windshield, Mom. It wasn't just his heart. It was...it was...everything. CPR shouldn't have saved him."

Her mother rubbed her face, smudging what was left of her makeup. She had turned forty earlier that year, and despite a few new wrinkles, was much younger than most of the parents of Louise's classmates. "Louise, please, it's late. And you're exhausted. Maybe you hit your head harder than you remember. And you were...hallucinating, or things were jumbled, or you were dazed. Let's just go inside."

Bobbie strode quickly toward the house without looking back.

By the time Louise made it inside, her mother was already in the kitchen, pulling bread from the pantry. She was usually too busy with evening showings or listing appointments to cook, and over the years she had perfected the art of a sandwich dinner. She called it her one true domestic skill.

"I'm not hungry," Louise said from the doorway.

Her mother picked up a knife to cut the loaf of bread, but she froze, holding it in midair.

"Mom."

She shook her head again. "Not yet," she said, the words so slight Louise wasn't sure if she meant to say them out loud.

She put the knife down, closed her eyes, and gripped the counter. The only sound in the house was the hum of the refrigerator and the distant night noises from the yard, chirps of cicadas and crickets, the occasional rumble of a car.

"You're right," she said at last. She opened her eyes, which shone under the kitchen lights. "It was real. And I believe you."

Louise let her mother guide her to a seat at the kitchen table. Her anger was gone, and her entire body felt hollow, exhausted in a way she had never experienced.

"I think I brought him back. He was gone and I brought him back."

"I know," Bobbie said. "I know you did."

Louise's confusion deepened at her reaction. There was no shock, no surprise, only a sorrowful kind of understanding.

"I should have told you. Years ago." Bobbie clasped her hands together on the table. "I didn't know if you'd be like me, or her," she said. "I tried to believe you wouldn't be."

"Be *what*?"

Bobbie took a deep breath, as though willing herself to say the words. "A healer."

Before Louise could respond, she reached out and set a hand on Louise's sore shoulder. At first it was just a small, hesitant gesture, uncertain. But then she increased the pressure, and warmth began to spread under Louise's skin, a trickle, and then a wave, until the pain was gone.

She gazed up at her mother, her mind shifting and rearranging a hundred memories from when they'd lived in Crozet, the sting of scraped knees and burns that lost their edge with a kiss from her grandmother, sore throats and stomach aches and growing pains that receded like a tide when her great-grandmother held her.

"I don't understand," she said.

"I know," her mom said sadly, withdrawing her hand. "I don't even really understand it myself, honey. I don't know if I can explain it to you." She steeled herself. "But I know who can."

Louise woke to the sound of tapping on her bedroom window. For one blissful moment, she rolled over, relieved. It had all been a horrible dream, the accident, the hospital, her conversation with her mother. But as she sat up, she felt the sting in her eyes from where she hit the airbag.

The tapping grew louder and more insistent. Louise pulled herself to her feet and crossed the room, glancing at her phone. It was nearly four in the morning, and only one person could be here at that hour.

When she opened the window, her eyes went immediately to the hospital band around Peter's wrist. She didn't want to see his face, picture him the way he had been on the ground.

"Are you okay?" he asked her.

She tried to nod but she couldn't look away from the band.

"Louise."

There was a rawness in his voice, and finally she made herself look up. She didn't know what she expected, but there was nothing out of the ordinary, no sign that they hadn't just spent the afternoon at the pool as planned.

"Are you okay?" he repeated.

She leaned against the window frame. "I'm okay."

A garbage truck rumbled by in the dark street behind them. "You don't look okay."

Louise didn't know what she could possibly say to him. It felt absurd to talk, to pretend she hadn't felt the absence of his heartbeat only hours earlier, and the explosion of electricity as she pumped her hands into his chest.

"I'm tired—that's all." She stalled, feeling the weight of the next question. "I'm the one that should be asking how *you* are."

Outside the window, Peter slumped against the opposite side of the frame as her. "I'm fine. I don't know how. No one does. The doctors were so insistent on finding something wrong with me I'm pretty sure I got every test there." His eyes darted toward Louise. "They said it's because of you. That you did CPR. That you saved my life."

Louise pressed her forehead to the cool window frame. "I don't know."

"I'm here, aren't I?"

For the first time since she came home, Louise felt an order to her thoughts, a sense that the world could right itself. He was there. He was alive, standing at her window, and they were acting the way they did as kids in the summer, sneaking out to play in his tree house with flashlights and scare each other with ghost stories. Did it really matter how he was alive? Or was it enough that he simply was?

She wanted to tell him everything. He was the only one in her life she could always be honest with, who knew about the stretches of darkness that consumed her house in the years after they moved, who had always been there waiting in the chaos of his own loud, messy home, ready to welcome her in. But she felt the words lodge inside of her. She didn't even understand yet what her mother had told her in the kitchen, or all of the implications. So, she told him the one true thing she could. "I thought you were gone. But I couldn't let you go."

Without a word Peter leaned through the window and wrapped his arms around her. He held her so tight that it hurt, but Louise didn't care. She breathed deeply into his shoulder, the smell of his laundry detergent mixing with the smell of hospital, alcohol, and bleach and plastic.

"Thank you," Peter murmured into her hair. "It feels so stupid to say that. It's not enough. It will never be enough. But I still have to say it."

The weight of his arms, the pressure of his chest against hers, she wished desperately she could reverse time, go back before the accident, to the party, to when he told her he loved her. If she could change that one moment, she could change everything that had followed.

Abruptly, Peter let go. Louise could sense his embarrassment, as though he too were remembering the party, what he said, what she didn't.

"It's a little blurry," he said without meeting her eyes. "But, in the car, before the crash. I don't remember exactly what I said, but I know I was being a jerk."

It seemed irrelevant now, to argue about college. Peter was alive. It was all that mattered. "No, I'm the one who should be apologizing. I should never have said... I don't think you're a screwup, Peter. You're one of the smartest people I know. I just wanted you to shut up and—"

"Why don't we just call an asshole truce?" he said, waving her away before she could finish.

Louise could tell he was uncomfortable with her attempts to smooth over what she'd said earlier. Nothing made Peter more self-conscious than his struggles in school, especially when he always compared himself to Louise and his older brothers, one of whom was in law school and the other premed.

"I wasn't at my best either," he continued. "And I know you can decide what you want to do. You don't need my advice.

I'm an idiot. I shouldn't have brought up the stuff with your mom... It wasn't—"

"It's fine," Louise interrupted. She didn't need him to rationalize it or try to apologize. She only wanted to pretend the conversation had never happened, tuck his words away in a dark, secret place where she wouldn't ever have to wonder about them. "We don't need to talk about it."

"Okay, so then what do I owe you?" Peter said abruptly. "I mean, would a cheeseburger do? Gift card? I think twenty-five dollars is probably sufficient for saving my life, right?"

"I think I deserve at least fifty dollars."

Peter nodded and played with his hospital bracelet. "I'm exhausted. I need to go to sleep, and my mother will kill me if she knows I broke out of invalid jail. I just wanted to check to see how you were."

"I'm okay, really. It's just been a long night." She motioned toward the sky, the lighter shade of blue at the edges. "Almost morning." She didn't know what else to say to him, how to lie, pretend the landscape of their relationship hadn't drastically shifted.

"Well, after I sleep until at least noon, I'll call you. Maybe we can try the pool thing again." He winced. "Only my car is totaled...so..."

Louise started to nod, but then recalled her conversation with her mother. *I'm a healer. And your grandmother. And you, it seems. She can explain it better than me.* "I'm not going to be here later, actually. I'm going to Crozet with my mom."

Peter cocked his head in confusion. "To...?"

"To visit my grandmother."

"With your mother?"

"Yes."

"Are you sure you don't have a concussion?"

Louise rolled her eyes. "I am not concussed. It was my mom's idea." She paused, aware that she would have to lie to him. Peter knew that her mother and grandmother had almost no relationship, that they barely spoke to each other.

"She wants to try harder," Louise said as she chewed on her lip, hoping he wouldn't see through the lie. "I think it was the accident. Shook her up. So yeah, I said we could go see her."

He watched her closely. "Okay, that's weird, and random, but fine. What about the plans we made for this week, though? Midnight movie at the Byrd. Float night at the pool. This is our last week together... I mean..."

Louise was surprised to hear the urgency in his voice. Peter had never needed her the way she needed him. He had other friends, people he could easily call up to grab a meal or go see a movie. "I'll be back tomorrow night, at the latest. I promise. I just have to take care of some family stuff."

She knew how vague she was being, but she didn't know what else to say to him, how to explain that she had to see her grandmother to find out why he was alive.

Peter remained unconvinced, but finally he nodded. "Call me when you get back?"

"Of course."

When he was gone, Louise lay back down on her bed and absently rubbed her shoulder. The pain was only a distant echo, like the last soft rumbles of thunder after a storm. She stared at the ceiling, at the glow-in-the-dark stickers she'd put up years earlier, her own private sky, littered with stars.

ROUEN, FRANCE
1942

4

HELENE

Rouen rose in vertical lines, its ancient spires and towers soaring toward the sky. As Helene made her way off the train and out of the station, the city stretched before her, with cobblestoned roads that curved past in graceful arcs, elegant stone buildings stacked neatly in shades of cream. At the edge of her line of vision cars rushed by on one of the main boulevards.

Her hand was sweaty as she gripped her suitcase.

"Helene? Helene Paré?"

She startled at the sound of her name and shielded her eyes from the sun as she looked around for the source of the voice. There was a tap on her shoulder. She turned to find a young woman standing there, her round face flushed, a few brown curls visible from the white cap that covered most of her hair. She wore a gray dress cinched at the waist, with a stiff high-buttoned collar that went all the way to her chin.

"Yes," Helene said. "I am Helene."

"Then follow me, please," the girl said, her expression bored, and pivoted toward the street.

"Sorry," Helene said, her feet throbbing, her dress itchy and uncomfortable under the summer sun. The bustle of a larger city disoriented her, and she had been expecting a family greeting, not some rude stranger. "I was expecting my cousin, Cecelia."

"Sister Cecelia is busy. Like the rest of them. That's why they sent me."

"And who are you?"

"My name is Elisabeth," the girl said. "I'm a probate nurse at the Hôtel-Dieu. Please follow me."

For several minutes they walked down the city streets in silence, Elisabeth's pace brisk. As they moved farther from the station, the street grew quieter and older, the modern stone buildings giving way to peeling old houses, their facades streaked with crooked wooden timbers.

"Are you from here?" Helene asked as she tried to keep up.

"No," Elisabeth said.

Helene waited for her to elaborate but nothing else came, and so they lapsed back into silence. After several minutes Elisabeth stopped abruptly. "And here we are," she said in a flat voice.

They stood next to a pair of iron gates, the rigidity of the city giving way to a lush, park-like space beyond the fence, a sprawling courtyard dotted with trees and formal gardens. Helene peered closer through the bars of the gates, unable to comprehend that the building in front of her was a hospital. It looked more like a castle, with three vast, stately wings that surrounded the courtyard in a perfect U-shape. Its stone facade held what seemed to Helene like a thousand windows, tidy rectangles that swept out in all directions. She let her hand rest on the cool metal. This place was nothing like the modest country hospital she'd envisioned. It was a fortress, an entire city unto itself.

Elisabeth cleared her throat. A German soldier was walking toward them from the courtyard.

Helene hadn't expected soldiers to be stationed at a hospital that housed a convent. In the days leading up to her departure, her grandfather, a devout Protestant, had said she would likely be at one of the few places in France the Germans had left alone because of the Catholic Church's cooperation with the Nazis.

"They allow evil at their door as long as they can keep their churches protected. They are as bad as Vichy," he had muttered. "Puppets. All of them."

"Don't be stupid. Just do what he says, answer his questions," Elisabeth said now.

Helene nodded.

"Mademoiselles." The soldier was short, not much taller than Helene, with a lean build. He gave a brief, perfunctory nod toward Elisabeth before turning to Helene.

"She's a student nurse," Elisabeth said, her gaze on the ground. "Here for training."

The soldier eyed Helene. "Identification papers?" he asked in French, the words mangled by his thick, heavy accent.

Helene removed her creased papers from her pocket. She had been told so many times she would be safer in Rouen, and yet it seemed her mother had sent her off to a place where Germans would dictate her every movement. If anything she was less safe here, miles from the protection of her family.

She passed her papers through the gates. After studying them he handed the papers back and swung open the gate. Helene and Elisabeth stepped into the courtyard.

"You are here as a nurse? And only a nurse?" His expression was hard, and Helene was suddenly aware of the pistol that hung at his side, its black metal, the long wooden point at the end.

"Yes, sir."

A large scar ran down the side of his face, covered in places by the strap of his helmet. It was still red, the flesh not fully healed. There were dark circles underneath his eyes, but his skin was smooth, unlined. He couldn't have been much older than twenty-five.

The soldier leaned so close that Helene could smell his breath. "Open it," he said, gesturing toward Helene's suitcase.

Helene's mind immediately went to her mother's journal. Would he be able to read the French? What would he think of the pages of notes, the detailed family tree of healers that went back generations, or the description of their magic itself, her mother's words, written on the very first page: "We don't heal the body. We heal the soul."

"They fear what they don't understand," her mother always whispered to her, whenever she held open the journal under candlelight as she mixed up broths or cups of tea for her sleeping patients, or when she placed her hands on sweaty brows to ease fevers. "What they can't control. Men. Doctors. Churches. Governments. They're all the same."

Helene gripped her suitcase tighter. She knew she couldn't trust anyone besides Cecelia with this information, much less a German soldier. Even if the days of witch trials were over, their legacy reverberated. It was the reason Helene's great-great-grandmother had fled from her ancestral home in Normandy to the mountains, a lesson passed to each generation with the same care as the magic itself.

"Bonjour," floated a gentle voice from the other side of the courtyard. A nun in a flowy white habit approached. She was one of the most beautiful women Helene had ever seen. She seemed more like a movie star dressed as a sister than an actual nun.

Her eyes moved between Helene and the soldier, who didn't seem to show her any deference in relation to her status as a sister. "Is there a problem with our new probate, Lieutenant Vogel? Something I can offer my assistance with?" She gestured at Elisabeth. "Did she forget her papers?"

"No, Mother Superior."

The nun addressed the soldier again. "Sir?"

The soldier watched Helene closely, then finally shook his head. "There is no problem."

He stepped aside and allowed them to enter.

"Good day, sir," the sister said, politely, although Helene noticed her shoulders stiffen as she turned away.

They walked in silence for a few moments until the nun fell into stride beside Helene. "Welcome, Helene," she said quietly. "I apologize for the delay."

"Are you Cecelia?" Helene asked, hopeful that this beatific, efficient woman was her cousin.

The nun smiled. "I am nowhere near as talented as your cousin. Hopeless truly when it comes to an operating theater. Some call me Mother Superior. But we don't stand much on ceremony in these times. You can also call me Sister Beatrice."

They reached an edge of the courtyard, near a large, tiered fountain, and Beatrice stopped. "Elisabeth will take you the rest of the way." She squeezed Helene's arm. "We are so happy you are here. Cecelia said you would be a quick learner, a natural."

Helene didn't know how to respond. She had never studied a real anatomy textbook, or learned sterile technique, or how to administer antibiotics for an infection. Despite her mother's brief experience as a combat nurse, the medicine Agnes practiced in Honfleur, the medicine Helene had been taught was the old way, a system entirely anachronistic to the modern world.

Aside from some rudimentary skills, Helene had no training as a hospital nurse.

"I'll do my best, Mother Superior," Helene said, trying to match her expression to her words.

Beatrice smiled again. "Of course, you will."

She nodded to Elisabeth and headed back through the courtyard.

Elisabeth led Helene down a narrow path along one wing of the building until it opened onto a square garden, where several women in white habits picked small red and green peppers and tomatoes from the billowing plants. Helene couldn't remember the last time she'd had a fresh tomato.

They turned away from the garden and walked through a large arch and up a set of covered stairs. Finally, they entered the hospital through an imposing wooden door. As they trod down a long interior hallway, Helene could feel the cool stone beneath the thin soles of her shoes.

"The living quarters are inside here," Elisabeth said as they approached the first door on the left side of the hall. She shoved it open with a groan of metal hinges.

They stepped into a cavernous room lined with metal cots on three sides. On the fourth side were a washbasin and several small tables with lamps.

Elisabeth pointed to a cot near where they stood by the door. A thin white sheet was tucked in tightly, a gray wool blanket folded at one end. "This is yours then." She hesitated before nodding to a cot a few spaces down. "I'm in here too. Not that it matters much. You'll mostly be in here to sleep."

Helene surveyed the cot, the enormous room, the tall arched ceiling above them. It was too big, too formal, too clean. She was embarrassed to feel burning at the edge of her eyes as she tried not to think of home, of her little attic bedroom, the dust on the bookshelf and old socks crumpled in a pile on the floor.

"You'll get used to it," Elisabeth's voice echoed as she walked toward the door and left.

Helene sat on the cot and lay back onto the scratchy sheets, her feet and back aching from the journey. She didn't want to be here, in this massive, vaulted room. She didn't want to be a nurse, to panic and flounder without the steady hands of her mother nearby. Her mother wasn't scared of anything. She would stand in place, never flinch. She was the moon for her patients, lighting up even the darkest of their nights.

Helene closed her eyes as her own inadequacy washed over her, but in the end, the exhaustion won out and she felt herself pulled toward sleep.

"Nurse Laurent may not have informed you of this, but we don't sleep during the day here," a loud voice rang out.

Helene's eyes snapped open, and the room came into focus, the white stone ceiling high above her. She shifted her weight and the hard cot creaked.

"Sleep during the day is only permitted if you have worked in the wards the previous night," the voice continued. It was deep and throaty, with a rustic cadence that reminded Helene of the way her mother spoke.

She rubbed her eyes and sat up. At the end of her bed stood a woman in a long white robe and white veil. She was tall and broad shouldered, in her late thirties or early forties, with oval blue eyes that softened an otherwise stern face.

"Helene."

"Yes?" Helene said, reaching down to loosen her shoes, which she hadn't even bothered to take off before falling asleep.

"I'm Sister Cecelia. Your cousin."

Helene quickly unfolded herself and rose from the cot. "I'm sorry, I didn't realize it was you."

"You were able to get settled, I see," Cecelia said without any warmth.

Helene tried to smooth out the wrinkles in her dusty dress.

"Your matron, Madame Durand, will go over everything with you when you meet with her in her office later. However, I felt that as a courtesy to your mother, I would also offer my assistance."

Helene nodded, her cheeks hot under Cecelia's intense gaze.

"This is a hospital, but it is also a convent, formed many centuries ago by the Canonesses of St. Augustine of the Mercy of Jesus. You may be here to volunteer as a lay nurse, but every single soul who lives and works within these walls follows the teachings and rules of our order. We are a Catholic hospital, run by Catholic men and women. We care for the poor and the sick, because we recognize the face of Jesus in every person who comes through these doors. You may not have been called to a cloistered life, but your calling as a nurse reflects that same divine imperative. Do you understand?"

Helene nodded again. She wondered what her mother had told Cecelia, if she knew Helene hadn't been inside a church in years, not since her father died. Her mother had continued to attend. She always said she believed in God in the same way she believed in the power of the moon cycles, a gravitational tide she could feel even if she couldn't see.

But Helene never could bring herself to go back. God hadn't saved her father. And God hadn't eased his suffering in the last, excruciating months of his life. Her mother had.

"We value humility here," Cecelia continued. "And obedience. You'll begin your training on the wards tomorrow night after supper." She stopped, her lips pursed as she inspected Helene. "The following will result in immediate dismissal from the hospital. Smoking in uniform, alcohol use, inappropriate conduct with a patient, or—" She paused once more. "Incompetence."

She spoke each word with such sharpness that Helene had to chew the side of her lip to avoid flinching.

"Yes, Sister."

Cecelia finally looked away from Helene, her eyes traveling to the small suitcase on the floor. "Your mother said in her letter that she has given you some training at home."

"When I can, I go with her on home visits. Mostly with births. But sometimes other things, people who are ill, or hurt. I help, as much as I can. I've been practicing, trying to get stronger…better. But I also gather herbs and plants that—"

"Has she taught you anything of nursing care? Not herbs. Not home remedies. I'm speaking of modern medicine. Nursing as a profession," Cecelia asked in a stern voice, cutting Helene off.

"Not very much," Helene said quietly. "A little," she added at the disapproving look on Cecelia's face. "Bed changes and some wound care. But she hasn't worked as a nurse since the last war, in Belgium. Mostly she works as—"

Cecelia took another step forward. "I know what she is. A *healer*."

"Well, yes...like you," Helene said, her voice faltering. Her mother had said she hadn't seen Cecelia since they were children, that she only knew of her whereabouts through Helene's great-aunt. Agnes had put blind faith in this woman because of their shared blood, but how much about her did she really know?

Cecelia watched her for a long moment. "This is a hospital," she said. "A modern one. We are nurses here. We practice medicine. We value science and technology. And this is also a Catholic institution. Where we abide by the natural laws of God. Whatever your mother has taught you, this is not the place for it."

Helene took a step backward, almost involuntarily. She knew Cecelia was a formally trained nurse, working in a modern hospital. And yet she was a healer by lineage. Surely, she hadn't abandoned her own birthright?

"I took you in here as a favor to your mother. Because she is family, despite—" her eyes narrowed "—our differences. But what your mother does. What you believe you can do, none of that is a part of God's plan for us. It's unnatural, and wrong."

"But my mother said you—"

"She told you I was a healer," Cecelia said, her blue eyes impossibly bright against the white of her veil, the only color, it seemed, in the entire room. "And I was, or I thought I was, for a long time. I was told that by my mother the same way you were told by yours. But then I became a child of God. And I learned that He is the only healer. The abilities in our blood, the so-called magic we have been given is not of His making. That touch is something else, something dark, and I will not have it used in this hospital. Do you understand me?"

Helene's heart pounded. "Y-yes, Sister," she stammered.

"Good," Cecelia said. "You'll need to wash up then. And join the other nurses for the evening prayer." She glanced at the clock that hung on the wall next to a silver cross. "It starts in twenty minutes, and we don't tolerate tardiness."

CROZET, VIRGINIA
2019

5

LOUISE

As the sky gleamed a cerulean blue over the rolling mountains, Louise and Bobbie pulled onto the dirt road that led to her grandmother, Camille's orchard. It had been over a month since her last visit, and in that time the orchard had transformed as it always did, from bare and brown in late spring to a lush, green, summer landscape dotted with peach and apple trees. On one side of the road were strawberry and blueberry patches, where several people picked the plump fruits off the vines, baskets at their feet. On the other was a small market. Louise caught a glimpse of Caroline, her childhood friend, standing near the outdoor register as she handed a family with two small toddlers a basket and pointed them in the direction of the peach trees.

"Trees are looking healthy," her mom muttered as they entered the gravel parking lot next to the market stalls. She had grown tenser with every mile.

Louise's instinct was to give her mother an escape route. She always tried to be a buffer between her and her grandmother, because anytime they were forced to interact, her mother seemed to dim like a collapsing star. Only now, there was no alternative, because Louise needed them to sit down together, explain to her what it meant that she was a healer, that they were all healers.

At the warehouse behind the market, Jim, the orchard's general manager, stacked crates. He had been an immovable presence there Louise's entire life, usually off among the trees, inspecting each one for signs of disease. He was quiet and gruff, and barely tolerated the tourists who streamed in from Charlottesville or Richmond. But he loved the orchard as much as her grandmother, had been there since Camille was a teenager, and was devoted to the family as much as to the fruit trees. Jim didn't have a spouse or children and practically lived at the orchard, often stopping by the house after his shifts for dinner with Camille. When Louise was younger, she used to wonder if Jim was a little bit in love with her grandmother. Even as a child, she could sense there was something tender about their relationship. She had hoped they would fall in love like in a movie, that Jim could move into the house so her grandmother wouldn't be alone anymore. But that had never come to pass.

"Is that Jim? Oh, come on. We have to go say hi. I haven't seen him in ages." Bobbie unbuckled her seat belt.

"That's because you've refused to come here ever since I got my driver's license," Louise said under her breath.

"I heard that, Louise."

"Mom."

"What?"

"We came here to see Grandma. You can't stall forever. We've already stopped twice."

"I'm not stalling," Bobbie said, obviously lying. "I just want to go say hi, see how he's doing. You know I used to be so terrified of him when I was a little kid, but I think I wore him down over the years. He started to talk to me when I was in college. I finally realized he's just not big on children. Or teens, I guess."

Bobbie got out of the car. Reluctantly, Louise followed.

The market had expanded over the last few summers from when it had been a simple folding table loaded up with baskets of fruit. There was now a large tent set up beside the storage barn, under which were multiple wooden tables, along with a sign advertising prices for pick-your-own fruit as well as gallons of cider. Louise hung back at the first table alongside her mother, noting boxes of doughnuts and baked goods, jugs of peach cider and jars of preserves.

"Local peach jam, fresh-baked peach doughnuts, blueberry honey..." Bobbie murmured as she put her sunglasses on her head. "There's no way your grandmother is making any of this stuff."

"We outsource," came a gravelly voice from a few yards away.

They both looked up as Jim walked toward them. When Louise usually saw him in passing on her visits to the orchard, he'd give her a small nod or a few mumbled words of greeting. But he approached Bobbie with a genuine smile on his leathery, bearded face.

"Hey, kiddo," he drawled. "It's about damn time I see you around here."

"Nice to see you too, Jim," Bobbie said as Jim wrapped her into a quick embrace. "I know, it's been a while."

His gaze traveled to the bruise beneath Louise's right eye. "Pretty nice shiner there. I heard about the accident. You okay?"

"A little bruised but okay."

He turned to Bobbie. "How about you?"

Bobbie put her sunglasses back on. "A little emotionally bruised, but also okay."

"Got it. No need to say more." Jim picked up one of the jars of preserves. "Apparently there's a market for local peach chutney." He emphasized the word *chutney* in his lilting country accent. "Lots of changes here, Bobbie. We also have interns from the university." He rolled his eyes. "I guess we get some kind of tax credit."

"Are they that bad?"

Jim cocked his head to the side. "You should know. You used to be one of those yahoos."

"Wahoos."

Jim waved his hand dismissively. "Same difference." He rolled the chewing tobacco to the other side of his mouth. "They're not like I was when I was a kid." He glanced over at the register where Caroline stood. Louise waved in greeting. Though Louise rarely ever saw her except in passing, they had remained friendly over the years, though Caroline now studied the screen in a way that made Louise feel like she was being ignored. "She's not so bad though." He put his hands in his pockets and surveyed Bobbie. "You're here to drop off Louise?"

Bobbie's expression immediately tightened.

"She's here for a visit, actually," Louise replied at her mother's silence. "She's staying."

Jim's eyes widened. "Well, isn't that something."

"It is," Louise said before her mother could disagree, or diminish it. Despite the accident, she also felt the tiniest spark of hope, that maybe after all these years, this would be enough to bring them back together again. Her mother was there, at the place that had been their home, and for once, she couldn't run away.

Jim leaned toward Bobbie. "It's a good thing you're here, kid. She misses you. And she needs you, even if she's too damn stubborn to admit it."

Bobbie looked up at him, her mouth half-open, forming a question, but Jim just patted her arm and strode away.

Louise turned to her mom, grateful for Jim's words. "No excuses now. Let's go."

After a short walk up the gravel drive, the square white house came into view, nestled into a clearing at the base of the mountain.

There was a long and never-ending list of updates the old

farmhouse needed, central heat and air, new windows that didn't let in every single draft, a new front porch to replace the one that practically hung off the house, half its boards loose or rotting. Whenever Louise would gently try to ask her grandmother about it, Camille shook her head and said she liked things as they were.

And so, the house stayed as it was, as it had been for almost a century, before Camille, before Louise's great-grandmother, Helene, before Helene's Irish father-in-law bought the land in 1922.

"Would it really kill her to pave this thing?" Bobbie said as they stepped over large puddles on the driveway from the previous night's rain. "It's like some kind of contest, isn't it, like she wins a prize for letting her house collapse around her. God forbid she hires someone to do anything. You know my uncle Daniel told me that the last time he visited, he found her up on a ladder cleaning out the gutters. At nearly *seventy*. She's as stubborn as a mule."

"Mom."

"What?"

"Please be nice to her."

"I'm always nice to her."

Louise made a face.

"I always try to be nice to her."

"Try harder."

Just then the screen door slammed. Camille walked out onto the porch, her curly white hair loose and long around her shoulders. She wore green linen pants, an oversize white button-down top, and tennis shoes, her face lined and freckled from years working in the sun. She hurried down the stairs, her movements, even at seventy, athletic and confident.

Camille gripped Louise's shoulders and looked her up and down. "You've got a black eye."

"Just from the airbag."

"Will it hurt if I hug you?"

Louise smiled. "I think I'll survive."

Gently, Camille pulled her in for a hug. Then she turned to Bobbie.

"Hi, Mom."

"Hi, Barbara. It's good to see you here."

There was a long pause that seemed to hold the weight of years.

"Come, come," Camille said. "It's not even noon and it's hot as hell out here."

They followed Camille up the wooden stairs, careful to avoid the board on the second step that had been missing since Louise was in middle school, and the others that were loose or splintering.

The porch was crowded with an assortment of Camille's shoes, mud-caked boots and flip-flops and garden clogs, as well as umbrellas and a stack of unopened packages.

"You want me to bring any of these in, Mom?" Bobbie asked with a nod to the packages. Her eyes narrowed as they traveled over the rest of the porch, the rocking chairs with peeling paint, the mugs of coffee and iced tea glasses left on tables.

"Oh, no, no, leave them," Camille replied as she opened the screen door. "Most of them are for Jim anyway. They tend to get lost when he sends them to the business PO box." She motioned for them to come inside. "Come on, I'll get you something to drink."

They trailed Camille through the living room, with its worn couches and chairs and window air conditioning unit blasting in the corner.

As they passed through the old dining room, which Camille had converted to an art studio that spring, Bobbie stopped. "What...?" she began to ask, looking around at the canvases stacked all over the room, the brushes and jars of paint scattered over a folding table, the paint-splattered drop cloth on the floor under a large easel. Her mother hadn't seen the room since

Camille moved the table and chairs out a few months earlier. Now, every time Louise visited there were a dozen new canvases lying out to dry.

"I told you about this," Louise said beside her mother, whose eyes were trained on a large canvas propped against the fireplace. It was an abstract landscape of a mountain, a swirling world of color, blues and greens and pinks.

Camille followed Bobbie's gaze. "Oh just thought it made sense, I have more time now with—" She stopped abruptly. "I don't do as much gardening because of my back. And you know I've always liked painting. I just used to keep it all in the shed when you guys..."

For a moment, they were all quiet, transported back to a past where they had been together in that same room, gathered around the table for Louise's early birthdays, the space filled with balloons and glitter and streamers, or for holiday meals, Christmases with carols blaring from the speakers, Thanksgivings where Jim always brought a massive turkey he deep-fried at his house, only to wave away all the fuss her great-grandmother tried to make about it.

"Anyway," Camille said hoarsely, moving on. "Excuse the mess. It's all very amateur."

They reached the kitchen at the back of the house. "What would you girls like to drink? I have iced tea, coffee, water?"

"Iced tea would be great, Grandma."

"I'll take some coffee," Bobbie said. She walked to the window and looked out toward the little two-bedroom guest cottage near the creek, where they had lived until they relocated to Richmond when Louise was six.

Camille handed a mug of coffee to Bobbie and a glass of iced tea to Louise. "How about we go sit on the back porch?"

The porch was cool and dark, shaded by the large magnolia tree in the center of the yard. Louise sank down onto the wicker couch, which shuddered slightly with the weight. Many of her recollections of her early life at the orchard were faded, blurred at the edges, but she had vivid, Technicolor memories of sitting on that wicker couch after she got home from kindergarten, on the days her mother was at work. She would play with dolls or color as her great-grandmother, Helene, sat in the rocking chair across from her, listening to country music or thumbing through the pages of an old red journal, talking to herself in French, which always sounded to Louise like a song. It wasn't until years later that Louise understood that her great-grandmother was already sick with dementia by that point, that this was the reason she never went out by herself, why Jim would sometimes appear in the house, musing about orchard business when in reality he was there as a favor to Camille, to sit with Helene when she and Bobbie were both gone.

"Thanks for the tea," Louise said, her throat tight at the sight of the familiar stenciled brown leaves of her iced tea glass. All these years, and nothing here had changed, not a single detail. Camille had been living by herself in this crumbling old house for nearly twelve years. Her brother, Daniel, a dentist who lived in Pennsylvania, helped the orchard financially, but the day-to-day operations of the orchard, and care for Helene, had been left entirely to Camille. Louise felt a rush of gratitude for Jim, for the fact that he had at least been present, when her mother couldn't be.

Her grandmother glanced between Louise and Bobbie, the expectation of what needed to be said so thick it felt like something solid between them. "Barbara," she said at last, "why are you here?"

"The car accident," Bobbie said. "Her friend Peter was in the car too."

Camille stilled, her eyes almost vacant, but then she blinked and focused again. "He was hurt," she said. It wasn't a question.

"He was gone," Louise said. "He was thrown from the car. He...he died."

Camille's face registered a thousand emotions before finally settling into understanding. "And then..."

"He came back," Louise said, as the numbness again descended like a curtain, the knowledge of what she had done clouded by the certainty that it was impossible. "I brought him back."

Camille rested back in her chair and folded her hands on her lap.

"I told her you could explain it," Bobbie said. "Because it's your truth after all, isn't it?"

Louise watched her grandmother carefully.

"I wasn't expecting this," Camille said. "You could have warned me over the phone."

Bobbie shook her head. "You don't get to decide how this happens."

Camille visibly blanched. "Barbara, I'm not... I'm simply trying to process all of this. You've sprung this on me, without any warning, without—" She stopped abruptly.

"Hard, isn't it?" Bobbie said quietly. "To not have any warning."

Louise felt a rush of frustration at both of them, for not being able to put their issues aside, just once, for her. "Stop, please. Both of you." She addressed her grandmother. "Mom said I'm a healer. That we are all healers. So please, explain it to me. Tell me what that means."

Camille cupped her glass of iced tea and looked at Louise, her eyes searching. "You really brought him back?"

Memories flickered across Louise's vision like lightning strikes, Peter on the ground, the angle of his neck, the blood at the corner of his mouth. She nodded slowly.

"I'm not..." Camille looked at Bobbie, almost pleading. "I'm sorry but I'm not feeling quite well."

"Mom, you don't get to do this. You don't get to avoid it, not with her. Not this time."

Her grandmother's eyes grew unfocused again, and her hands trembled as she reached for her tea and then put it back down. "I think you know what you did. I think you knew from the minute you felt it."

Slowly, Louise nodded. "I saved his life."

"You healed him."

Her grandmother's words sunk into her skin, filled her lungs up like smoke, heavy and almost unbearable. "How?"

Camille raised her hands. "Touch," she said as she turned her palms to face Louise. "You put your hands on him. That's where it is, where it all comes from, the gift you have carried since the day you were born."

Louise inspected her own hands. They seemed ordinary, unremarkable.

"I can't explain it." Camille leaned forward. "I could talk for hours but it's not really going to mean anything. But if you'll stay here tonight, I promise I can *show* you. I have a home visit scheduled. Tomorrow. You can come with me. Would that be okay, Barbara?"

Bobbie bit her lip. Louise knew she was struggling with the idea. In the years since she quit nursing, if the subject of her former career ever came up, Bobbie immediately shut down. Louise learned to never mention it, to pretend as if that part of her mother's life never existed. She stopped carrying around her mother's old stethoscope. And even though it was always her favorite make-believe game, something she used to occupy herself with for hours at the orchard, bandaging up her dolls and stuffed animals, she was careful to never play nurse or hospital unless she was at Peter's house, away from where her mother could see.

But Bobbie had brought her to Crozet for a reason, and Louise knew that for once she couldn't say no, even if it meant letting Louise enter the world she had long ago walked away from.

"Please, Barbara," Camille asked at her daughter's silence. "Stay here. One night."

Louise could feel all the years of silence accumulating around them like snowdrifts, the holidays and birthdays spent apart, the awkward interactions at Louise's piano recitals and school events.

"It's why you came here," Camille continued. "Let me help. Let me show her."

Louise faced her mother. She refused to let their history stand in the way of her learning the truth. Her mother's happiness, and comfort, couldn't be the driving force behind every decision.

"Please, Mom," she said. "Do this for me. I never ask you for anything. I'm asking for this."

Bobbie's features softened. "Fine. We'll stay. One night." She turned back to Camille. "You promise you'll be able to show her, explain it all?"

Camille nodded. "I promise."

ROUEN, FRANCE
July 1942

6

HELENE

The Hôtel-Dieu was quiet and mostly empty as Helene, Elisabeth, and the other first-year nursing students walked from their dormitory in the convent to their wards in the hospital. Their stiff brown shoes clicked on the stone floor of the enormous, arched hallway that connected the two wings of the building. It was Helene's second night there, and a waning moon cast a pale blue light through the edges of the blackout shades of each window.

A young German officer with his arm in a sling was stationed halfway down, but he only nodded as they passed, his expression vacant.

"Handsome, isn't he?" one of the second-year students in front whispered with a smirk. A nurse beside her made a hushing noise.

Helene hadn't interacted much with the other nursing students since her arrival the previous afternoon. Mostly she kept to herself, eating in nervous silence while the girls who had been there longer chatted and gossiped in tight, impenetrable groups.

"What?" the same girl said to her friends as they giggled nervously in response. She stopped and turned back toward Helene. "You think so, don't you? I can tell. You think the German is handsome." She smiled at the friends beside her. "You know most of them are sent here from the Russian front, the ones who are sick or wounded. They let them heal, get their strength back, and then send them right back. I'm sure he'd appreciate some female attention before he leaves, don't you think? Someone who will thank him for his bravery." She took a step closer. "They're proper soldiers after all. Willing to stand for what's right. Defend our country when so many here would rather be cowards, let it fall into ruin." Her eyes were hard as she searched Helene's face for a reaction. "The least we can do is let them know how much we appreciate their service."

The student wasn't much older than Helene, but she reminded her of the older girls at her school before the war, when she'd attended regularly, the confident, pretty ones who thought it was fun to tease Helene, to whisper loudly that her father was a drunk and her mother had to work all hours of the night to support their family.

"Why don't we ask the matron?" Elisabeth muttered, coming up behind Helene. "I'm sure she'd like to hear your thoughts, Denise."

Denise narrowed her eyes at Elisabeth until one of her friends set a hand on her arm. "We'll be late," the friend said.

Denise glared at Helene and Elisabeth before continuing on down the hall, her friends flanking her on either side.

"Thank you," Helene murmured as she walked beside Elisabeth.

"She really thinks that, you know," Elisabeth said, voice full of disgust. "That we're better off with them here."

"I don't," Helene replied.

Elisabeth crossed her arms. "You think that's noble? You think I'm impressed by your heroism to our national cause?"

Helene felt a surge of anger, days and weeks of frustration

at her mother's decision to send her away building up to the point where she wanted to scream at Elisabeth's rudeness, at her judgment.

"I don't care what you think," Helene said, enunciating each word clearly. "They took everything from my family."

Elisabeth's brown eyes softened for a moment, but then her expression closed off once more. "Not *everything*, Helene."

There was something unspoken behind Elisabeth's words, but before Helene could ask what she meant, Elisabeth moved on.

When Helene caught up with the other girls at the end of the hallway, they were met by a surprisingly old woman, white hair visible beneath her nursing cap. Her eyes were wrinkled but sharp and clear as she surveyed the group of teenage girls.

"Good evening, Matron Durand," Denise said in a sickeningly sweet voice.

The matron looked her up and down with barely concealed disdain. Helene stifled a smile.

"Come now, girls," she said. "You're tardy."

They followed the matron down another long, arched hallway with wood paneling. Helene tried to absorb her surroundings. Several empty, unmade stretchers lined the sides, along with large metal carts filled with linens. There were heavy wooden doors spaced out in large intervals, each with a small sign in German and French beside it. At the second door, two of the nursing students broke off from the group and stepped inside.

Every so often, another group of two or three girls entered through a door. Helene craned her head as they opened, catching vague glimpses of beds and curtains.

The matron strode quickly, several paces ahead as the group dwindled. At the very end of the hallway, she didn't turn to offer any explanation but went through another door that led to a narrow stairwell. The remaining girls trailed her up the white stone stairs until they reached the second-floor landing, where another German officer was stationed.

The matron pushed the door open and motioned for the girls to follow down a hallway identical to the one beneath it. "Arnaud, Clement," she said as they all came to a halt.

Two girls stepped forward, smoothing down their starched dresses.

"You'll be with Sister Marie in the surgical ward tonight." She pointed to the door nearest them. "Aprons on as you enter."

"Yes, Matron," the nurses mumbled before walking through.

"Fournier, Adrien," the matron continued, her voice echoing in the long, empty hallway.

Two other nursing students stepped forward.

"Venereal ward with Matron Renaud," she said.

Helene noticed that only she, Elisabeth, and another new girl named Anne were left. There was a long silence as the matron looked between them. Her eyes rested on Elisabeth. "Laurent, very few of my girls have to repeat their probationary term. I am disappointed to see you here again."

"That's two of us," Elisabeth muttered, her eyes cast down.

"Pardon?" the matron asked.

"I meant to say, I am disappointed as well, Matron." Helene saw the effort as Elisabeth tried to rearrange her features into some semblance of piety. "Disappointed in myself."

The matron crossed her arms. "As you should be. However, God sometimes gives us trials that are unexpected. He has a purpose in challenging you in this way. And I expect you to do your best to overcome this particular test."

"I will, Matron," Elisabeth said with a small bow.

"Paré and Corbin then?" she asked.

They nodded.

"I am Matron Durand. I will be your head matron for the next month. You will be considered probationary for your first six months of training. We have sixteen wards at the Hôtel-Dieu. The first floor is women and children. Second floor, where you are currently standing, is for men only, dedicated to medicine and postoperative surgical care. The third floor is our isolation wards." She straightened even further. "We are also, as I'm sure you know, currently functioning as a military hospital. Those wards are in the west wing, along with the operating theaters.

"By the end of this six-month period you will have spent time in each and every part of this hospital. From there you will complete the rest of your training, and eventually specialize in one area of nursing. The nurses who graduate from this program are some of the most well equipped in France. That level of training requires discipline and sacrifice," she said. "It requires hard work and the strictest obedience. Understood?"

"Yes, Matron," all three girls said in unison.

"All of our girls start exactly where you are. But you'll learn quickly. You'll have to. We begin with our basic preliminary training. Fresh linens for every bed. Cleaning the wards. Organizing and refilling supplies. Washing instruments and bedpans. Invalid cookery. It's not glamorous, but it's essential, and no one here is above it."

Shouts came from down the hall. Helene swiveled in the direction of the sound, but Matron Durand didn't react at all.

"Are we ready to begin then?"

Helene reached up to loosen the tight collar that rested right beneath her chin, her skin itching underneath it.

"Yes, Matron," they said.

"Wonderful." She clasped her hands together. "Then follow me, girls. I walk quickly, so please do keep up."

Without another word she set off, her starched dress swishing around her wide hips, each step brisk and confident, her white cap a fixed beacon in the darkening hallway.

By the time the dawn arrived, Helene could barely keep her eyes open. Her back ached with every movement, and several blisters were forming on her feet from the stiff uniform shoes.

The night had passed both excruciatingly slowly and at times all too fast, with rapid bursts of instruction that Helene struggled to retain as her mind swirled in the fog of exhaustion.

Nothing Helene had done felt anything like actual nursing. She hadn't even gone near a patient. Instead, they had spent hours in the toilets, scrubbing bedpans until their hands were raw. When the toilets were finished, Matron Durand had the girls clear every supply cabinet and scour the bottoms with pumice soap. She felt far more like a maid or orderly.

When the sun was nearly up, Helene sat beside Anne and Elisabeth in a supply room near the operating theaters, cutting and folding gauze into small, different-sized shapes and packing them in cylindrical metal drums. She could think of nothing but her bed at home under the eaves, her family sleeping soundly in the house beneath her.

Elisabeth placed a folded piece of gauze into the drum and dropped her scissors with a clang onto the tile floor. "I can't do another," she said as she leaned her head back against the peeling white wall. She looked at Helene.

Helene placed her own scissors on the floor and toyed with the gauze in her hand. "Won't the matron be upset if she finds us?" she asked in a tone of mock worry as Anne continued to fold and cut with meticulous attention. "We were warned to keep up."

"No one on earth could keep up with that old crow."

Helene tried to stifle a laugh as Anne glanced up from her work, horrified.

"She is relentless, isn't she?" Helene asked as she rolled her neck, feeling the ache in her shoulders.

"That's one word for it." Elisabeth's eyes were tired and red, strands of her dark, curly hair hanging down from her cap. She seemed miserable here, and if she had already failed once, why hadn't she simply gone home?

"Did you ever think about leaving?" Helene asked. She tried to choose her words carefully. "I mean, after you...after..."

"After my abject failure?"

Helene shook her head and started to apologize but Elisabeth waved it away with a wry smile. "Of course, I think about leaving every single day."

"Then why haven't you?"

Elisabeth rubbed her shoulders. "Long story." Her eyes were distant for a moment, but then she blinked. "Why are you here? It's pretty obvious you don't want to be."

"My mother was the one who wanted this."

Helene rolled the gauze around in her hand and thought of her mother. Where was she at this exact moment? Likely with a patient, called to a bedside for a death or birth, working in candlelight, blackout curtains drawn, without even the moon to guide her. If Helene were with her, she would be in charge of the red journal, searching for remedies to supplement her mother's magic touch, herbs that could speed along protracted labor, or tonics to ease the agonal breathing of death. Helene had always suspected her mother had the journal memorized, that she only made this request of Helene to give her something to do. She still encouraged Helene to put her hands on the patients, to ease their pain, always promising it would come back to her, but no matter how many times Helene tried, she never felt the full force of her ability. At the first glimpses of suffering, she recoiled. She couldn't visualize their pain, hold on to it for long enough to take it away. All she could see in those moments was her father's face, the relentless agony of his last months, when her mother spent nearly every hour with him, her hands on his belly, keeping his pain at bay as though she were trying to will away a gathering storm.

"Mothers are funny that way, aren't they?"

"Yours, too?"

Elisabeth nodded slowly.

They watched each other across the small supply closet as some thread of understanding wove its way between them, until the door behind her opened with a loud bang and they all jumped.

"Just checking on our progress," Matron Durand said crisply as she entered. She noticed their idle hands and the scissors on the floor. "Girls, is there a reason why you have delayed your work?"

Helene quickly picked up the scissors and another roll of gauze, and Elisabeth scrambled to do the same.

Matron Durand dragged over one of the wooden chairs from the center of the room to where they were sitting against the wall. "Perhaps I should sit in for a while and supervise." She checked her watch as she sat down and picked up an extra pair of scissors along with a basin and roll of gauze. "There's an hour left until end of shift. Plenty of time to finish our work. Agreed?"

"Yes, Matron," Helene replied.

"Well then," Matron Durand said, her uniform spotless and unwrinkled, her hair still neatly pulled back. "Let's continue."

Five weeks later, Helene walked down the hallway to her assigned ward with a stack of clean linens in her arms. Her movements were automatic, tracing the same path she had taken a thousand times since she'd arrived.

She was used to the dark, from working at night with her mother. But she wasn't accustomed to so many days without sunlight, a life spent mostly indoors except for weekly treks to the church on the other side of the grounds for mass. The nursing students had one shift off a week, but Helene was often too tired to do much on her day off besides sleep. And so, darkness and exhaustion were the only constants in her life. The entire month had passed in a haze of endless instruction, hours upon hours spent stocking supplies or folding laundry or dusting shelves. Her hands were raw and her back ached from shifts spent scrubbing floors and helping prepare patient meals in the kitchens alongside Elisabeth and Anne.

Helene had hoped things would be different after the first month, that once she was assigned to the wards, there would be more to her training than the monotonous slog of cleaning and organizing and listening to lecture after lecture from the elderly French doctors who had been permitted to keep their roles in the hospital. But the tedium of grunt work had only been replaced by the tedium of rudimentary patient care, bed changes and baths and temperature checks. She had written to her mother, soon after she arrived, trying to explain the situation without using the plain words.

> Our cousin has changed from when you knew her last. She doesn't care for our family resemblance. I don't think she even wants me here. Please, Maman, this is not the place for me. Allow me to come home.

Near the middle of the hallway, she stopped by a large arched window, a hint of light coming through the blackout curtain, and closed her eyes. The words from her mother's reply flashed before her.

My dear Helene, I am so sorry to hear of your problems with our cousin. But please be patient. You will make a wonderful nurse. You are needed exactly where you are.

Helene opened her eyes. The one and only bright spot the last few weeks had been Elisabeth, who despite her initial attempts to remain aloof, had softened as each long night passed. But as much as her friendship with Elisabeth sustained her, she longed for the wide sky over the harbor in Honfleur. She wanted to see the size of the moon, mark the days by its waxing and waning the way her mother had taught her.

She only needed a few seconds. She reached for the thick rough fabric of the blackout curtain, slid a small portion to the side, and hungrily pressed her face into the glass, gazing out over the rooflines at the wide black sky that shimmered with stars. The moon was round, nearly full, casting a gorgeous glow on the city beneath it.

"Mademoiselle," came a male voice from Helene's left, and she jumped, releasing the curtain as though she had been burned.

"I'm sorry, I was only…" she started, but as she turned to face the man who had spoken, her entire body went cold.

Lieutenant Vogel stood watching her from a few feet away. His short, sinewy body was held with calm precision, but his features, even in the dark hallway, betrayed a taut energy. He didn't frown, or smile, only waited for Helene to continue.

"I wanted to see the stars," she said, her arms at her sides. He cocked his head slightly, as though she were an interesting specimen, an object to be examined. "But I know I shouldn't have opened the curtain, sir."

Vogel took a step toward her, that detached curiosity still apparent on his face. "No, you shouldn't have," he said, his French accent all sharp angles, flattening the beauty of her language.

Helene shifted the linens in her arms. She could feel Vogel's eyes on her, but she refused to meet them. She looked past his shoulder. The doors to the wards were still, the night deep.

"You are the girl from Honfleur?" he asked abruptly. "You have family still there?"

Helene tried to nod. "Yes, sir."

"Do they conduct themselves well, follow orders, do as they are told?"

Helene had the nauseating feeling that he saw her the same way a cat would see a mouse, as a toy, there to taunt at his will. She had heard whispers from the other girls about him, unsettling encounters in the hallways, questions that felt probing.

Just then, the door at one end of the hall creaked loudly on its hinges. A matron in a white nursing uniform appeared, carrying a tray full of empty glass medicine vials. Her sense of purpose reminded Helene of Agnes, walking down a quiet Honfleur street, her gray skirt skimming the sidewalks, her leather bag slung over her shoulder, off to homes all over town, called, as always, by death or illness or new life.

"Back to your ward, Paré," she said sternly. "Off you go then."

"Yes, Matron," Helene said, and she moved quickly away.

Vogel didn't try to stop her, but she could feel his eyes on her, his hard, calculating stare following her long after she was out of sight.

CROZET, VIRGINIA
2019

7

LOUISE

Louise lay awake in the old wooden spool bed in the guest room, watching her mother's face on the pillow next to hers. Her grandmother had offered to sleep on the couch so Louise could take her bed, but Bobbie had refused, unable to accept any peace offering, no matter how small.

Louise had tossed and turned the entire night. Being back there with her mother had brought all of the old memories back, flitting through her consciousness like a slideshow: driving away from the orchard in the moving truck, her mother silent beside her as Louise cried, begging her to let them stay. Her monthly visits after she left, when her mother dropped her off but refused to get out of the car.

Her great-grandmother's funeral, sitting in a folding chair at the community center in town, the space packed full of people Louise had never met, men and women from all over Virginia, driving hours to say goodbye to the nurse who had cared for their loved ones. Bobbie had been unwilling to bend even then, sat stiffly beside Camille without touching her, stayed out on the porch at the reception.

As though she could feel herself being watched, Bobbie's eyes opened with a start. She blinked several times before pressing her cheek into the worn yellow sheets. "I forgot how uncomfortable this bed was." She groaned as she sat up. "Spring beds were not made for someone middle-aged."

Louise sat up too and leaned back against the wood frame. "How long have you known you could…that we could heal people?" She had to say it quickly, before she lost her nerve. Though her mother told her the basics after the accident, that healing touch was an ability passed on to each new generation through the female line, Louise still couldn't wrap her mind around the fact that her mother would have quit nursing if she were a healer, that she would hate the profession so much if she had such an extraordinary, innate skill to use as a nurse.

"A while," Bobbie said. She pushed herself up and out of the bed and walked to the dresser for her glasses.

"How long is a while?"

"It's complicated. More than you could know."

"Why didn't you tell me?" Louise asked in a small voice. Of all the questions that crowded her mind, that had kept her awake for hours the previous night, this one was the most painful for her. But she had to know.

Bobbie's face sagged slightly. "I didn't… It was complicated."

"Stop saying that. It's an excuse."

Bobbie wrung her hands, and the vulnerability in her features made Louise's anger subside slightly. "I promise we can talk more later. But I have some work calls to make this morning. One of my clients wants to make an offer on the house we saw yesterday morning, before…before the accident. The internet here is terrible so I'll have to go to the coffee shop in town."

"You're leaving?" Louise was incredulous. Her mother was

going to leave her there alone without answering a single one of her questions, after everything that had happened?

"Just for a little bit. While you spend time with your grandmother. And then we can all talk more later before I take you back home."

Louise's mother was running away, refusing to put her anger in the background, even for Louise's sake. "What about Grandma? What about me?"

"Your grandmother doesn't need me here." Her expression softened. "And you'll be okay, honey. It will...it will all be okay." Bobbie turned away and opened one of the dresser drawers. "I guess I'll have to wear what I wore yesterday. All that's in here are my old field hockey uniform and some cloth napkins."

"Mom."

"I'll call you, when I'm on my way back. Shouldn't be later than noon."

"Mom!"

"I can't stay here," Bobbie said, her back still to Louise. Above her was one of her grandmother's newer paintings, an impressionistic portrait of the orchard in the spring, dashes of pink against green ripples. "I'm sorry, honey, but I can't. I want this to all make sense to you. I want you to understand what happened, and why I didn't tell you, why..." Her shoulders rose and fell, and she shifted around to face Louise. "I want to tell you all of it, Louise. But I can't. *She* can. And she will. She owes me that. She owes us both that. Grandma will tell you everything. Answer any question you have. I promise. I thought I could be here. But I can't... I just need to get out of this house. Can you understand that?"

Louise wanted to question her mom, yell at her, make her explain, stay. But their roles were too ingrained, and after all this time Louise didn't know how to be anything other than what her mother needed her to be.

"Okay."

∞

After her mother left, Louise found her grandmother in the kitchen. She sat with a crossword at the kitchen table, her forearms already stained with paint, a pair of red-rimmed reading glasses balanced on her nose.

"Mom's really busy," Louise said, hovering near the table. "With work. I'm sure she would have liked to stay."

Before Louise could come up with more lies to explain Bobbie's absence, she noticed the smell of something burnt and slightly sweet. "What is—" There was a small plume of smoke rising from the range against the wall.

"Oh, damn it," Camille said loudly as she got up to grab a towel and moved an old cast iron frying pan off the heat. She sighed as she waved away the smoke. "I wanted to make you French toast. Like I used to. Our little tradition."

Whenever her mother worked a night shift at the hospital, Louise would stay up in the big house with Camille and her great-grandmother, Helene, and in the morning, her grandmother always made French toast, slathered in butter and oozing with syrup. "It's no big deal," Louise told her now. "I don't even usually have time for breakfast before school."

"You should always eat breakfast. Especially when you're away this summer on your own. If that's still the plan?" Camille turned from the stove. "I didn't know, with the accident, with what happened…" Her eyes searched Louise.

"Of course it's still the plan," Louise said.

Camille waved away a wisp of smoke above her. "I've been meaning to ask you though, how is your friend?"

Louise pulled out a kitchen chair and sat down. Peter had called her several times the previous evening. Every time she answered, he asked her to go over the accident again, explain it in more detail. With each telling, she felt herself spinning more lies, glossing over a new detail, minimizing things to make it more logical for him.

"He's fine," Louise said. "Completely fine. That's why I'm here, isn't it? Because he's alive. Because I brought him back."

"Of course," Camille said. She walked to the table and patted her arm. "I promised I'd explain it. Would you still like me to show you?"

A trickle of anticipation ran down Louise's spine. She had been so caught up in the fear of all that she had almost lost, that she hadn't let herself think much of what she had *gained*. But at her grandmother's words, she could feel an unspoken world blooming before her. All she had to do was enter it.

Camille went to the small bookshelf near the door to the back porch. The top was scattered with papers and sunglasses and cans of bug spray, and the shelves were full of books, mostly paperbacks.

Camille squatted and removed a thin leather journal from the bottom shelf. "I wanted to show you this first." She carried it across the kitchen and sat down.

Louise examined the red leather cover. There was no inscription, but it looked decades old.

"This was my mother's. Her mother, my grandmother, Agnes, started it in France. About halfway through, my mother added to it when she was working in Virginia as a home hospice nurse. And then I even have a few pages at the end, although nothing I wrote in here is as useful as what they wrote." Camille's expression softened. "I should keep it in a safe, or under glass. To protect it. But I also like it to be nearby."

"What is it?" Louise asked, mesmerized by the tender way her grandmother traced the cover with her finger.

Carefully, Camille opened it. The yellowed paper inside held drawings mixed with words and phrases that appeared to be in French. She thumbed through a few pages, revealing additional illustrations, flowers and herbs and trees. There were even a few dried flowers pressed between the pages, so fragile they would blow away in the wind.

"A guide, of sorts. My grandmother and mother wrote about herbal remedies and plant medicine, a heritage that was passed down in writing and word of mouth from generations before them."

She touched the faded ink on the page with her fingers.

"But they also wrote about the magic in our blood, what you just experienced with your friend, the gift of our touch. Healing."

"What does that mean exactly?" Louise asked as she craned to get a better view of the journal. She recalled the power she had felt when she brought Peter back, the raw intensity of it.

Camille was thoughtful for a moment. "What my mother always taught me is that the foundation of our healing, the very essence of it, is taking away someone's pain." She looked at Louise intently. "You can do that, my dear. Put your hands on someone who is suffering. And make it go away. It's a tremendous gift."

"But what about the rest of it?" Louise asked, thinking of the way her mother had erased the bruise from her seat belt. Her mother hadn't only healed the pain, but the injury itself. "What else can we do?"

"There are limitations to our touch, Louise. It's not a magic wand. There are little things we can 'cure' or 'fix,' yes, small cuts or scrapes or burns. But cancer, heart disease, diabetes, strokes, those are beyond our abilities." She paused. "I didn't really understand this myself, when I was your age, but healing and fixing are not necessarily the same thing, not always. And much of what we do, our touch, has nothing to do with curing."

She looked down at the journal, then up at Louise, her eyes full of both grief and pride. "I'm a hospice nurse. I've spent my career caring for people who are dying, and there are times medicine isn't enough. When no amount of opiates will grant someone peace. And I've been able to help people who are suffering, give them some small respite from the pain, some dignity in their final days. I know to you it could seem like it's not enough. But...to them, it's everything."

Camille closed the journal. "Here I said I would show you, and all I'm doing is blathering on. Come with me out to the garden. That's where we begin."

The ground was warm as Louise stepped out from the screen porch. She was barefoot, the way she'd always been as a child here, when the land and the mountains and orchard had been Louise's home.

She followed her grandmother out into the wide, sprawling garden behind the house. At one point, the area had been nothing more than a blank slate, mostly grass, home to the chickens they used to keep. But Helene had started a garden in one corner and Camille eventually took over. Between the two women, nearly every inch of soil had been cultivated, with a small, winding walking path that ran through all the color and greenery. Each pocket of the garden was full to the point of bursting, with containers and raised beds exploding in color, a high wire fence tangled with vines and weeds.

"What are all these?" Louise asked as she approached the bed where Camille had stopped.

"Lavender, bergamot, pokeweed, peppermint." Camille leaned in toward a large, sprawling plant that was nearly her height, with huge heart-shaped green leaves and prickly pink flowers the size of grapes. She plucked off one of the flowers, and turned it in a slow circle.

Louise tried to focus on her grandmother's words and the flowers in front of her, but she didn't want to talk about plants. She wanted to know about healing. She wanted to know everything.

"Are there still other people like us?" she asked as Camille straightened up beside her on the garden path. "Have you ever met other healers?"

Camille nodded. "Yes, there are. And yes, I have. But there are fewer and fewer with every generation."

"Why?"

Camille let the pink flower drop to the ground. "Smaller families. Not as many daughters to pass the genes on."

Louise shivered. It was strange to hear something that seemed like a fantasy described in such practical terms, as though her grandmother was talking about eye color or any other hereditary trait.

"And some choose not to practice it," Camille continued. "Pass it on. There's less of a need for it now, of course. Communities have doctors and hospitals. It's not like it used to be, when it was all midwives and healers, when these women were all that people had from birth to death."

"But you chose to practice it?" Louise asked, turning to observe her grandmother.

"It never really felt like a choice for me. It was always who I was." Her eyes were distant as she spoke, as though lost in the remembering.

Louise tried to make sense of it all, rearrange the parts of her past, all the way back to her earliest memories with her great-grandmother, Helene, who had been revered in Crozet. People would talk about her like she was a saint, the French nurse who used to run the old Winston orchard and spent her career seeing patients deep in the mountains and valley. She hadn't simply been a nurse. She was also a healer.

Camille motioned for Louise to follow her toward the edge of the garden, where the land began to slope down to a creek at the base of the mountain.

"I haven't gotten around to cleaning up over here yet," Camille said as she took in the gray-and-brown plants that peeked out from the soil. She squatted and pointed to a shriveled, nearly black collection of stems. "This is a daylily. Has no medicinal use. I just think it's pretty. It looks like this because of rust, a kind of fungus."

Louise didn't know why they were talking about plants again, but it did seem messier here than she remembered.

Camille's eyes were intent. "I want you to try to heal this."

"I'm sorry, what?"

"You heard me." She gestured toward the garden bed. "Revive it. You asked me how it works. This is how you practice. It doesn't work quite the same with a flower as a person. But it's a good place to start. They're living things too after all."

Louise fought the instinct to argue that it was ridiculous. A small, stubborn part of her was still unwilling to submit to the new reality right in front of her. However, at her grandmother's encouragement, she crouched beside her and reached out toward the daylily, let her hand brush its soft petals as a little bumblebee zoomed up from the ground.

Around them, the sounds of birds and insects deepened.

"I don't feel anything," she said.

"Close your eyes," Camille requested, just as Louise started to draw her hand away. "Do it with intention. Picture it in your mind, not as it is now, but how it was, green and upright, the petals bright yellow."

Louise did as her grandmother suggested. She knew, on a logical level, the ability was inside of her. She could still feel echoes of the electricity that surged through her body when she'd saved Peter's life. She remembered how she had willed his heart to beat, begged him to come back to her.

A warm breeze tickled the back of her neck, and the noises of the garden came into focus again, the low vibration of hummingbirds at their feeders, the rustle of leaves as blue skink lizards darted out from rocks, the cries of birds as they swooped in and out of the rows of peach trees.

And then Louise felt it, a little heat inside of her skin, pulling her toward the lily as though a tide toward the moon. She opened her eyes as it spread into her hand and flowed into the plant, all the places inside of it that weren't dead, but simply silent.

The lily curled further toward the ground, as though stooped by a heavy rain, and then in one swift motion righted itself, stretching toward the sun as its leaves turned green, as the flower fell to the earth, replaced instantly by a delicate, new yellow bud as soft as a marshmallow. Faint lines of red spread along the edges of the bud.

Louise let go of the flower and lowered herself the rest of the way to the ground. Even after what had happened with Peter, even after everything her grandmother had explained to her, a part of her had still not been able to truly believe it, to accept this new, wilder world.

"That's healing?" she asked, overwhelmed.

Camille knelt beside Louise and grazed the lily with her fingers. "It's a small part of it. That energy you just felt, and heat. A flower requires much less from a healer than a person does. You could bring nearly any plant back, as long as there's a bit of life left in it. A plant has a much fainter life force. It's a living creature but it doesn't have a soul, desires, wishes, fears. Same for animals, although they have a stronger life force than a flower of course. But with people, it's different. We can't simply cure someone if they are too sick or too hurt."

Despite the awe Louise felt at seeing her ability in action, she sensed a tug of confusion, a contradiction between her grandmother's words and what she had experienced. "But Peter. I fixed him. I brought him back. He was dead."

Camille didn't answer at first, her hand still caressing the lily.

"My mother told me stories. I knew it was possible, what you did, but it's incredibly rare. It must have been years of pent-up abilities. It's not something you could repeat."

Camille finally looked at Louise, and her expression was serious. "You need to understand, despite what you did, that healing isn't about cheating death. There's a reason why healers are usually nurses and not doctors. Because the people who want to be doctors tend to be people who think that death is a failure. They spend their careers chasing it away." A faint smile slipped onto her lips. "Nurses know better. We treat the whole person. In sickness. And in death."

Before Louise could say anything else, a loud alarm went off on her grandmother's phone. "I'm supposed to be at Sarah's house. The home visit I mentioned." Camille stood and wiped the dirt off her hands. "I hadn't gotten around to telling you this, but since the last time you visited, I actually have... I retired. I was only part-time anyway the last few years with the hospice agency, barely worked enough hours for that. It was overdue really. Not many nurses doing bedside care in their seventies. I was ready. Now I have time for painting. It used to just be something I dabbled in from time to time, a mental break from hospice work, a place where I could always find some beauty and peace. And now...now I can do it every day."

Louise thought of the dining room, the sudden decision to transform it into an art studio a few months earlier. How long had her grandmother waited to tell her she had retired?

"I've put it off for years." She reached out a hand to Louise, who accepted it and climbed to her feet. "But it's a good thing. I'm thrilled about it really."

Her grandmother was rambling, and the lightness of her tone wasn't enough to convince Louise she believed her own words. Nursing—and healing—had been the most essential part of her being, like something she would be practicing forever. Louise couldn't imagine her grandmother existing without her life's work.

"I was going to tell you both," Camille said. "I just hadn't gotten around to it. I'm still seeing a few of the people who were in my care, before I retired. Just as a favor to them and their families. Today is Sarah. You know her actually, I'm afraid to say. You remember Caroline Henley's mother?"

Louise did have memories of Sarah. She was tall and muscular and tan and used to run races with Caroline and Louise down the hill to the creek, her arms strong and sure as she showed them how to catch tadpoles, her feet bare and muddy.

"She's in hospice?" Louise asked, although she already knew the answer.

"Unfortunately. Colon cancer. She was diagnosed a few years ago, went into remission but then it came back. Everywhere." She studied Louise. "I'm sorry. I didn't really think about how hard it might be for you, to see someone you know in that state. I sometimes forget what I do isn't normal for everyone."

Louise wiped red clay dust from the back of her pants and looked toward the magnolia tree as a wind chime hanging from one of its dense branches chimed in the breeze.

For a moment, she saw herself at five years old, balancing on the largest branch that ran along the ground, watching her mother's headlights light up the dusk as she arrived home from her long shift at the hospital in Charlottesville. Louise would race to her, jumping into her arms, inhaling the smell of hand sanitizer and hospital lotion. Her mother was always exhausted after work in the ICU, her hair messily piled into a bun, whatever makeup she had applied that morning worn off. But she was also content, her expression full of pride as she told Camille stories from her day. Louise had been certain she wanted to be just like her mother when she grew up, take care of people the way she cared for the animals at the orchard, the chickens and barn cats she pretended were her patients. But so much had changed. Louise had grown up, and her life had veered in a completely different direction.

"You don't have to come with me," Camille said gently. "It's okay if you've changed your mind. You can wait here for me to come back. And then we can talk more about all of this here, spend more time in the garden."

Louise brushed her hands off, letting a tiny cloud of clay disperse through the air. She couldn't deny the tiny tug inside of her, the curiosity to see her grandmother work, to practice her healing abilities on a person.

"No, I'm ready. I want to go."

Caroline's father, Jake, answered the door in a baseball cap, flannel shirt, and work pants. He seemed shorter than Louise remembered, and thinner, his gaunt cheeks visible beneath his unruly, gray-flecked beard.

"You remember my granddaughter, Louise, don't you?" Camille asked him. "She's here visiting, and asked if she could come along, to say hi to Sarah. If that's okay with you?"

Jake's tired brown eyes were emotionless. "Fine," he grunted. "Just make sure Sarah is okay with it."

"Of course," Camille replied as Jake stepped aside for them to enter.

When they reached the back of the house, Jake stopped at the doorway that led into the den, its ceiling framed by large oak beams. There was a low hum and rhythmic clicking from the IV pump set up next to a large hospital bed, as well as a faint hissing noise from the oxygen. The sharp, acrid scent of alcohol mixed with a cloying lavender from a diffuser on a bookcase in the corner.

Louise stayed in the doorway, but Camille walked to the bed and squirted hand sanitizer from a bottle on the plastic bedside table. "Morning, Sarah," she said warmly.

There was a rustle of movement. "Hi, Camille."

The voice from the bed was the same voice Louise remembered, only faded.

"How are things this morning?"

"Oh, can't complain," Sarah said. "Or I guess I can, technically."

"How is your pain?" Camille asked with a glance up at the pump hanging on the IV pole.

"I'm doing okay."

"I have to get to work," Jake said, checking his watch. "The day nurse, Gena, can't be here until ten. I usually go in later on Thursdays but there's this meeting with the electrician."

"I'll stay until she gets here," Camille said.

He leaned down and kissed Sarah. "I'll call if I hear anything back, from Duke," he said, gentler than he had been since they'd arrived.

After he left, Camille sat on the edge of the bed. "What's at Duke?"

There was another rustle from the bed. "Oh, you know. Some trial or treatment that's too expensive or too experimental or that will reject me outright because I don't have the right genetic markers. He thinks it's something promising. But he always does."

"I can't believe I forgot," Camille said, her eyes bright as she motioned for Louise to come around the bed. "My granddaughter, Louise, is here. Is that okay with you?"

"Oh my God, little Wheezy," Sarah said, and Louise could hear her shift her weight in the bed. "Oh please, yes, I'd love to see her, Camille."

Louise made her way into the room and to the other side of the hospital bed.

"My goodness," Sarah said as her chapped lips softened into a faint smile. "Is this really sweet little Louise?"

Louise tried to speak, to say hello, to do anything but stand there.

"Impossible, isn't it?" Camille said, and Sarah nodded slowly, her eyes still on Louise.

"Hi, it's nice to see you again." The words hung in the air, meaningless and awful, but Sarah only smiled more.

"You too, honey," she said, wincing as she pushed herself up in the bed. "You too." She shook her head at Camille. "I can't handle these little girls growing up into beautiful women. She's supposed to be four years old and sitting at my kitchen counter eating a tuna fish sandwich."

Louise felt a little of the tightness in her chest loosen at the memory.

"I completely agree," Camille said.

Sarah looked back up at Louise. "How are things, hon? Graduation? Getting ready for college? Do you know where you're going?"

"Things are good," Louise said. "I'm going to NYU. I leave in a few days actually for their freshman summer program, for students who want to get a head start, get some course credit and settle in to the school early. I'll be taking a Calculus II course, since I did AP calculus this year."

Sarah beamed at her with a pride that made Louise feel strangely uncomfortable, as though it weren't fully earned. "Wow, that's incredible, Louise. Although you always were such a bright, curious kid."

Camille went back around to the foot of the bed. "I'll go get some towels and water. Be back in a few minutes."

Sarah nodded and turned back to Louise. "How's your mom doing?"

"She's fine." Louise's gaze lingered on the clear tubing that ran out of the top of Sarah's chest, the oxygen pressed into her nostrils. "She's back home, in Richmond."

"Is she still working in a hospital?"

"Oh, no. She's not a nurse anymore. She's a Realtor."

Sarah's eyes widened. "Bobbie is a Realtor?"

"She changed careers when we moved."

"That's surprising. Nursing seemed to always fit her so well."

Louise's mother had never explained the reason she left nursing. Louise only knew that for a month before she quit, her mother had been quiet and worried, her mood dark. And then one day she simply never went back. They moved to Richmond a few weeks later.

"I guess she just wanted something different," Louise said, pushing back the memories of that time in her life, her mother adrift, Louise confused and lonely in a new city.

"Honey, do you mind handing me my water?"

Louise picked up the large plastic hospital pitcher.

"Thank you," Sarah said as she put the straw to her dry lips and took several gulps. She started to cough and her face contorted with the movement, her body tensing as she squeezed her eyes shut. She gripped the bedside rail so tightly that her knuckles turned white, and Louise waited for it to end, for her to open her eyes, but she seemed trapped.

Without thinking, Louise set a hand on her back, letting it rest on the thin fabric of her T-shirt. She felt nothing at first, only the rigid muscles of Sarah's back.

Louise watched the door, wishing her grandmother would come back, to help. She tried to remember her grandmother's words: *Do it with intention.* She closed her eyes as Sarah let out a low moan. Louise tried to visualize Sarah's pain melting away, but she felt only panic.

For an agonizing moment she was no longer in the room in Crozet but on the side of the road again, standing above Peter, willing his heart to beat—

"Breathe," came a voice from far away.

Louise's hand shook as she rested it on Sarah's back.

Camille stood a few feet away, a plastic basin of water on one hip. She looked straight at Louise and repeated herself. "Breathe."

As she exhaled again, Louise felt her body grow heavy, her weight sinking down toward Sarah as she pressed into her hand. She closed her eyes again, felt a familiar heat spread into her fingers, only this time it wasn't a surge or jolt, like an electrical shock, but a slow warmth, like dipping beneath the surface of a hot bath.

It took Louise several moments to notice the silence of the room, the softening of Sarah's body.

She opened her eyes. "I'm so sorry," Sarah said, her voice hoarse. "Muscle spasm. From the cough." She looked up at Camille. "I probably scared her to death."

"She's fine," Camille said, her gaze moving past Sarah, finding Louise again. "Aren't you, Louise?"

Louise's hand on Sarah's back was still heavy as the heat dissipated. "I..." She glanced from her grandmother back to Sarah.

Camille put the basin of soapy water on the bedside table. Beside it she set a stack of clean linens, sheets and towels and pillowcases, the smell of fabric softener wafting toward her.

Sarah leaned forward as Camille began to clamp and unhook the IV tubing. Camille helped lift her shirt over her head, covering her with a clean sheet as she moved the washcloth over her back in slow, smooth circles.

"It's okay, Louise," Sarah said. "You can help. I stopped being shy about all of this a long time ago. And who knows, maybe your grandmother will convince you to go into nursing, carry on the family legacy."

"She's kidding, you know," Camille said gently as Louise hesitated, unsure of how to reply. "But you can still help me. If you'd like."

For a few minutes, Louise only watched her grandmother work. Each time she touched Sarah, Louise could sense some of the tension leave her body. After a little while, Sarah's breathing turned to snores.

"Would you like to try it again?" Camille asked.

Louise felt herself nod. Easing Sarah's pain was a sensation unlike any she had felt before. Terrifying. But also in a strange way, like a release. As though her body had been waiting eighteen years to serve its purpose.

Camille dropped her washcloth into the basin, took Louise's hands, and guided them to Sarah's back. Her skin was cool, the bones beneath palpable.

"Go on," Camille said in a quiet voice.

Louise closed her eyes as a gentle flush once again settled into her palms like the first pale streaks of morning sun. Her hands moved toward Sarah's pain as though controlled by an invisible magnet.

And with every flicker of heat across her skin, Louise understood just how much of herself had been hidden, lying beneath the surface like a dormant spring.

ROUEN, FRANCE
1942

8

HELENE

In the gray, muffled predawn hours of August, Helene rested in the sluice at the back of the German military ward. She wiped the sweat from her forehead and tried to loosen the collar of her uniform. Each shift there were more soldiers, fresh, unshaven faces to replace those who had left. The fortunate ones returned to their postings in France, and the others were sent like fuel to feed the endless fires of vague and distant fronts.

Even though she knew Matron Durand was waiting, Helene stopped and let her hands idle on a stack of linens. Everything in the military ward was spotless and new, vials of medicine and glass thermometers, shiny black combs and razors still in their packaging. The linens were never stained or torn. There was always strong coffee for the patients in the morning, the smell so pungent that it made Helene's eyes water. The soldiers had cigarettes with real tobacco, and there was local apple brandy in the evenings for the officers. Their dinner trays were full with fresh bread and good meat and cheese. Helene sometimes found herself watching them eat, trying not to think of her grandfather back home, standing in line in the early morning in his suit and hat to beg for whatever meager rations were left.

There was a muffled sound behind her, a man's voice speaking in German, another answering it. She had been so sure they would all be like Lieutenant Vogel, would look at her with the same cold eyes, make every hour spent there feel like walking a tightrope, always an inch away from falling into an abyss. But they were mostly just boys, young men who were hurt or sick and a thousand miles from their mothers. They were quiet and they were scared, their jaws clenched as the nurses cleaned their wounds or adjusted their splints or administered medicine to bring down fevers.

She hated the kindness she sometimes heard in her voice when she talked to them, the gentleness in her hands when she helped them down the hallway to the bathroom. She tried so hard to shut it out, to close her eyes and think of her uncles, of her grandfather's boat and livelihood, seized from him, of the yellow stars on the clothes of her Jewish neighbors or plastered on shop windows, of a thousand other crimes they owned, no matter how polite or young they were.

She wished she could be like Elisabeth, whose hardness hadn't slipped once in her time on the ward, who was brisk and stony as she performed whatever task she was assigned. Helene searched the ward for her friend now and found her near the door, shoulders rigid, speaking in hushed tones with Matron Durand, who had one hand on her forehead, clearly frustrated.

Helene wondered what slight she had committed, a missed medication, perhaps, or forgetting to document a temperature or blood pressure on a patient's chart. She tried to catch her eye, but just as Elisabeth looked up, Cecelia strode into the room, her normally perfect habit slightly askew. Helene's body stiffened at the sight of her cousin. She had seen her occasionally since their first conversation, during meals or at mass, but they hadn't spoken. Helene had been grateful to avoid her.

Helene had tried to heal once, two weeks previously, on her second shift on the military ward. It had been a rash moment of resentment, toward Cecelia, toward her mother for not allowing her to come back home, for sending her there in the first place. There was a soldier from the front, his back torn up by shrapnel. Despite the morphine, he continued to writhe in pain each night. She was assigned to baths that night, and when she reached him, every movement was clear agony. His entire body shook as she turned him, his face pale. And without really thinking, she tried to take away his pain.

But she couldn't. Her hands were cold as she touched him. All she could see as she closed her eyes was her father, who had once been a boy just like him, a wounded soldier in the muddy field hospital where he met Helene's mother.

"Something's happening," Elisabeth said beside Helene, who was so lost in her thoughts that she jumped at the sound of her friend's voice. She hadn't even noticed her approach.

Cecelia and Matron Durand were huddled in conversation, their backs to the ward. Helene didn't want to imagine what they were discussing so urgently, but she felt a deep sense of foreboding. Helene could only understand the war in fragments, information passed in rumors or whispers through the hospital, the Germans advancing farther into Russia, reprisal killings for resistance in a Czech village, the mass arrest and deportation of Jewish people throughout France, each piece of knowledge more dismal and catastrophic than the last. There was never positive news in France. Only defeat and surrender and collaboration.

The door swung open and the German head of the hospital, Dr. Weber, entered, his usually clean-shaven face covered in white stubble, his skin as pale and anxious as Cecelia's.

Cecelia broke away from Matron Durand to meet the doctor. A few soldiers stirred in their beds at the sound of so many footsteps.

"What are they saying?" Elisabeth whispered.

They were too far away to hear anything. "I can't make it out."

"I'm going to try to get closer."

"Are you sure you should do that?" Helene asked. She didn't like the thought of Elisabeth being subjected to Cecelia's wrath.

Elisabeth rolled her eyes. "I'm not as scared of your cousin as you are."

She walked toward Weber and Cecelia, her posture confident as she carried her tray of medicine cups toward a cabinet near the door. Weber's and Cecelia's heads were bowed together, their voices indistinguishable but urgent, and they didn't seem to notice Elisabeth as she carefully placed the tray inside the cabinet. She hovered there for several moments, rearranging vials and syringes, trying to appear busy, until finally Cecelia caught on and cleared her throat loudly.

"Thank you, Nurse Laurent. That will be enough. Please go and make sure the clean linens are ready for the day shift."

"I think there's been a landing," Elisabeth said when she returned to Helene, the words tumbling out of her mouth, her expression almost giddy.

For years Helene had waited for news of a landing, so long that the hope of an end to the war, so bright inside of her in the early days of occupation, had waned like a once-full moon.

"Did you hear me?" Elisabeth asked. "I heard the doctor tell Cecelia to ready nurses for an influx of wounded. He mentioned Dieppe." She let out a shaky breath and then to Helene's surprise leaped forward, embracing her with so much force Helene was almost knocked off her feet.

Helene had never seen her this way, like the girl she was under the layers of guardedness.

A feeble hope stirred in Helene's chest. And it remained, tiny but persistent, as they finished their work and left the ward at the end of the shift, as the hospital came alive with whispers and rumors and talk of the coast. They could all feel it, their small, insular world stretching and shuddering toward the expansive, imminent dawn.

Shortly after Elisabeth and Helene returned to the dormitory, Mother Elise, followed closely by Cecelia, walked through the doors.

Mother Elise never came to the dormitories. She rarely spent time in the lay side of the Hôtel-Dieu, was mostly cloistered in the convent except for mass and shared meals.

"Gather, girls," Cecelia announced, her stern voice cutting through the babble of excitement.

The nursing students lined up and faced the nuns at the front of the room. Some of the girls giggled or linked arms as Mother Elise stepped forward to speak, but Helene was focused on Cecelia, the emptiness in her eyes. She felt the last, tattered remnants of her hope extinguish.

Mother Elise was quiet for a long moment, her elegant features hesitant. A few girls still whispered to each other. They didn't understand the look on her face. But Helene knew it well. She had seen it on her grandfather the day after the Armistice, when she'd walked down to breakfast in one world only to have it taken from her by supper, when news of the surrender reached their town, solid ground replaced by a bottomless void.

Mother Elise steeled herself. "As you girls may have heard, there was an Allied landing in Dieppe this morning. We don't have much information, only that the fighting began early, before sunrise." She paused. "And that it appears to now be nearly over."

She clasped her hands at her waist and stared out at their faces. Expressions changed slowly, as one by one the girls understood what Helene had known immediately, that if there had been an attempt at an Allied landing, the only way it could already be over was by a catastrophic defeat.

"Of course, we are grateful," she continued. She glanced down, as though she couldn't look at them as she finished her sentence. "We are grateful for a swift end to the fighting." She pursed her lips and looked up again. "And for the continued security of our Vichy government."

"Grateful," Elisabeth muttered beside Helene, her jaw clenched. Her voice was so low Helene wasn't sure she meant to say it out loud.

Cecelia took a step forward and raised a hand as a few of the girls turned to speak to each other or cry out. "Silence now, girls."

Helene tried to read her cousin, to search for some sign of the fear that reverberated across the rest of them. But Cecelia didn't betray any emotion.

"They have asked for nurses to come to the field," she said. "We will ask some of you to stay here, to help the sisters and nurses prepare for the arrivals of the wounded. The ambulances will begin arriving any moment with the first of them." Her gaze flickered to Helene's. "The rest will go to Dieppe, to help treat the casualties on the beach and assist in whatever way you can."

"Blanchet, Allard, Moreau, Chastain, Vernier, Bassett, Adrien." Several of the girls looked up at the sound of their names. "Report to your assigned wards. Your matrons will direct you." With a soft, scurrying of feet and a rustle of their gray uniforms they left the dormitory together.

"Corbin and Laurent. Shower and dress and report to your wards."

Anne and Elisabeth stepped forward. Elisabeth caught Helene's eye, questioning.

"The rest of you," Cecelia said, surveying the small group that remained, most of them the more experienced nursing students, girls like Denise, who had been there at least a year, "report to me near the west entrance of the Hôtel-Dieu in fifteen minutes. Bring your aprons and caps."

Helene didn't move at first, unsure she had heard correctly.

"That includes you, Paré. Dress quickly and come down with the rest," Cecelia said.

Helene opened her mouth, but no sound came out. She had only been there two months. As a nurse, she had been tasked with nothing more complex than bed changes and baths. What could she possibly do on a battlefield?

"Why?" she finally managed to ask.

Cecelia's expression didn't waver.

"Come now. Do as you've been told."

Helene's body flooded with fear, to be in a position where she would have to face death and suffering on such a staggering scale, to have no idea if she would even be able to help. But she knew at the look in Cecelia's eyes she had no choice. And so with a shaking hand, she picked up her clean uniform from the end of her bed and followed orders.

The truck jostled its way down the long road that led into Dieppe. The space underneath the canvas cover was shaded and silent, clouds of dirt kicked up by the oversize wheels occasionally floating through the wide opening in the canvas flaps in the back. As they churned through the countryside that separated Rouen from the coast, the flaps revealed farms and small villages, churches and schools, little shards of normalcy scattered along the route clashing with the sounds of aircraft overhead, the procession of armored cars, military vehicles, and ambulances that screamed past in the opposite direction.

Everything inside the truck had a dreamlike quality, the girls around her, vague and interchangeable, hands fidgeting relentlessly in their laps; the sisters seated across from them, almost comical in their oversize white habits and veils, their heads bowed as their lips moved in prayer.

The only person who appeared to her with any clarity was Cecelia. She didn't bow her head or pray like the other sisters.

She simply looked forward, her blue eyes almost glowing in the darkness.

After they'd been on the road for at least an hour, the truck stopped with a lurch. The driver idled for several moments before making a sharp turn to the left, the engine groaning as it picked up speed once more. Out the back of the truck Helene saw that the countryside had given way to the outskirts of a larger town, wide fields replaced by narrow streets and larger buildings, shops with darkened windows, shuttered homes and apartments. Helene knew their destination couldn't be much farther.

"Do you smell that?" came a voice from her left, Adeline, one of the nursing students from a town on the coast not far from Honfleur.

"Do I...?" Helene started, but before she could finish, she knew what Adeline meant. It hit her like a wave. It was home, the scent her father once carried back from the docks, woven into the fabric of his jacket as he twirled Helene in great circles, her face buried into his neck. It was the rain outside her bedroom window at night, her first breath in the morning, the way the scent changed, softened or deepened with the winds and tide. It was the throughline, the horizon, the light that filtered through every one of her memories.

The salt air rose, taken in by warm gusts of air. Outside, the streets grew crowded with other trucks and ambulances. They passed tanks with enormous guns stacked to their roofs, an armada of vehicles, what seemed like thousands of men, Germans in uniforms with guns, Allied prisoners sitting on street corners with dirty faces or bloody bandages watched by more Germans with guns, an entire village full of men adrift.

As they inched through Dieppe's city center, a group of Allied soldiers marched slowly past the back of the truck. A few were limping, their shoulders slumped, bandages soaked with blood tied around arms and legs.

There was a loud exclamation, and a German soldier came

into view, his large, black gun shoved so hard into one man's back that he fell to the ground. Beside Helene the other girls let out moans and clutched each other. Across from her the sisters prayed, their hands folded.

Helene watched numbly as the German towered above the other soldier, screaming, until the truck picked up speed and they faded into the background, the boy curled into a ball with his hands over his head.

"Was that an American?" Helene whispered to Adeline as they turned down a narrow side street away from the congested plaza. Her throat was dry and irritated from the dust.

"Canadian," Cecelia said before Adeline could answer. Helene was surprised to have been heard over the commotion outside. "Most of them are." It was the first time Cecelia had spoken since they left the Hôtel-Dieu.

"It's nearly time now," Cecelia said to the group as the truck rumbled to a stop. Over the noise of the other trucks and aircraft, Helene could just barely make out the soft crash of waves in the distance. "Stay close to me. Do as they tell you. We are here to serve, but we must also be safe. Remember your training."

The truck was flooded with light as the driver lifted the flaps to the side. The street was full of men, an endless sea of soldiers walking to and from the beach, some Germans, others in Canadian fatigues, their arms behind their backs, their postures collapsed.

"Go on now, girls, report to the medical tents. They're bringing the men there from triage. Make yourselves useful in whatever way you can," Cecelia said. The women began to climb out of the truck, but Cecelia put a hand on Helene's arm to stop her before she could follow.

"You'll come with me, Helene. Down to the beach."

Helene couldn't move or speak or even form a coherent thought. There was no anger in Cecelia's expression, or disappointment. Her normally composed features were clouded with apprehension.

Cecelia flinched as a gunshot rang out in the distance. Then she leaned forward and gripped Helene's wrist. "Help them," she said. "I brought you here so that you could help them."

"I'm not a nurse."

"I know that."

Helene looked up at her, comprehension dawning. "You said…"

"I know what I said." Cecelia held Helene's wrist so tightly now it was painful. "And we will both reckon with the consequences of our actions." She turned her head toward the beach. "But for that, there is time. Now, we must help them. True mercy. Not at the end of a rifle. Not cold and wet and alone. Find the ones at the end. And take away their pain. You can't save them, Helene. But you can give them grace in their last moments."

She lifted Helene's wrist up until it was at her chest. "Can you do what your mother taught you, Helene?"

Helene trembled. She thought of the last time she was able to use her gift, the last few weeks of her father's life, when her mother needed to sleep or see a patient. She was thirteen years old, watching her father die, unrecognizable, his mind delirious. She had tried to save him. She didn't care what her mother told her. She pressed her hands onto his chest, begging him to live, but she couldn't bring him back. She wasn't strong enough.

"I… I don't know that I can," she said.

Cecelia's gaze was so penetrating Helene felt every failing of her past exposed, cast into the glaring light of day. There was no compassion in her eyes, none of the gentle understanding of her mother. She didn't look at Helene like a helpless child. She looked at her like an equal.

"You can, Helene. And you will."

Something deep in Helene's body seemed to come alive at

Cecelia's words. A current of energy ran down her arms, a sensation she had once known innately, one she had believed she might never feel again.

Without another word, she stepped down from the truck and followed Cecelia toward the beach.

CROZET, VIRGINIA
2019

9

LOUISE

Louise didn't speak on the short drive back from Sarah's house. She didn't know what to say to her grandmother, how to express how wonderful it was to have helped Sarah, but also how confused she felt. She watched the mountains on the horizon, laced with veils of mist despite the blue skies overhead.

She didn't know how to simply go on with her life, tuck away the knowledge that she could help people who were suffering, focus on college math courses and a career in finance when this vast, undiscovered world now existed. It had always made sense to her, to choose a career where she could support herself. It was a lesson drilled into her by her mother for as long as she could remember.

"Don't make my mistake," she told Louise. "Make enough money where you never have to ask for help, rely on your father to pay your rent. It took me years to build my career into a place where I could support us alone. And look at your grandmother. If it wasn't for my uncle Dan she couldn't keep the orchard going. It's massively expensive to run that place, and the profit doesn't cover it."

And Louise had agreed with her mother. She would follow the path laid out, make enough to support herself and her mother, pay her back for all she had sacrificed, the late nights and constant weekends spent working, the struggle to balance a career and being the only available parent.

But now, she felt that path shift beneath her feet.

"Penny for your thoughts," Camille said from the driver's seat.

Louise squinted into the bright sunlight as she looked out the windshield. She didn't want to tell her grandmother what she was thinking, as though saying the words out loud would give them a power she wasn't ready to face.

"Can I tell people?" she asked finally, settling on the question that had pressed on her the most, every time she struggled to explain to Peter what had happened after the accident or contemplated a future in which she would always have to lie to him. "People outside the family?"

Camille didn't respond at first, her eyes on the road as they passed a pasture filled with grazing cows. Finally, she shrugged. "There aren't any rules to this, Louise. It's not like we have a handbook. I took my lead from my mother. She never told my father or brother. I think it was always easier for her, to keep the two things separate, her role at home and her role as a healer."

She checked the side mirror. "She didn't trust the world. She had seen too much evil, and suffering."

Louise thought of Helene, of all she'd endured during the war, the loss of nearly her entire family. She understood why she had lived in fear, and she felt an enormous amount of grief for her, for how lonely it must have been not to be able to trust anyone.

Camille turned off the main road once they reached the orchard. The apple trees swayed in the wind, their twisted limbs weighted down with unripe fruit. "And she always told me that I had to protect myself, protect this ability, because people would find a way to break it if I allowed them in. And so I never told your grandfather either."

Louise's grandparents had been divorced since before she was born, so it was harder for her to imagine them together than apart. They were so different too. Her grandfather was incredibly social, friends with half of Charlottesville, where he lived and worked as a lawyer. Whenever Louse visited him on her way home from her grandmother's house on her monthly visits, it wasn't unusual for him to have a friend or two over at the house. He divided his time between his tidy, perfectly maintained house in the city and Farmington, the country club right outside of town, and seemed to exist in a different world than the wild orchard and messy house where her grandmother lived.

"Is that why…?"

"Why we got divorced?"

Louise wondered if she had gone too far, but when Camille looked at her, her face was contemplative.

They passed the farm stand and headed up toward the house.

"Part of it, yes. Not the only reason. When we were in college, he was this cute, preppy rich kid and he probably thought I was exotic because I wore Birkenstocks and didn't have a trust fund." She winked at Louise. "That was back in my rebellious phase, when I made every decision as long as I thought it would horrify my mother."

Louise couldn't picture her grandmother rebelling against Helene. They had always seemed so similar, devoted to their work, and to the orchard, both so strong and independent.

"You had a rebellious phase?"

Camille nodded. "It was brief. But I made it count. I went to school in Richmond. Met your grandfather and broke up with the boy my mother would have chosen for me if given the chance, someone who spent less time at the club and more time working outdoors." Louise could sense her considering how honest to be. "I also smoked a lot of pot. And to my mother's greatest shock, I decided to be an art major. I came to my senses about the career stuff, switched to nursing senior year, even though it meant an extra two years of school. But it took me longer to realize how wrong I'd been about your grandfather. He is a good man, Louise. I would never disparage him to you. But he was never meant for me. And our differences got more pronounced as we got older. And I was never as good as my mother at being two people. She had years of practice after all, during the occupation. I think your grandfather always sensed that I was holding back. He was patient, for years, but in the end, he needed more from me than I could give him."

Camille parked the car next to the house and shifted in her seat. "It's a lot to process. I know. But you were wonderful back there, Louise. You really helped Sarah. It seemed very natural, for you to take care of her like that." Camille's smile faded. "But of course, you took care of your mother. For all those years. When I couldn't."

Louise didn't respond at first. Camille never mentioned that time in their lives. It had become an unspoken agreement between them, and Louise was shocked to hear her grandmother bring up the old wound, to acknowledge her part in it.

"You tried," Louise said simply.

"I could have tried harder."

The crunch of gravel sounded behind them as Bobbie pulled in the driveway.

"Well," Camille said with a glance in the rearview mirror. She wiped her eyes quickly. "Time for lunch."

A few minutes later, Louise sat stiffly on the screen porch across from her mother while her grandmother busied herself making lunch in the kitchen.

"I got back here as quickly as I could," Bobbie said. "I probably shouldn't have... I could have rescheduled the work stuff.

I'm sorry. I panicked. You know that's sort of my thing in these situations. Remember when I volunteered to be on the PTA and didn't even make it through the first meeting?"

Louise tried to smile, but she couldn't force it. She was so unaccustomed to being angry with her, not like this, not in a way that felt suffocating. But after that morning, seeing the journal, healing Sarah, Louise also couldn't deny how hurt she was, by her mother's choice to keep it all from her, to act as though this essential part of Louise was irrelevant, to let her make plans for her life, create an entire future without the basic facts of her existence.

"How was your morning?" Bobbie asked gently.

A slight breeze rippled through the porch. Louise heard the twinkle of wind chimes in the backyard, the soft rustle of tree branches.

"I helped Sarah Henley," she said bluntly. She wanted to see the shock on her mother's face, have her feel what it was like to have your world upturned. "She's dying of cancer and I helped her."

Bobbie went rigid. "What do you mean?"

Louise sat up taller. "I touched her and took away her pain."

Bobbie grimaced. "That's too much for you to take on. You're eighteen. You shouldn't be thinking about death or suffering. I know I agreed, but clearly that was a mistake. I don't want you to be…"

"Like Grandma," Louise finished for her.

"That's not what I was going to say. That's not fair. Don't put that on me."

"Fine." Louise leaned back in the wicker chair, completely exhausted. She thought of the journal on the bookshelf, the flowers in the garden, the missing pieces of her life that had been given to her that day. All that her mother was willing to keep hidden, locked away like old family photo albums in an attic.

"I think I'd like to stay here with Grandma," Louise said. She tried to keep her voice steady but she knew her mom would see right through her. She wasn't ready to leave, to pack for college, shop for her dorm room, pretend nothing had changed. "For another day or two."

Bobbie's face showed a concerned surprise. "But you're leaving on Friday."

"I'll be back before then."

Bobbie opened her mouth to argue but then seemed to stop herself. "Okay, Louise, if that's really what you want."

Louise gazed past her mom at the garden as Bobbie got up and kissed Louise on the cheek, once. "I love you, you know?"

Louise nodded but didn't reply.

"What do I tell Peter?" Bobbie asked as she straightened up. "He's going to be looking for you. You guys have plans tonight, don't you?"

"I'll call him." Louise felt a twinge of guilt. She knew Peter would be disappointed, maybe even hurt, but she wasn't yet ready to face him. She didn't know what to tell him about the accident, if she was ready to be honest. But she also didn't know how to be around him and openly lie. "He'll understand."

Bobbie put a hand on Louise's arm. "I am sorry, for all of it. For how this all happened. You know that, right?"

Louise nodded again, biting her lip.

"I'll be back tomorrow," she said, squeezing Louise's arm before making her way back through the house.

In the silence of the porch, Louise heard her stomach growl. After her grandmother burned the French toast earlier, they never ended up eating breakfast.

She waited until the front door slammed before going inside. The house was quiet, her grandmother likely down at the market or warehouse, checking in with Jim. She grabbed a bag of open pretzels off the kitchen counter. She needed to walk, clear her head, sort through all the confusion and noise. She was turning to leave when the red journal on the table caught her eye. She grabbed that too and went back outside.

She dialed Peter's number and headed into the orchard. He answered after only one ring.

"Are you back yet?" he asked, a tentative hope in his voice.

"No, I'm still in Crozet."

"What time are you getting home?"

She came to a stop as she reached the edge of the yard, where the land sloped down and the rows of fruit trees began. "I'm not coming home. Not today."

There was a long silence on the other end of the phone.

"What's wrong? Are they fighting?"

Peter knew the details of her mother and grandmother's broken relationship as much as anyone. He had been there, a few months after they moved to Richmond, as Louise sat coloring in the kitchen while Peter's mom fixed them an afternoon snack.

Peter had just gotten back from a week at the beach with his grandparents and extended family, and was sunburnt and full of stories, the hours spent playing in the waves with his cousins, catching crabs off the dock with his grandfather.

"Do you have plans with your grandparents this summer, honey?" Marion asked Louise as she set a plate of apples and peanut butter in front of them. She was always gentle with Louise, her tone dramatically different than when she was talking to her three rowdy boys, who were usually either wrestling or jumping off of furniture.

"My mom is in a big fight with my grandma," Louise said, the truth spilling out. There was something about Peter's boisterous, chaotic house that made her feel less guarded, at ease in a way she wasn't even in her own home. "My mom won't even answer the phone when she calls," she blurted.

She had been immediately horrified that she had told them, that it was somehow a betrayal of her mother. Louise felt her eyes sting in the bright kitchen at the silence that followed.

"My uncle Dan drinks too much beer," Peter said. "Right, Mom? And my cousin Ellie has her tongue pierced. And...and sometimes my other cousin, Henry, wets the bed, even though he's nine."

Peter's mother had smacked him gently on the head, even though she smiled as she did it, and Louise giggled. After that, she knew she would always be safe with him, that he would always find a way to make her feel better. But now something fundamental had shifted.

"Nothing's wrong," Louise finally said, trying to keep her voice light. "I just needed a little more time with my grandma. I promise I'll come back tomorrow or Thursday at the latest. And we'll be able to make the midnight movie at the Byrd before I go."

There was another pause.

"Okay," he said, though she could hear disappointment in his voice. "You'd let me know, though, if something was wrong?"

"Of course I would," Louise lied. "I'll talk to you tomorrow."

Louise hung up and went down the aisle between the first two rows of peach trees. Bees and flies swarmed the peaches that had fallen. Louise remembered collecting the intact fruits from the ground as a child, the ones they used for cider and cobblers and pies. Her great-grandmother was especially fond of peach cobbler. She'd told Louise that during the war it would have been considered the height of decadence, a prize fit for a queen, a sentiment that always made Louise giggle, because nothing about peach cobbler felt extravagant in the parameters of her safe, easy life.

She reached the end of the row and turned toward the next. She wanted to walk for hours, lose herself among the tangled branches of the orchard, pretend life was as simple as it had been when she'd played in these same places as a child. And so she did, weaving her way between the apple and peach trees, cutting through the strawberry and blueberry fields planted in the clearings on the other side of the road, pausing occasionally to rest, her mind drifting and wandering like the wispy clouds in the afternoon sky.

When the sun was directly over the mountains in the west, Louise finally let herself stop. She lowered herself in the middle of a row of unripe apple trees. It was quiet in that section of the orchard, away from the distant noises of the farms bordering the property.

Louise leaned back against a tree, its thick, squat base still warm from the day's sun. The canopy of branches curved and twisted above her, each heavy with green fruit the size of baseballs.

It had been twelve years since Louise lived at the orchard full-time, but she was comforted by how little had changed, how if she closed her eyes it felt possible that she was still five years old, chasing Caroline up and down the long rows as they played tag or ghost in the graveyard, their faces flushed, shrieking as they darted in and out of the trees. Or in the springtime, when the peach trees blossomed, and she, Camille, and Helene would twirl in circles, as every gust of wind made it rain a thousand petals of pink.

At the vision, Louise remembered the thin journal. She withdrew it from the back of her waistband and held it out in front of her. It was warm from the contact with her skin, the old leather stained and discolored in spots, remnants of water or coffee spills, maybe.

She flipped gently through the first few pages. The writing was all in French, but she studied the illustrations, drawings of flowers and herbs, a chart depicting different phases of the moon, short paragraphs that looked like diary entries. She turned a few more pages, pausing to examine an image of the human form, surrounded by symbols and divided into four quadrants, each labeled with a different word: *Flegmat*, *Sanguin*, *Coleric*, and *Melanc*.

A breeze rustled Louise's hair as the handwriting became

more fluid and slightly less embellished. She guessed it was when Helene took over from her own mother. She felt a little wave of grief as she touched the pen marks on the page, trying to imagine the elegant old woman she knew from memory as the young one who would have written these words.

The journal continued in French, before English began to appear, hints that Helene was now in Virginia, names that were familiar: ginseng and jewel weed, drawings of flowers that grew wild along the hillsides. There were also dosing charts for penicillin and morphine and Pitocin, patient names and addresses, inventory lists of dressings and IV needles, clues of Helene's transition to home health nursing after she married in the early 1950s.

Louise adjusted her legs beneath her as she reached the point in the journal where Camille's handwriting began to appear, small and exact, more of a shorthand than the formal script of the women before her. There were drawings interspersed with the written entries, delicate watercolor depictions of flowers and herbs that hinted at her passion for art. But mostly she left notes about patient encounters, a patchwork quilt of the moments in her career that had shaped her.

August, 1979
First day on my own at work after orientation. Working with Hospice of Shenandoah—assigned to Ms. Nancy, a seventy-nine-year-old mother of three, grandmother of nine, with lung cancer. Her family is wonderfully kind, and opinionated. Didn't much care for the first nurse the agency assigned them. Apparently, she whistled. Have to wonder what they think of a brand-new graduate. But Ms. Nancy knows Mama from town. She was in a lot of pain when I got there—we adjusted her morphine dose but she still struggled. I offered a bath and bed change, and was able to bring her some peace as I worked. Her daughter, Ellen, asked me if I was praying when I put my hands on her. I told her

that no disrespect to the Lord, but human touch brings comfort much quicker than prayer. I think she likes me. I hope they like me.

Louise smiled. She enjoyed hearing her grandmother's voice in this way. It was hard to imagine her ever being new, or nervous, but she followed this thread through her early entries until gradually her passages became more confident, and she sounded more like the Camille Louise had always known.

The orchard grew quiet and distant around her as Louise read her grandmother's words, tracing the dates. A young woman's death that hit Camille particularly hard the year Bobbie was born. A long stretch of no entries that coincided with her divorce. There were also mentions of another healer named Naomi. Louise vaguely remembered meeting her as a little girl when she visited the orchard, but she had no idea the richness of her past. Camille described Naomi as descended from enslaved healers, part of an ancient line that went back much further than their own family.

As the years went on, the entries became sparse, and less confessional, until finally she reached the last page. There was a date at the top: August 19, 2007. And underneath, one short paragraph.

It's yours. All of it. When you are ready. I wasn't. Please forgive me. But know I always loved you first. Before everything else. That love guided every choice. Every mistake. And it will remain, always.

Why was her grandmother asking for forgiveness, and from who? Was it a man, someone she had been with after her divorce?

Louise searched her memory. She'd been six years old when her grandmother wrote those words, the same year they left Crozet and her mother and grandmother's relationship had shattered. Louise always knew something horrible must have happened to make her mother so rigid in her anger. But no matter how many times she asked, her mother always refused to give a clear answer, say anything other than it was complicated. Could Bobbie be the "you" in the diary entry?

She turned the page and pulled out a photo that had been tucked into the back cover. It was of Helene holding a small baby underneath the magnolia tree in the backyard. Her expression was serene, her blue eyes bright as she gazed down at the infant in her arms. Louise felt a tug inside of her chest as she realized the baby in the photo must be her, taken shortly after she was born.

Louise squinted into the late-afternoon sun. She felt full with the magnitude of their words, the power of three lifetimes, this long and winding road that had led to where she sat at that exact moment. She studied her hands, which looked so ordinary and unremarkable, and yet held the weight of a long legacy. It hit her with a renewed force, how if it hadn't been for the car accident, she never would have known. All of this beauty would have remained hidden in that book.

She placed the journal beside her and uncrossed her stiff legs, stretching them out on the soft, red clay soil. Little bees flew in and out of patches of clover, and for the first time that day, her mind became blissfully empty. She sunk into this feeling, letting it envelop her until nothing existed beyond the rows of the orchard.

Then there was a loud crack of branches directly behind her, followed by a low, animal-like sound, part growl and part moan. A thud so close the ground beneath her vibrated.

Louise got up quickly, her heart racing, and peered into the long row of apple trees, trying not to make noise. She couldn't see anything, her view clouded by tangles of apple branches, but a low rasp came from a few feet away, like air blowing through a straw. Her heart beat harder.

When she was finally able to force her legs to move, Louise stepped forward into the row of trees. She scanned the wide clearing that ran between the rows, until she noticed the unmistakable black mound only a few feet away.

Louise had only ever seen a bear that close once. She was seven years old, visiting her grandmother. They were driving home from the ice cream shop in town when they passed a huge black bear crumpled on the side of the road. Louise had pressed her face into the window as Camille slowed the car, muttering under her breath. The bear tried to rise to its feet, but its legs gave out and it collapsed again.

Her grandmother had called animal control, said they would put it down, and Louise had cried the rest of the way, asking why they couldn't help the bear, take it the vet, find a way for it to live. When they got home, Camille had squatted down next to Louise outside the car and held her shoulders. And she told her words that Louise had never forgotten, even if she only now began to understand their meaning: "Death isn't a tragedy, Louise. Not always."

Back in the orchard, Louise's mouth was as dry as sandpaper. One of the bear's back legs was mangled, there was a large patch of fur missing near its neck, mange probably, and bright red blood matted the fur of its injured leg.

She held her breath, frozen with fear, as the massive animal rolled over onto its side. It whimpered, its eyes wide with panic.

She should run. She should go back to the warehouse, find Jim. He would know what to do.

But her feet wouldn't move.

The bear released another low, soft moan, almost a cry. Louise stepped out from the shelter of the apple trees, and the bear turned its head slightly at the movement.

Louise's legs shook, but she walked forward. Dimly, she was aware of her actions, of how reckless she was being, but she also knew that a wild and beautiful creature was dying in front of her, and that letting it happen felt unbearable. Her grandmother's words echoed in her mind about animals and plants, how the magic was simpler—*You can bring it back, as long as it has a little bit of life left in it.*

Its long claws stirred feebly at the dirt, its eyes glassy, staring out toward the apple trees. She felt the bear's breath on her legs as she knelt beside it.

Her palms were hot before they even met the bear's sticky, matted fur. It was surprisingly rough, almost like pine needles, but she pressed her hands firmly into the thick flesh surrounding the leg wound.

Distantly, Louise heard a human voice, a visitor to the orchard nearby most likely, but she ignored it. She closed her eyes as a jolt of electricity raced along her nerve endings. It was fainter than the explosion she had felt with Peter, but still powerful as it accelerated through her arms and into her hands and surged into the bear.

Louise opened her eyes as the bear shifted beneath her. The ragged edges of the wound were closed, leaving only soft, slightly puckered skin visible among the fur.

The bear was still for a long moment, its head resting on the ground. But then it blinked, and its eyes grew focused, alert.

Louise stumbled to her feet. It was too late to run. The bear rose up with surprising agility, several hundred pounds of muscle and sinew and raw power. It turned its head in her direction, its round black eyes wide and curious as it sniffed the air between them. Then it lumbered away with a slow groan and ambled down the row, its body swaying side to side as it occasionally stopped to sniff at the fruit above, and eventually crossed into another row and disappeared.

She stood there, half-dazed, until the sound of new footsteps broke the silence.

It was Jim, his eyes on the spot where the bear had been moments earlier, sunlight streaming through the branches above him.

DIEPPE, FRANCE
1942

10

HELENE

As Helene's eyes adjusted to the brightness of the sun outside the truck, they found the channel. For as long as she could, she held onto the pale blue horizon of the world she knew, the waves that broke in gentle white swirls, the sea birds that dived recklessly toward the surface, the sights and sounds of her childhood, of every memory in her heart that was good and solid and beautiful.

But she couldn't prevent the new, broken world in front of her from crashing into swift, unstoppable focus. The avenue before them was clogged with a web of machinery. Military trucks lurched past, spewing fumes and smoke, making slow progress through the crowds of soldiers, a sea of men in black and olive and brown. There were groups of German officers in clean uniforms, their heads high and faces smug as they marched prisoners past, boys with filthy cheeks and shocked expressions. There were horses tied up near carts, their coats shiny, and dogs and cats that anxiously followed the men, lured by the promise of food.

When they reached the promenade, the full view of Helene's coast, her ruined home, hurtled toward her. There were only the sounds of the channel, the cries of birds, as Helene looked out onto the gray stone beach fringed by cliffs.

Even from a distance, the bodies were unmistakable, dark clusters strewed along the shore like driftwood, some half in the surf, others floating in rhythmic motions in the shallows of low tide. There had to be dozens, hundreds even, some in piles, others alone. There were too many of them, abandoned on the shore like debris from a shipwreck. But for every lifeless body there were many more wounded, dozens on stretchers, others crouched over on the hard pebbles of the beach. Still more walked in groups away from the sea front, hands over their heads.

Helene's eyes traveled along the length of the beach, lingering on the ruined tanks, their twisted metal frames pouring smoke into the clear blue sky, the piles of guns and packs and equipment, the ruined landing craft, smoldering and useless, the only signs there had been any kind of battle. Everything else pointed only to a slaughter, a thousand men pushed off boats to be mowed down before their feet even reached dry ground.

"Come now," Cecelia said behind Helene. "Move, Helene."

Helene followed Cecelia down a set of stone stairs and onto the pebble beach. Up close, the channel seemed more violent, its waves pummeling wrecked ships and gear as the tide flowed in.

"There," Cecelia said, her steady voice cutting through. She turned Helene by the shoulders. "Start on the other side of the tank. The boy there." She pointed toward a figure lying by the wreckage of one of the Allied tanks.

There was a film over everything, a shiny haze that muffled all the color and light. She tried to take a step and stumbled.

"Go," she commanded herself. And with great effort she moved forward past a body, and past another one, past men she told herself were sleeping, past boots blown off their owners, packs and canteens scattered over the rocks.

She forged forward until she was right beside him. When she knelt down, she saw that his face was gray, his blond hair matted with ash and dried blood. Beneath it all he was very young, maybe twenty. A little stream of blood bubbled out of his mouth.

"Are you here to help me?" he said in English, his voice hoarse. "Please help me."

Helene could only nod as she felt his wrist for a pulse. After several moments she found it, rapid but barely detectable. His hands were cold, the skin waxy.

"I'm a nurse," she said, dredging up the rusty English from her former life as a schoolgirl, when things like the proper way to conjugate a verb in a foreign language mattered.

"Please don't let me die," he said, his eyes blinking in and out of focus. His muscles bulged beneath his skin as he writhed. "Please," he said again, barely a whisper, the whites of his eyes laced with red. "I want to go home."

The boy was beyond saving. Helene had seen death enough to know what it looked like, the rattling sound lungs made as they gasped for air, the waxy sheen of skin. She thought of her father, how at the end there was so little left of him, to the point where he felt like a stranger, nothing like the man whose arms were so strong, who sang to her at bedtime and brought her home chocolate at the end of the day. She felt the tug in her chest to run. She couldn't do what Cecelia had asked. She would fail again. But then the cadence of the waves filled her ears until it was all she heard, the crash of the water against the smooth stones, a sound she had known before she could even comprehend what it meant.

And suddenly she was six years old again, petulant in the kitchen as Agnes held out a tiny robin wrapped in a towel. Helene had found it on the street, lying listlessly near a shop window, and she had brought it home, breathless, so excited to give it to her mother to fix.

"We can help it," Agnes had said gently, its red chest visible beneath the white fabric. "Just not the way you want."

Helene's shoulders shook as she looked down at the kitchen

floor. She hadn't understood why her mother wouldn't simply make the bird better, touch it and heal it and let it fly away.

"You're old enough now." Agnes had shifted the bird into the crook of her arm and took Helene's hand. "It's not just a scratch or broken wing. She's very hurt, Helene. But you, you are special, my love, because you can make the pain go away, help her go peacefully."

She guided Helene's hand down to the bird, until her fingers brushed its delicate feathers. Helene had felt it then, little sparks in her fingertips, like touching candle wax. After a few seconds, the robin stopped its fruitless attempts to free itself from her grip. Its body softened, then went rigid.

"It may not seem like it now," Agnes said. "But that was kindness. That was healing. It's a tremendous blessing, to be able to help a creature die with dignity."

Back on the beach, Helene tried to hold on to Agnes's face, her voice, her composure. Without another thought she reached out her hands. The warmth spread through her before she even touched him, and she was overcome with an almost unbearable sense of relief, finally, as though after years of gray silence, her world had once again exploded with sound and color.

"Breathe," she said kindly as she pressed into his bloodstained shirt, as the heat grew, until she could feel it leave her and pour into him. With a gasp, the boy's body relaxed and his face went slack. He tilted his head up toward the sun that shone above them.

Helene kept her hands on the soldier's stomach as his breathing slowed.

"I don't want to die here." His eyes were filled with understanding as the desperation drained out of him with the pain. "Will I go home? Will they send me back home?"

"Where is home?" she asked. The blaze in her hands intensified. She willed it to go deeper, to seek out every last devastated nerve cell, every shattered bone, the arteries and organs still at war inside of him, to flood every part of him with peace. She tried to hold on to the image of the bird, the way her mother had stopped its suffering.

"Canada. Elora," he said, his voice nearly lost in the noise around them. "Do you know it?"

Helene shook her head, trying to remember the English words. "I never leave France."

He nodded slightly. "I had never left, before this."

Helene pulled a piece of gauze from her medical kit and wiped his bloody lip. "You have family? Brothers, sisters?" she asked as she adjusted her hands back on the wound.

"Two sisters," he said, the words now slurred. "My parents own a seafood restaurant. Right on the water." He looked at her, but his eyes were becoming unfocused again, heavy. "It's nice. You should come. After all of this."

The blood flow from the wound beneath her hands slowed. "Tell me," she said. "About home. Your papa. And mama."

The force began to reverse, out of his body, into her hands. She knew what she was doing. She had seen her mother help people die, elderly men and women whose bodies clung to life even as they begged for it to be over. It was what Agnes had encouraged Helene to do with the little bird, not simply take away its pain, but help it to die because its death was inevitable.

Helene had always been terrified of this kind of healing, of what it must feel like to end a life. But as the warmth from his body flooded her own, as images of the boy's life flashed across her mind, a mother's face, a sister's laugh as they played as children, she understood that it had nothing to do with her. She wasn't taking his life from him. She was helping him find peace.

"I want you to think of them," she said in French, fervent, the closest to a prayer she had spoken in years. "Your sisters. And parents. Think of them all, waiting for you together at the table, so happy to see you again. Because it's over now. It's all over. You can return to them."

Her hands were cold as his chest stopped moving. She knelt there on the rocks, the bottom of her dress wet with sand and mud and blood, his vacant body beside her.

After seconds or minutes or maybe even hours, she felt a firm hand on her shoulder.

"There are more of them," Cecelia said, the words a plea.

Cecelia took her place beside the soldier, her eyes closed and lips reciting as she made the sign of the cross on the boy's forehead.

"You think that matters?" Helene asked, unable to stop herself. They were surrounded by countless dying men. If there was any proof God didn't exist, they were living inside of it. "Here?"

Cecelia made another sign of the cross on the soldier's forehead and gently shut his eyes. "I think it matters here more than anywhere," she said.

Repeatedly that afternoon, as the sun crested above them, Helene followed the screams. She lost track of how many she tended, their faces indistinguishable, soldier after soldier, boy after boy. She was vaguely aware of the other sisters and nurses working near her, the living carried off on stretchers to medical tents, the walking wounded hustled up the beach at gunpoint.

With each soldier, she found it quicker, the source, the pulsing fatal wound. She worked without conscious thought, the heat palpable as it transferred from her skin to their cooling bodies, until the screams eased, and their bodies stopped trembling, until they were able to speak again, for a few moments, look up at the sky, feel the sun on their skin.

Eventually, Helene took a break. Beneath her dress her knees were raw from kneeling on the hard rocks. Her back ached and her head pounded from the sun. She hadn't had any water or food in hours.

She wanted only to rest, to stop kneeling beside dying men. But then, out of the corner of her eye, Helene caught a flicker of movement. A man, a dozen or so meters away, so close to the water that his feet were covered by the rising tide. He was almost completely still, but whenever a wave washed over his legs, he twitched.

When she reached him, there were no obvious wounds on the soldier's abdomen or chest, no signs of major trauma, just occasional moans as he stirred. She shifted him carefully onto his back, her hands tingling, but there was nothing visible there either, no bloodstain even in the fabric of his coat.

His eyes were closed but his eyelids moved rapidly, as though he were dreaming. As Helene's adrenaline slowed, she really looked at his face, something she had avoided with the others. His skin was pale but not ashen, his cheeks still pink. He had thick, wavy brown hair and dark, long eyelashes. His features were round and soft, almost childlike, but he was tall, nearly six feet, with broad shoulders, as though his face hadn't quite caught up to the rest of his body.

"Where are you hurt?" she asked, her fingers finding a bounding, energetic pulse in his wrist. She inspected his legs, and this time a dark bloom of crimson on his right leg caught her eye. She felt the fabric behind his knee, soaked from the waves, and searched until she brushed a piece of something sharp and metallic protruding from the skin.

Relief washed over her. He wasn't dying. He was hurt, wounded, but nothing that couldn't be fixed in a hospital. She rummaged through the medical kit Cecelia had given her for a bandage. She knew enough from watching her mother to apply a basic dressing. Her hands shook as she pulled it out, clumsy in a way they hadn't been for the last few hours.

As she tied the tourniquet above his knee, she eyed the beach ahead of her. It was quieter now, with groups of mostly uninjured men and a dozen or so on stretchers in the direction of the large seafront casino. Before the war it had been a grand destination. Now it stood like an uncaring monolith, blank and empty and blackened by smoke.

"Who are you?"

Helene jumped and found the soldier staring at her as he tried to lift himself up.

"Christ," he said, wincing. "Still here then. Never going to get off this godforsaken beach, am I?"

He spoke in fluent French, the words easy, but his accent was unfamiliar.

"I tried to pull it out, you know." He looked down at his wounded leg. "They kept telling me to wait, the German medics, said they'd get to us eventually, although not as politely as that. And I thought I could just do it myself." He grimaced as he propped himself up on his elbows. "I gave a little yank and that's the last thing I remember." His eyes, pale silty gray, nearly the same color as the channel, met hers. "You didn't answer my question."

Though his wound was minor, it felt impossible that he could be speaking to her, that such a thing as conversation could exist in this space. "I'm sorry, what was your question?" she managed, her voice sounding very far away.

"Who are you?" he asked.

But she was gripped by dizziness. She held a hand to her temple to fight it.

"Here, drink this." Something hard and cool was shoved into her hands. "There's only a little left. But it's something. Come on now, drink a little."

Helene fumbled with the metal top of the canteen and took a long drink of the lukewarm water. Her mouth and throat were so dry she could barely swallow. She resisted the urge to gulp the last drops, wiped her mouth, and returned the canteen to him.

"Thank you," she said. "And I'm a nurse."

He was watching her closely, his gray eyes reflecting the sun. "And I do speak French. You're not hallucinating." He smiled. "You're not the only ones who do. I'm from Montreal."

Helene shook her head. "Of course." She leaned over to examine his wounded leg again, remembering why she was there. "You need to be seen by a surgeon."

"So it seems."

Helene straightened and searched the area for a soldier who could transport him to the medical tent, but there was no one nearby. "They'll just need to remove the shrapnel. Maybe some sutures. You'll be fine."

The boy winced at that and lay back down. "I look forward to my convalescence in a prison camp."

Helene didn't know how to respond. He wasn't wrong. She had seen countless men that day marched off at gunpoint, had heard the stories of what happened to captured paratroopers, sent off to the same work camps or prisons as her uncles, or worse, executed in cold blood.

"I'll go and get help. They'll need to bring a stretcher. Get you to the medical tent."

He sat back up abruptly and gripped her wrist. "Please don't."

She tried to ignore how soft his palm was, how smooth his skin. She wanted to be professional, clearheaded. "You need medical care."

"Didn't you just say you're a nurse?"

"Oh, no. I mean, yes I am. But like I said, you need a surgeon for this, someone to remove the shrapnel." She looked around again for transport. "I'm only supposed to be doing triage."

To her surprise, the corner of the soldier's mouth twitched. "They finally send us some nurses but ones who are useless. Wonderful—I'm sorry," he said immediately. "You should know that I can be an idiot. I'm sure you're a wonderful nurse. All of you. My leg just hurts is all."

Helene reached for her medical kit. "It's fine. But I do need to get you some help. That wound will get infected. It's wet and filthy."

"Please don't leave," he said. "Please just stay. For a little while?" She couldn't help him further, but when she looked at his face again, beneath the charm, she saw real vulnerability. "What's your name?" he asked.

Her hand was still on her medical kit. If she stopped working, stopped moving, allowed herself to exist as herself again and not simply a nurse, she didn't know if she would be able to get up. But his expression was so kind, and trusting, and Helene couldn't unsee it. "Helene," she told him.

"Helene," he repeated. "It's probably stupid, but I thought it might be nice to have a few more minutes. Before all that. Just to sit here in the sun and talk to a pretty girl."

Helene felt her cheeks flush. She had never been called pretty by a boy. She had hardly even talked to a boy. Even before the war, she'd never lived the kind of life that some of her neighbors or classmates did, where she could put on a nice dress and go to a dance and talk to a handsome boy. By the time she was old enough to go to dances, her father was already sick, and after his death, she never had much interest. Music reminded her too much of him, of the way he sang to her, the old fisherman's ballads he knew by heart.

"There's no reason for you to leave, Helene. There's no one left to help," he said quietly as his eyes scanned the beach. "The Germans are taking care of anyone too injured to be brought to the tents."

Gunshots echoed in her mind. She had been ignoring the sound all afternoon, but she knew he was right.

At this reminder, some last, remaining prop inside of her collapsed. It was all over, and for what? All those men, all those bodies, and nothing had been gained or changed.

"I'm Thomas." He offered his hand and she accepted it. "It's a pleasure to meet you, Helene."

"You as well."

He peered straight at her, his gray eyes curious. "How did you end up here exactly?"

Helene set her arms back at her sides and crossed her legs.

Her arms were covered in sand and dried blood. Her hair was loose from where it had been tied back that morning, sweaty and sticking to her forehead. She smoothed the wrinkles in her lap, automatically, but stopped when she saw the dark red stains on her apron.

"Why did you decide to be a nurse?" His voice was softer now.

"I..." She thought of giving him a vague, polite answer, the kind of agreeable pleasantry told to strangers. But for some reason she couldn't bring herself to lie to him, not after what'd she witnessed today. "I didn't. My mother. My mother wanted this for me."

Thomas nodded. "Why is that?"

"She was one. In the last war. She sees people in our town now. Helps with the pain of childbirth. Takes care of people who are sick. Anything people need. I assist her. Or try to at least."

"What is the name of your town?"

"Honfleur." Something inside of her loosened as the word left her lips. It was almost like saying the name could bring it closer, her grandfather's rough wool coat, her mother's dried flowers hanging in the closet, the creak of the loose floorboard on the stairs, the light through the windows in the afternoon.

Thomas cocked his head. "Is that near here?"

Helene gazed out toward the channel. "Not too far. It feels far, though, sometimes." She knew she was only a short train ride from Honfleur, and yet Rouen felt like its own continent, separated from her old life.

"I know what you mean."

Helene looked back at Thomas. She couldn't help but note how handsome he was as the sun kissed his skin. She felt awkward, unsure of how to talk to him. She settled on the simplest question she could think of, an easy one. "How old are you?"

He squinted at her. "Why do you ask?"

Had she embarrassed him? "I'm sorry, I didn't—"

"I'm eighteen, nineteen in October," he said before she could finish. "Why? Do I seem young to you?"

"No," she said. "Or, I mean, yes. Not too young." She felt herself blush.

Thomas studied her in a way that made Helene's stomach somersault. "How old are you then?"

"Seventeen."

"Ha!" Thomas exclaimed. He tried to shift his weight but grimaced at the movement. "Knew it."

"Knew what?"

"That I was older than you."

"That's a strange thing to be excited about."

"I'll take whatever victories I can get today."

Helene started to smile. "What's it like?" She wanted him to be light again, to keep pretending. "Your home. Montreal?"

Thomas shook his head. "No disrespect intended, but a hell of a lot nicer than what I've seen of France."

Helene couldn't argue with that.

"I'm from just outside of Montreal, a little town called Saint-Jean-sur-Richelieu."

"That's quite the name."

Thomas removed the top of his canteen, swigging the last few drops before wiping his mouth. "We can't all be from lovely-sounding places like Honfleur."

Helene wanted to steer the conversation back to Thomas. She much preferred to ask him the questions, to learn about his life. Her own existence had been filled with the hopelessness and tedium of occupation for so long. She needed to remember a world away from the war, one with the possibilities only peacetime could allow. "What is there to do in Saint-Jean-sur-Richelieu?"

"There's a river," Thomas said. "And a canal. A fort and a railroad. It's all quite grand as you can imagine."

"And your parents?"

Thomas opened his mouth to speak but then hesitated. He

looked down at one of his hands and picked at the dirty nailbed. "My father owns a textile factory. My mother was a nursery school teacher, before they met."

"They must be proud of you. For coming here."

Thomas swallowed. "No, not really." He looked back up at her. "I enlisted, right after I turned eighteen. My mother cried when I told her. My father left the room."

"I don't understand." Helene had never seen her grandfather prouder, even through his sorrow, as when his sons went off to fight the Germans before the surrender.

Thomas picked up a smooth, black rock and tossed it out toward the water. It landed with a splash. "They don't think it's our war. Not my father. Not most of the people where I'm from. When my father finally did speak to me, he said I was being reckless, acting like a child, fighting someone else's war."

So many in Helene's country, too many, believed the same as Thomas's father, that as long as their lives continued in a faint outline of what they had been before the war, it wasn't their business, that collaboration was preferable to fighting. It was why France's leaders had surrendered so easily, chose capitulation to Germany. Thomas had lived on the other side of the world, in safety, and yet he was willing to fight for the good of the world.

"I don't think it's childish," she said.

Thomas picked up another rock and turned it over in his hand.

"I think it's brave," Helene continued. Her voice was shaky but she plunged forward, the words inside her suddenly urgent. Because he was kind and held her gaze when she spoke. Because soon they would take him away. "It's not childish. Your father was wrong. No one is fighting here. We're all just living beside them and letting them do whatever they want and take whatever they want." She paused. "And you all tried." She could still hear the sounds of the dying soldiers in her ears, all those boys who would never see their homes again. "And that matters."

"Does it?" Thomas asked.

Helene wanted to memorize his face, the way his nose curved slightly at the bottom, the scar on his chin, the swirls of white in the gray of his eyes, the crease on his forehead as he watched her.

"I think it's all that matters," she replied.

There were footsteps on the rocks behind them, a nurse perhaps, or a German soldier, rounding up the last of the walking wounded. Thomas eased himself onto his back. "It's time to leave now, isn't it?"

"Yes, I think it is," she said as she shifted her weight to look over her shoulder.

Her body went rigid. Lieutenant Vogel stood a few feet away, one hand on his pistol as he blinked into the sun.

Helene tried to rise to her feet, but her legs were unresponsive. She put out a hand as Vogel stepped toward them and raised his gun. She scrambled onto her knees, trying to place herself between them. But Vogel was focused on Thomas, who lay on his back, eyes closed, his chest rising and falling.

"No," Helene heard herself say.

Thomas opened his eyes and lifted his head, his mouth half-open in surprise.

"Get out of the way," Vogel said through gritted teeth. He pointed the gun at Thomas, whose face drained of all color.

"Stop!" Helene screamed, so loud it ripped through the air like an explosion. "He's not dying. He's barely hurt. Please."

Vogel ignored her, his gun still outstretched. He set his finger on the trigger.

Thomas lifted himself to a seated position and raised his hands in the air. "Please," he said in English. "Don't."

Vogel's finger twitched. Helene felt the world around her slow and draw inward, pulled toward the long black barrel of the pistol.

But before Helene could plead again, her vision was obscured by the full white skirt of a sister's habit, covered in dirt and blood.

Cecelia stood in front of Vogel, her chest inches from his gun, her arms at her sides and body as rigid as a wall.

Vogel registered her presence, but he didn't lower his gun. "Get out of the way," he said to Cecelia, his chapped lips barely parting.

Cecelia's head was held high, even as Vogel's gun waved in front of her. "No."

Vogel sneered. "That wasn't a request." He took a step to his right, but Cecelia again placed her body between his gun and Thomas.

"There's only been a misunderstanding," Cecelia said calmly. "This soldier has minor injuries and is ready for transport. Your services are not needed."

Helene braced herself for a torrent of anger, but to her surprise Vogel's mouth twisted into a grin. It made him appear even more ratlike. "You think you get to tell me that?"

He raised his gun until it was in her face. The white fabric of her veil rippled slightly in the breeze, but her body was still.

"Listen to me now, Sister." He leaned forward, his gun shaking. "I am doing more for these men than anyone else on this beach. More than they deserve. You say you're a woman of faith. Well, what does your God think of leaving someone to suffer and die like a wounded animal?" He put his free hand on his chest. "So, I will ask you, once, and only once more, to move and let it be done."

She shook her head again. "No, I will not."

"Then you've made your choice."

Helene sprang to her feet, even as she felt Thomas reach out to try to stop her, and stepped directly beside Cecelia, her legs shaking violently underneath her skirt.

"You're hurt."

There was a long, unbearable silence.

"You're injured—your arm," Helene continued. She pointed to Vogel's left arm, where she had noticed a small, black hole in the fabric near his elbow, raw skin visible underneath. "It doesn't look bad, but it could get infected." She knew only that she had to keep talking. "It needs to be washed out, the sooner the better."

Without moving his gun, Vogel inspected the hole in his sleeve, perplexed.

"You were here then?" Helene asked. "You were here for the battle?"

There was a faint flicker of recognition in his eyes. "Only the end of it."

"You served bravely then," Helene said. She couldn't look at Thomas or Cecelia. "You saved all of us. It's not even your home and yet you fought for it. That takes tremendous courage. Thank you, Lieutenant." She tried to make her features neutral, smooth out any of the fear left in her voice. "Now let us tend to him. Get him ready for transport. His delay getting to the medical tent was our fault, our mistake, an error in the triage, and you were so kind to offer your help. But you need medical attention yourself now."

Vogel glanced at Cecelia and then back at Helene. For a horrible moment, his face hardened.

But then he nodded and lowered his gun. "Fine then." He eyed Cecelia for a long moment, hatred radiating from every inch of him, before turning and walking briskly away.

Once Vogel was gone, Helene crouched beside Thomas. "Are you okay?"

"Of course. Was never worried. Just another German trying to kill me today." He studied his hands, covered in dirt and dried blood. "Still, thank you," he said softly. "For that." He squinted into the sun at Cecelia. "And you, Sister."

Cecelia inhaled through her nose, as though it were her first real breath in hours. "I was only doing God's will."

"God's will was for you to put yourself between me and a Luger?"

Helene tried to stifle a smile as Cecelia narrowed her eyes.

"Go," she said to Helene. "Have them bring a stretcher."

Helene leaned in so Cecelia couldn't overhear. "I'm sorry," she said to Thomas.

"For what?"

Helene could see the afternoon sun reflecting in his gray eyes. He seemed lit from within, despite the events of the day, with a brightness, a hope Louise hadn't seen in years. She had spent hours surrounded by death, by the destruction and carnage of war, but something about her proximity to Thomas, simply being next to him, made her feel like not all was lost.

"That you have to go."

Thomas's right hand toyed with a rock next to him, then he looked up and smiled. "Don't worry about me."

Helene tried to return his smile, the profoundness of the moment welling up inside of her.

Cecelia's hand clamped down on her shoulder, the final axe falling. "Go on now, Paré. Back to the tents. Send along help."

Helene smoothed her skirt as she rose. "Good luck, Thomas."

He reached out his hand. "You as well, Helene."

She tried to memorize the feel of his skin against her own, the weight of it, both nothing and everything all at once.

CROZET, VIRGINIA
2019

11

LOUISE

Jim strode toward Louise, lit behind by the late-afternoon sun. He had always seemed like a giant to her, as though he were carved out of the same mountains that surrounded the Shenandoah Valley.

One of his cheeks was puffed out with a wad of chewing tobacco. "Bears are wild animals," he said finally. "In case you forgot."

Louise's hands shook, still tingling with energy. She slid them into her pockets. "Of course. I should never have… I wasn't thinking," she mumbled, unable to explain why he had caught her kneeling so close to an injured bear.

But he didn't push. He peered down at Louise, his brow furrowing. "Come on then, I'll walk you back up to the house."

"Sure," Louise stammered. She looked over her shoulder. "I just need to…to grab something." Quickly she walked back to where she had sat earlier and tucked the small journal into her waistband before falling into step beside Jim.

They were both silent, the only sound the gravel under their feet once they made it back to the main road, the orchard running in long, lush rows of green on either side of them. She felt ten years old again, caught by Jim eating her weight in peaches, his features stern as he led her back to her grandmother's house.

"You shouldn't mess with things like that," he said, his accent thick. Even after so many years on the other side of the mountain, he carried the lilts and intonations of the valley. "You should know better. And your grandmother wouldn't be happy about it. Not about the bear. Or the healing."

She stopped walking, sure she had heard him wrong. If her own grandfather and great-uncle hadn't known about their abilities, certainly Jim wouldn't know. "What are you talking about?"

Jim removed his hat and wiped at his brow. His eyes were softer than she remembered, two gentle ponds in the otherwise rugged terrain of his features.

"I've been around this orchard since I was a lot younger than you, kid. My mama worked as a nurse in the valley, until she moved here after she got married. Then she met your great-grandmother, Miss Helene." He set his hat against his chest, almost reflexively, as though all these years later he still felt the need to show respect. "You're not the only family with *abilities*."

Louise was stunned. Even though her grandmother told her there were other healers, she hadn't considered the possibility they were so close to home. "Your mom was a healer?"

He showed the ghost of a smile. "She was one of the best."

Louise bit the side of her lip as she tried to process the fact that Jim had known her family's history years before she even did. She didn't want to show the hurt this realization caused.

"Miss Helene took my mama in, after my daddy died. She treated me like a son. She was a great lady. And I grew up with your grandma. Knew her back when she was Cami, all wild hair and moody." There was a real tenderness in his voice, and Louise recalled her earlier conversation with her grandmother about her rebellious phase, how she'd turned down the boy her mother preferred. Had Jim been that boy? She wondered if that was the reason he had always stayed with the orchard, never married, if he'd spent his life waiting for Camille to choose him.

"Not my place really." Jim's voice cut through her thoughts. "It's a family matter, but…with all that's been going on, you know, getting it all ready for sale, and all of it, are things sorted? Between your mom and your grandma? I saw she was here with you. Seems like a step in the right direction."

Louise looked up sharply. "What sale?"

Jim inspected her face for a moment, but then glanced at his watch. "You know I best be getting on. Have someone coming by for ten crates of strawberries."

Louise's worry expanded. "Jim?"

He started to walk away but turned before he got far. "Don't be stupid, kid. It's not a magic trick. It matters, what you do with that gift of yours." He held her eyes intently. "Do you understand?"

There was a seriousness in his tone that jarred her. But before she could parse it, he was gone.

It was nearly dusk by the time Louise reached her grandmother's house, the sun low over the indigo mountains.

To her surprise, her grandmother wasn't waiting for her in the living room. The kitchen was empty as well, except for a teakettle boiling over with a loud hiss. Louise quickly removed it from the heat and then went upstairs to talk to her grandmother.

She looked up from the landing as her grandmother's voice floated down.

"Thanks, Sam, I'll stop by sometime tomorrow to sign it."

Louise knew she shouldn't be eavesdropping, but her grandfather's name piqued her interest. Even though they had stayed cordial, fine to come together for her graduation and other major family events, as far as she knew they weren't in regular communication.

"I will," Camille said. "I appreciate that, and your help with all of this. And with...everything. I really do...bye now."

There was silence and then footsteps as Camile headed her way. She stopped short when she saw Louise.

"Sorry, I didn't..." Louise said. Her grandmother's eyes were bloodshot. "Is everything okay?"

"Fine!" Camille said brightly. Louise noticed her grandmother's hands shaking slightly at her sides.

"Just some business odds and ends."

But Louise knew her grandfather no longer had any business ties to the orchard. "Grandma, what—"

Before Louise could finish, there was a loud knock on the door. Camille moved past Louise down the stairs and went to open it.

"Hello, Mrs. Winston. I'm Peter, Louise's friend. I'm sorry to just show up like this but is she here?"

Louise was halfway to the door before she was aware her legs were in motion. She didn't care if things were uncomfortable. She didn't care if she had to lie to him. She realized, with a force that almost knocked her over, that what she had needed more than anything was to see him, to know that he was alive and whole, that he couldn't be taken from her again. She threw herself into his arms.

"You didn't sound like yourself," he managed to say as she buried her face into his chest and held him in a way that felt necessary for her survival. "On the phone."

She let go and looked up at him, then nudged him playfully on the shoulder. "You could have let me know you were on your way."

"Thought I should keep both hands on the wheel this time." He didn't smile despite the joke. Instead, he looked at her the way he had at Kyle's party, with clarity and intention, and she felt suddenly self-conscious, embarrassed by the way she'd embraced him.

Camille cleared her throat from behind them. "Louise, you're being impolite. Please invite your friend inside. Why don't you two go have a seat in the garden and I'll bring you something to drink."

Camille set two glasses down on the picnic table as the sky glowed orange over the mountains. Even with the sun low, the air was unrelentingly humid, so thick that even the frogs and crickets were listless, punctuating the early evening with thin croaks and chirps.

"Can I get you kids anything else?" Camille asked as she swatted a swarm of gnats. "You sure you're not hungry, Peter?"

"No ma'am, thank you, though," Peter said politely.

Louise felt herself fidgeting with her hair and put her hands in her lap. She was suddenly nervous to be alone with him, worried they would fight again like they had in the car, or that he'd see right through her, discern that she was lying about the accident.

"Thanks, Grandma. I'm fine too."

"Yes, truly, thank you," Peter added. "I'm sorry again I just showed up at your house."

"No need to apologize, sugar. We're happy to have you." Camille patted Peter's shoulder and left.

The buzz of gnats and mosquitos grew louder as the sun sank deeper. The breeze from earlier was gone, the stillness seeming to hold the entire orchard in place, tethered to this moment in time.

"She must like you," Louise said. She didn't know what else to say to Peter. She was unsure how to go back to being friends after everything that had happened between them the past couple of days. "She doesn't ever call me sugar."

Peter flicked a mosquito from his forearm.

"How are you feeling?" she asked, trying to draw him out. Despite his attempts to act normal, she knew something was bothering him. He could never hide a single emotion, wore every feeling on his face. When he found out he didn't get into Virginia Tech, he had tried to pretend it didn't matter, but Louise knew he was devastated. He was so sure that his track performance would be enough to get him accepted, that it would be enough to counter his grades. But it wasn't enough, not for Virginia Tech or the other four state schools to which he had applied.

"Why are you here?" Peter asked, picking at the wooden table. "Can you just tell me what's going on?"

For a long, tantalizing second, Louise wondered if she should simply tell him the truth. They could face it together, the accident, their fight, her family's abilities. They only had a few days left together. But as she tried to form the words, she realized she wasn't ready. She needed to keep her friendship with Peter, one of the foundations of her world, steady. Too much else in her life was in motion.

"It's nothing with us. I promise."

He let out a long breath and leaned back.

"I just needed to come here," she insisted.

Peter chewed his lip. "Fine, okay. You don't owe me an explanation for visiting your grandma." He leaned forward again, placing his palms flat on the table. "But you've never been any good at lying. I know something is wrong."

"I'm not lying. And it's just..." She searched for a half truth, something she could give him. "It's family stuff. My mom and grandma. Things aren't good."

Peter shook his head. He still didn't believe her. "I get it. I literally died in front of you. It freaked you out. Don't you think I was scared, too?" He grabbed her hands. "My heart stopped. I don't know how to process something like that. And that you... you were the one—"

"To bring you back," Louise said. It was both the truth and a lie, the two woven together with heartbreaking simplicity.

Louise studied her hands in Peter's. It was the second time that week he had held her hand, such a basic act but entirely new. She wanted only to sit there in the quiet garden and hold his hand for hours. She could still hear his words in her mind, that he loved her. Impossibly, he loved her.

"Thank you," Peter said. "I know I already said it. But I should have probably said it again." He paused. "I probably should start every single conversation with that."

Louise tried to smile. "Might be a little weird."

Peter didn't return her smile. "So come back home then. If what you say is true and you're okay, then just come home."

Louise wished she could say yes, go back with him and pretend that everything was fine, go see a midnight movie and eat at their favorite restaurant in Carytown. But she still had more questions. She thought of the journal, her grandmother's plea for forgiveness, if it was meant for her mother like she suspected. She had tried so many times in the early years after they moved to force her mother and grandmother to interact, invited her grandmother to as many events as possible where her mother would be, birthdays and recitals and debate tournaments. But it never worked. Her mother was always civil, but unwilling to bend or soften. Yet, if she could find out the truth behind her grandmother's words, discover the root of their fracture, maybe she could finally mend it.

"I can't. Not yet. One more day. Just one, okay?"

He looked up at the darkening sky. "Okay, so you stay, I stay. I'll give you a ride home tomorrow, whenever you're ready. If everything really is fine, then that shouldn't be a problem, right?"

His request, and her pending reply, felt loaded. It would make things harder, to have him there. She wouldn't be able to speak openly with her grandmother, would have to find opportunities to talk to her in private. But she didn't want to hurt him again by sending him away. And a small but insistent part of her was comforted by the idea of having him there, someone on her side.

"Okay," she said. "Yes. You should stay."

Louise woke at midnight, unable to fall back sleep. She crept past Peter, snoring loudly on the couch in the living room, and made her way out into the yard. Her feet were bare and the ground was wet from dew.

The night sky was cloudless, a black curtain, and studded with stars. Louise was grateful for the full moon as she walked along the edge of the orchard toward the small guest house down the hill.

The little cottage sat near a cluster of peach trees. Her grandmother had rented it out occasionally over the years, to college students and orchard workers, but it was currently vacant.

Louise tried the door, but it was locked. It didn't matter anyway. She knew what she would find inside: the two small bedrooms and a kitchen and living room, now filled with bland department store furnishings. Her mother had brought baby Louise straight from the hospital to that guest house. She'd been only twenty-two when she got pregnant, when she was casually dating her father. Both were seniors in college and totally unprepared to have a child. Her father moved back to California to attend law school shortly before Louise was born, and though he provided financial support and visited once every summer, Louise saw him more as a distant uncle than a father.

Still, her memories of the cottage were nothing but warm and golden, and she preferred to envision it the way it had been then: the oversize leather couch in the living room, the antique floor mirror where her mother checked her reflection as she dressed in scrubs for work, the trundle daybed Louise slept on. She could see the round kitchen table, where there was always a puzzle or art project out and where they never ate, choosing the coffee table in the living room instead.

Louise sat down on the creaky wooden porch steps. One of the boards was rotted, and the exterior paint was peeling, but it still felt like home, because it was the only place where they had all been together, where her mother, grandmother, and great-grandmother had been so close it sometimes felt like they were sisters, drinking wine on the porch swing while Louise ran in circles in the grass. She was never scared, even as darkness fell and she ran down the rows of the fruit trees, the little cottage hidden by branches. She always knew the three most important people in her life were there under the lights, their heads together, talking for hours.

She looked out past the orchard, at the mountains, turned cobalt blue by the moon. Whenever she visited her grandmother and spent the night, she was always struck by how different Crozet was, how deep the quiet, how the darkness seemed more solid, vast and infinite in a way it wasn't in Richmond. She heard bird cries she never heard back home, songs she had known as a child, warblers and woodpeckers and whip-poor-wills. Her great-grandmother, Helene, used to sit with Louise and point out all the different birds as they landed at the feeder.

"Some of the old mountain people around here think that one, the whip-poor-will, is a death omen," Helene had told Louise one evening, as they sat in the yard waiting for Louise's mom to get off work. "That they arrive when it's time for a soul to depart, and carry it with them as they go."

Louise had watched the large, squat, brown bird as it pecked at the seed, feeling a shiver of dread. "Is that true?"

"No, Louise." Her great-grandmother had smiled. "They just like the night. They aren't afraid to sing in the darkness."

Louise made out the sound of footsteps. Peter walked toward her wearing the same clothes from the day before.

"Hey," Louise said as he approached. With Camille always

present, they had both acted normal the entire evening, though whenever Louise had glanced in Peter's direction he was already looking her way.

Off in the distance, a frog let out a low croak.

"Can't sleep?" Peter asked as he eased himself down onto the step beside her.

Louise shook her head.

"Me neither." Peter pointed back at the cottage. "Is this...?"

"Yep," Louise said.

Peter nudged her shoulder, and Louise felt a flutter in her stomach that she tried to ignore.

"I think it's nice." He smiled. "Better than a treehouse even."

She had told Peter about the cottage countless times. When they were eight, she said it was a tree house, set up high in the woods. Then it was a log cabin, with an outhouse for a bathroom. Over the years, the stories became less and less colorful, until finally the cottage was just a little house.

They sat in easy silence, gazing out over the orchard, which spread down the hillside and disappeared into the dark, watching as the air lit up with hundreds of glowing embers. She remembered catching fireflies with Helene and Camille, squealing with delight as she opened her hands to see them light up, impossibly bright for creatures so small.

"This place reminds me of camp," Peter said softly.

Their summer camp was in south Virginia, on a flat expanse of land alongside a river. There were no mountains or orchards, but she understood what he meant, how the sky there felt endless, the nights sweet with the smells of summer, how time was slower, more deliberate. Louise always liked camp, but Peter had loved it. He was a natural there, extroverted and funny, and when they first went in elementary school, before Peter grew a foot and joined the track team and got noticed by girls, it was his escape. It was the place where it didn't matter what grades he earned in reading or math, where he didn't have to be separated into a group for extra help, where people only knew him for his strengths. And even as he got older and made friends with the popular kids, when he didn't need camp in the same way, Louise knew it would always be his safe space.

"I can see that. Especially at night," she told him.

"Like when we all sneaked out to that abandoned cabin in the woods."

Louise couldn't help but smile. "When you *forced* me to sneak out to that abandoned cabin in the woods. I wanted to sleep!"

"It was our last summer as campers. That's practically mandatory."

"Remember the failed prank to bring the go-carts down to the lake?"

Peter leaned back against one of the porch columns and faced Louise. "God, those things were so heavy."

Louise laughed. "Not the best idea."

Peter smiled, and Louise leaned against the opposite column, her legs straight out in front of her. In the darkness of the night, it felt like just another blissful summer, the two of them up late, sleeping in a tent in Peter's yard, until one of them got scared and convinced the other to run back inside.

Peter's brow furrowed. "Aren't you going to miss it? Camp? All of it?"

Their eyes met, and Louise's breath caught in her throat. She had been so distracted by the events of the last few days—Kyle's party, the accident, the healing—that she had buried the cold, clammy fear that they wouldn't be spending the summer together, that in the fall Peter would stay behind in Richmond, and she would be living six hours away.

She nodded, an ache in her chest.

She wanted to say the words out loud, the ones that had been fighting to the surface. That he had always been what she wanted, that she saved his life out of sheer will, because there was no world for her in which he didn't exist. She almost let herself imagine the summer as it could be, full of nights like this one, under star-streaked skies, Peter beside her, not as her friend but as more.

But Peter was her family. His brothers were like her brothers, always teasing her, but in a way that made her feel included. His mom was there for her all the times her own mother couldn't be, the gingerbread decorating party in first grade, when Bobbie told Louise she would be there but either forgot or couldn't find the energy to come. Louise's eyes had stung with hot tears as she sat alone, knowing deep down she wouldn't show. But before the tears could fall, Marion swept her up in a hug, whispering in her ear, "Come sit with us, honey, we've got plenty of room."

At every point in her life when she had felt the absence of her family most acutely, the lack of a father, the chasm between her mother and grandmother, Peter and his family were there to fill the gap. It wasn't simply that Louise was scared. It was reckless, to risk losing Peter, endanger the world that had taken years to rebuild.

She realized, with a sadness that felt as vast as the night sky, that she would never be able to take the leap he wanted her to take, that this desire for safety was too ingrained in her, that it was better to minimize the ways the world could break your heart.

"I'll miss everything," she managed to say. "All of it."

ROUEN, FRANCE
1942

12

HELENE

Helene woke with a start. She blinked as sunlight peeked through the edges of the blackout curtains.

Her memories of the previous night were hazy and fragmented, the long truck ride back to Rouen, supper surrounded by a cacophony of voices, everyone talking at once. The entire hospital had transformed. Where before the long halls were heavy with a numb, tedious boredom, the entire Hôtel-Dieu had become infused with sound and movement and purpose. The landing was all anyone could talk about, different accounts of what had happened, of the arrival of the soldiers in the wards, chirps and whispers of news.

Helene had sat silently through supper, staring down at the deep red stains underneath her fingernails, resistant to all attempts to scrub them clean. Elisabeth sat beside her. Unlike some of the other girls, she hadn't pestered Helene with questions when she'd first returned that afternoon, as if she could sense Helene had neither the energy nor will to answer them.

"Matron Durand told me to let you know that you have tonight off," Elisabeth said when they'd reached the dormitory afterward.

Helene had climbed into her bed, fully dressed. "Fine," she mumbled. It felt like years had passed since news of the landing hit that morning. Whatever joy had been on her friend's face was gone now. "Sorry," Helene said. "I know you thought…"

"It doesn't matter," Elisabeth said. She hugged her arms to her chest. "I have to go get report from day shift. We've been given a temporary transfer to one of the new wards."

Helene looked up. She wasn't due to change ward assignments for another three weeks.

"They want all the staff nurses and sisters assigned to the German soldiers. Probates like us can take care of the prisoners. They're expendable, after all."

Helene knew her friend was disappointed by the failed landing, as was she, but this felt like a glimmer of good news. "At least we'll be away from the Germans?"

"Yes, of course," Elisabeth said dully. "Good night, Helene."

Helene turned onto her side and burrowed into the thin pillow. Instinctively, she reached for her mother's journal, which she kept hidden underneath the mattress. She couldn't use it in the hospital, but on the days she was most homesick, or whenever she needed comfort, she clutched it in her hands for a few moments, just to feel the solid weight of its presence. Yet, even with the journal, she couldn't close her mind to the events of the day. In the silence of the dormitory, she heard the sound of engines, the cries of wounded men, softly at first, but then building, until it was so loud she wanted to squeeze her hands to her ears to shut it out.

Breathe, Helene.

Thomas's calm, kind voice cut through the din. Helene held onto it, and the journal, like life rafts.

In the light of morning, Helene watched Elisabeth from her cot. Even in sleep, her friend was restless. Her hands twitched and mouth moved, as though she were having an argument with someone who wasn't there.

Helene knew she should try to sleep more in preparation for the night to come, but her mind revved to life like an old engine, playing the events of the previous day in an endless loop, each image sharper than the last. Before she could replay it all again, she grabbed her slippers and a clean uniform from beneath her bed and left for the washroom.

An hour later, Helene walked into the east wing. She had only ever visited this part of the hospital for supplies or to attend lectures in one of the spartan classrooms, outfitted with a few wooden benches and a chair for whichever elderly French physician had been chosen to speak to them. Now, the corridor was full of a charged, frenetic energy as nursing students and sisters streamed past, carrying stacks of linens or boxes of supplies in and out of doors. No one even glanced at Helene as she headed toward the nearest ward.

"Name, if you will, please," the guard at the door said in broken French.

"Helene. Helene Paré."

The young soldier checked his papers, then looked up and nodded. *"Eintreten."*

Nearly every inch of the ward's stone floor was occupied by a cot, one after the next stretching from wall to wall with only narrow aisles in between. Some men sat on the sides of their beds, talking and playing cards, and some struggled to test out crutches in the aisles or limped back and forth from the makeshift lavatory set up behind a curtain in the back. Others were still in their beds, covered in bandages, hands folded, eyes fixed on the cracked, peeling ceiling.

Whereas the German military ward had always felt calm and orderly, enough so that Helene spent most of her time folding linens or organizing supplies, the chaos here was overpowering. There were too many voices: English from the soldiers, French from the nurses and sisters who made their rounds, occasional loud barking from the German guards stationed at the front and rear of the ward. It all blended into one indistinguishable wall of noise.

Helene had no idea where to even begin.

Before she could ask, Matron Durand strode toward her with a large crate. "They've had nothing to eat today," she said, her face flushed underneath her white veil. She shoved the crate into Helene's arms. "Go on now."

Helene took a breath as she approached a soldier lying on a cot near one of the massive arched windows that ran the length of the ward. He was naked from the waist up, his abdomen wrapped in a large bandage.

"Hello," Helene said in English with a small smile. "You are hungry?"

The soldier propped himself up on his elbow. "Yes," he said. "Yes, please."

Helene handed him an apple and ripped off a chunk of bread from a dense loaf. He stared down at the food with an almost childlike awe before tearing hungrily into the bread.

"Thank you," he said, crumbs flying out of his mouth as he spoke. *"Merci."*

The soldier's dressing was covered with old blood. He needed a change, clean linens, soap and toothpaste, pain medicine.

"I will return," she said in her halting English. She motioned to the bandage. "When I give all the food."

The soldier smiled gratefully.

For the next hour, Helene offered what little she could. The men were appreciative, most in a state of shock as they accepted their food from her with dirty, bloodstained hands. Helene tried not to look at any of them too closely. It was strange, after what had happened in Dieppe, to be back in the role of a probate nurse. She felt as though a hundred days had passed in that one afternoon, and yet at the hospital time had stood still.

When she reached the far side of the ward, Helene's crate of meager food was nearly empty, save for a misshapen last loaf of bread and a few apples so brown and dented they were mostly mush.

"I thought maybe I made you up."

Helene's hands slipped slightly on the wooden crate as she turned.

Thomas sat up on his cot, his wounded leg propped on a pillow. He seemed even younger without his full uniform, his wavy brown hair unkempt. But his gray eyes were instantly familiar as they found hers. "But here you are."

"I didn't think you'd be here," she managed to say. "I thought you'd already have been..."

"Shipped off."

Helene nodded toward Thomas's bandaged knee. "I thought you'd be okay to leave as soon as they removed the shrapnel."

He shrugged. "So did I. But I guess it was more complicated than they anticipated. Damn thing was lodged near an artery." He glanced toward the crate she carried. "Is that food you have there, Helene?"

Helene set the crate down and picked out a small portion of bread and a tiny, dented red apple. "It's not much. I'm sorry."

Thomas smiled as he leaned forward eagerly. "I've only had water since yesterday. It's more than enough." He devoured the food in large bites, stopping only occasionally for air.

Helene looked toward the front of the ward. There was an endless amount of work to be done, and she would be scolded if she was caught talking to a soldier instead of performing her duties. "I should report back to the ward sister."

Thomas wiped his mouth. "Now why would you do that, when we just found each other again?"

Helene's cheeks flushed. She was almost sure she had imagined Thomas as well, or at least the way he'd looked at her, the way he'd made her feel. "You'll want a proper nurse. I'm not much of one."

"I don't really believe that. You saved my life yesterday, after all. I don't think I even said thank you." The lightness in his voice was gone.

Since the war had broken out, so many people had been willing to look away from brutality as long as they were safe. Even her mother and grandfather, the two people she most admired, had been shockingly complacent. Whenever Helene murmured about resistance, her mother had silenced her immediately, warning it was too dangerous. But, as terrified as she'd been on the beach, she couldn't be passive any longer in the face of so much suffering.

"What else could I have done?" she asked.

"Let him shoot me," Thomas said. "You could have just stepped aside."

"I couldn't have done that."

"Some would have." Thomas rested back on his cot and stared at the ceiling. "I know how I can thank you," he said abruptly. He sat up again, his mouth turning up into a grin. "Practice on me."

Helene blinked back at him. But he just smiled wider at her confusion.

"Sorry?"

"You said you're a terrible nurse."

"I don't think I used the word *terrible*..."

Thomas held up his hands. "Fine, maybe not in those words. But from the looks of it, you might be the best they've got."

She followed his gaze as he surveyed the room. A few cots down, Dominique, a teenager only a few weeks ahead of Helene in training, was bent over a soldier, her forehead drenched in sweat. The soldier in the bed grimaced as she fumbled to apply antiseptic to his wound.

"My bandage hasn't been changed since they operated. I don't know much about medicine, but I imagine it's not supposed to look like that."

Helene peered closer at his leg. He was right. There was blood seeping onto the fabric near his knee. "I'm not sure what we have in the way of supplies," Helene said as she checked over her shoulder. "I can try to find a clean bandage, some iodine."

"Perfect. This way you don't have to go away again." Thomas's cheeks were slightly pink. "At least not yet."

She wished more than anything she could put her hands on his wound and fix it with her touch. But his leg wound was far deeper than the simple scrapes and bruises she had mended with her mother. And in the crowded ward, with Thomas's eyes on her, there was no way to do it without revealing herself. Helene could feel the echoes of her mother's warnings in her body, the constant vigilance to not be seen for who she truly was.

Helene took a deep breath in through her nose. After Dieppe, she could no longer make excuses, or tell herself she wasn't equipped. She had survived a battlefield. "I'll go and get supplies then."

"You promise you'll come back?"

Helene nodded. "Promise."

The next day, Helene sat at the breakfast table and picked at the bland food on her plate. She had lost her appetite the moment she read her mother's letter, which arrived that morning. Helene withdrew the note from her pocket and read it again, trying to parse further clarity from her mother's vague phrasing.

Your grandfather isn't at home right now. All is fine. There is nothing to worry about. But he's been sent away for a while, for reasons that are difficult to explain in a letter. I'll write more when I can, and I'm sure he'll be back home with us soon.

Helene traced her mother's handwriting, the crisp precision of her elegant lines. *He's been sent away for a while.*

He had done something stupid. Or said something stupid. Broke curfew. Fear clutched at her chest. If she had been home, this never would have happened. Her mother was too distracted, too busy with her work. And now her grandfather was gone, in some prison or work camp.

Helene carried her plate to the bin. She knew it was useless to try to eat, and even though her shift didn't start for a few more hours, she decided to head back to the prisoner's ward. She needed a distraction from her mother's news. And if she were completely honest with herself, she also wanted to see Thomas again, to hear his voice once more before he was sent away. No one would question why she was on duty early. Since Dieppe, nurses and doctors were working twenty-four-hour shifts, scouring the hospital for what was left of dwindling food and supplies. The rigid order had dissolved, and they could use all the help they could get.

Helene was almost at the entrance to the hospital wing, when she heard her name called from behind her.

Cecelia stood near a door that led to the convent. She was dressed in a clean, pressed habit, her hair pulled back into a tight bun beneath her veil. But as she stepped forward into a beam of bright afternoon sun, Helene noticed how pale she was, her eyes lined with inky blue circles. Cecelia, like most of the other sisters, had been working nonstop in the German military ward.

"I was hoping to find you," Cecelia said. A few nurses walking down the hallway looked up as Cecelia's shoes made sharp clicks on the stone floor. "I tried your dormitory but you were gone already."

It felt strange, to see this cold, intimidating version of Cecelia again. She'd thought something fundamental had shifted between them in Dieppe. She was hopeful there might be an understanding, a truce of kinds, and Cecelia might even allow Helene to use her gift to treat the Allied soldiers on the wards, take away the pain from shrapnel wounds, ease the burns caused by explosive devices.

But Cecelia's expression was stern. "Can I speak with you a moment?"

Helene nodded.

"In private," Cecelia said as she motioned toward the door. "Follow me, please."

Helene trailed Cecelia into a small chapel within the convent that was off limits to the lay nurses. Compared to the vast, echoing Église Sainte-Madeleine, with its soaring stone arches and enormous windows, this chapel was modest and plain. Save for one lone stained glass window, the walls were made of rough, hand-carved stone. The space was tiny, but in a way that felt comforting instead of claustrophobic, as if the world had been contained to this simple room.

There were two small stone statues at the front of the chapel, of Mary and another saint Helene didn't recognize. Beside them a row of candles flickered, casting an orange glow. A few simple wooden pews lined either side of a central aisle.

"Sit," Cecelia asked, gesturing toward one of the pews.

Helene genuflected briefly at the aisle before she sat down on the wooden pew. Cecelia sat beside her, so close that the soft white fabric of her habit brushed against Helene's fingers.

"I feel I owe you an apology," Cecelia said, looking straight ahead.

Helene followed her cousin's line of sight to the candles. Did Cecelia regret her decision to bring Helene to Dieppe, or think Helene hadn't been ready for it? "What for?"

Cecelia clasped her hands. "I never should have... You see,

I lost control of myself, in Dieppe." She was completely still, like the statues at the front. "I was wrong, to ask of you what I did. To do what I did. What we did. I meant what I said when you arrived here. These…what you and I share, it is not of His making. And when I was tested, I not only failed, I failed you as well. And I am sorry, deeply sorry for that."

Helene felt the wind knocked out of her. She knew her cousin forbade healing when Helene first arrived, but she was so sure that had changed after the beach.

"We helped those men," she said. "It wasn't wrong."

Cecelia shook her head firmly. "What I did on that beach… what you did, is nothing more than blasphemy."

Helene could barely believe what she was hearing. Those men had been in so much pain, and so scared. The horror of the afternoon had felt all-consuming, and yet she could cling to the work she did, the men she comforted, the way they died in peace. After years of its absence, she was acutely aware again of the power of her gift. And Cecelia was trying to turn it into something ugly. "How could you possibly feel that way?"

"I didn't," Cecelia said quietly. "When I was your age. When I so freely sinned, following my mother's lead. But I…" She gathered herself. "I found my salvation here. They took me in, when I had nothing. This place saved me, Helene, and I owe it to the other sisters, and to my God, to abide by their laws."

Helene didn't understand what Cecelia was talking about, what she needed to be saved from, how an institution that had persecuted women just like her could be her deliverance.

But Cecelia raised a hand to silence her. "I didn't bring you here to discuss it," she said tersely. "I only wanted to apologize, for my lapse in judgment. What I said when you arrived remains the truth. These abilities are unnatural and have no place within these walls. And I forbid it. If it happens again, you will be dismissed from this hospital." She stood and moved out of the pew, pausing briefly to kneel in the aisle.

Helene rose, her heart pounding in her ears. She couldn't accept this. "I saw you out there. You helped those men." She had spotted Cecelia again and again that day, crouched beside the soldiers, her hands on their bodies. She didn't understand what had changed. "Why did you ask me to come?" Her voice wavered slightly. "You didn't have to bring me to Dieppe. There was no reason to choose me."

Cecelia lifted herself up from the floor and turned to face Helene. All of the formality was gone, and there was only a naked plea in her eyes, as though she had asked herself that same question. "I didn't choose you, Helene. I didn't chose any of this."

She held Helene's gaze for a moment before she pivoted and left. The distant thunder of church bells echoed through the convent, crashing into the silence.

Helene had spent the night in near-constant motion. Despite the transfer of a dozen soldiers to prisons in Germany during the day, the ward was still over capacity. Perhaps the chaos had become familiar after a few days, or perhaps she so desperately needed the distraction, but for the first time, she felt in control.

Elisabeth too worked with a new kind of efficiency. Even though she remained withdrawn, she seemed less tense as she tended to the British and Canadian troops. Their mere presence offered a sliver of hope, proof that beyond their occupied world, the war raged on.

When most of the men were asleep, as Elisabeth and the other probate nurses began to stock and organize supplies to prepare for the next day's shift, Helene quietly made her way to the far side of the ward to find Thomas.

"I was hoping you might come say hello." Thomas was wide-awake, his gray eyes watchful.

"I'm only making my rounds," Helene lied, careful to keep her voice low.

"Of course," he said with fake solemnity. He pushed himself up into a seated position. "Can you stay for a little while?"

Helene glanced toward the other nurses. She knew she should go assist them. Thomas followed her gaze and tilted his head thoughtfully. Then he loosened the edge of his bandage, unraveling it.

"What are you doing?" she asked, reaching out to stop him.

"You needed to redo my dressing," he said, as the unwrapped bandage fell into a pile beside his leg. "So now you can stay."

Helene crossed her arms, but she felt the tension in her chest release ever so slightly. "You shouldn't do that," she said.

"It's already done, isn't it?"

She sat down at the end of his cot and gathered up the bandage. Secretly she was pleased, grateful to have an excuse to stay with him, to live a little longer in the precious place they had created. It felt like standing in the sun when she was with him, a bright radiance even in the dark of night. "How are you feeling?"

Up close, his face was paler than it had been earlier in the night. His forehead was beaded with small drops of sweat at the hairline.

"Better now that you're here."

Helene rolled her eyes. "You don't really talk like that, do you?"

"You don't like it? I thought I was being charming." He smiled.

Helene straightened out the bandage. "Charming, maybe. Sincere, no."

"I feel okay," Thomas said, his voice less practiced. "Thanks."

"I thought maybe you'd be gone, when I got back today." She considered her next words. He had been so honest with her, about his home, his family. She wanted to be honest with him too. "I'm *glad* you're still here."

"Better than the alternative, isn't it?"

Helene shook her head. "That was a stupid thing to say."

"No," Thomas said. He looked down at his knee as Helene began to roll the bandage in slow circles. "It was a kind thing to say."

They lapsed into a comfortable silence as Helene worked. The skin around his knee was warm, almost hot. "Are you sure you're feeling okay?"

Thomas sighed. "The doctor looked at it earlier. The skin is a little red around the wound, but he put some sulfa powder on it. Said it should be better by the morning."

Helene felt a prickle of worry. She knew from shadowing her mother how quickly minor wounds could progress to sepsis. In her mind, she could see the pages of her mother's book that dealt with infection. If she were at home and had access to the ingredients, she could use dried oregano and sage to make a poultice, or brew chamomile tea. She tried to reassure herself that Thomas had been seen by a doctor, that modern medicine was just as effective as her mother's remedies, but she didn't like how pale he looked. "I should check your temperature."

Thomas waved his hand. "It's really nothing, no need to worry. Can I ask you something, though?"

Helene frowned.

"I'm fine, Helene, really. But I would like some distraction."

"Okay, but if—"

"I promise I'll ask the doctor about it, when he comes in."

"Fine, ask me your question."

"What do you want to do after all of this? If you could do anything?"

She fought to keep the skepticism from her expression, but all she could think of was her grandfather, likely in prison somewhere, of her shuttered hometown. "How do you know there'll be an after?"

"You don't really talk like that, do you?" he said kindly.

Helene wanted to be like Thomas, believe in a better future, but when she searched inside of herself, all she found was vacant space. "I didn't used to."

"What changed?"

"Everything."

Thomas shifted in the bed. "Has it been terrible here, since the war started?"

"Some of it. When it was new, especially." She began to wrap the bandage around his leg. "I remember my grandfather crying at the kitchen table the morning the Germans came to our town. I was fifteen and when I saw that, I knew with certainty that the world was ending." The thought of that same table empty, of her house without her grandfather in it, gripped Helene with such force that all the air left her lungs.

"And the rest of it?" Thomas asked.

Helene reminded herself to breathe, to concentrate on Thomas's dressing change, the correct way to weave the bandage so it would be secure but not too tight. "So much is the same," she said. "People go to work. And school. And if it's warm and sunny and the trees are in bloom, for a second, it can almost feel like before, like you don't even realize you're holding your breath."

"You'll have that back, Helene. Your before."

Helene nodded even though she didn't believe him. Whatever hope she held that there would be an end to the war had broken on the rocky beaches of Dieppe. And it had only been further fragmented when she learned her grandfather was missing. Even if a miracle happened and the Allies won, even if the occupation ended, nothing would ever be the same again.

Thomas held her gaze. "But what if you pretend for a moment. That you'll be able to do anything. Or go anywhere. Would you go back home, work with your mother?"

Helene grabbed the pin to secure his bandage. It had been years since she'd allowed herself to think of a future beyond Honfleur. When she was a little girl, she'd listen to her father's stories about places that existed across oceans, cities and deserts and mountains he described with such clarity she was sure he had seen them all, and she had wondered if she would ever see them for herself. But her world had slammed shut the day they buried him. She could never abandon her mother.

"Of course. My life is in Honfleur."

"Your life *was* there," Thomas urged. "It doesn't have to be always."

At his words, Helene felt a fragile thread of possibility unspool between them, a life that could be full, and safe, far away from the ruins of her home.

Thomas took Helene's hand, the movement effortless, as though he had done it a thousand times. "Close your eyes. Now picture what it is you really want, what you'd most like to do, what it is you want your life to look like."

Helene felt silly but did what she was told. At first she could see only the reality around her, Rouen and Honfleur, France. She had always expected she would stay there her entire life, work with her mother as a healer, marry a fisherman in town. It would be a quiet life of service, but she would find moments for herself, as she always had before the war, drawing, or bicycling out to the sea. But the war had made Honfleur claustrophobic, tainted by the German soldiers in a way she wasn't sure would ever fade. Now she felt the lure of the wider world, all the places that glimmered beyond them. She saw herself living somewhere new, across oceans, like America, a place that was expansive, with wide-open land that raced toward infinite horizons.

She saw herself as an adult. She wanted to live with the same kind of purpose as Agnes, to exist as a light for the people around her, but she wanted to be softer, more open to the world, less weighed down by duty.

"Is it beautiful?" Thomas asked. He gripped her hand tighter.

Helene nodded as more of her life played out in front of her, until she could see the same world Thomas saw, one where she could be happy, where everything could be whole again.

There was the bang of a door on the other side of the ward and Helene's eyes shot open.

"That'll be Dr. Weber for rounds," she said, reorienting herself. "I need to get back to work. And you should get some rest."

"Before you go, ask me," Thomas said, his grip on her hand still firm. "Ask me what I want to do."

"What do you want to do?" she said with a small smile. She wanted to share his optimism just a few minutes longer. "With your after."

"Go home first, for a little while. See my mother, because she worries about me. And my little sisters." He stopped, and Helene saw sadness pass through his eyes at the thought of his family. "I'll tell my father that I'm okay, that this wasn't the terrible mistake he thought it was. And then I'll say what I never could before, that I don't want to work for him, that I don't want to spend the rest of my life managing a textile factory, stuck inside every day, arguing about things that don't matter. And he'll be angry, for a while, but he'll understand, and then…and then I'll go somewhere."

"Go where?" she asked, wanting to stay in this dreamworld of possibilities.

"Everywhere. For a while." He let out a huge yawn. "Mexico. Asia. Africa even. And then I'll stop when I find somewhere by the ocean, where I can live on the coast, and it never gets cold."

Dr. Weber was making his way down the rows now. "I have to go," she whispered. As Helene released his hand, she could feel a resistance, as though there were a force holding them together. "Good night, Thomas."

Thomas leaned back on his pillow and closed his eyes. "Maybe California," he murmured. "You'll like it there too."

His features softened, and Helene sneaked away, careful not to wake him. As she left, she felt lighter, her body floating away on the strength of his hope.

CROZET, VIRGINIA
2019

13

LOUISE

Louise found her grandmother in the garden, pulling weeds in a bed at the back of the yard.

She yawned deeply as she walked along the warm brick path. Peter was still sound asleep on the couch. They had stayed out until nearly sunrise, when the sky was fringed with pink over the mountains. They had talked about a thousand little things, each topic inconsequential compared to the reality of their present. But for a few, lovely midnight hours, things between them were the way they had always been.

"Morning," Camille said as Louise approached.

"Sorry I slept in." Louise crouched down beside her grandmother. She spotted a wilted hydrangea and considered letting her hands rest on the bloom, to practice, but her grandmother's tense demeanor told her now wasn't the time.

"You needed the sleep." Camille removed her gardening gloves. She rose, acknowledged the pile of weeds, and sighed. "I garden when I'm feeling overwhelmed. Less now because it does a number on my back. But still, I find it therapeutic."

She looked pale in the light of morning. Louise was used to her grandmother working up on ladders pruning trees or hauling huge bushels in the orchard, but suddenly she seemed frail.

Camille shoved her gloves into her pocket. "It's a gorgeous day. Go up to the park. Take Peter. You can use my entry pass. Or Sugar Hollow. You remember that swimming hole up there from when you were little? It's not far from here."

The blurry memory came to the surface, a cool, clear river in the mountains, perching on smooth rocks, giggling as the water tickled her toes. Peter would like it there.

Camille smiled, but it was strained, like she was holding back. "Also, I asked your mom to come back here again. I'd like the three of us to sit down together before you leave for New York. There are things we need to talk about." She patted Louise's shoulder. "She said she could come this afternoon once she's done with some appointments. So you might as well do something fun in the meantime."

Without waiting for Louise to reply, she got up and headed back toward the house.

"I don't want to talk to Mom. Not right now." And anyway, she had Peter to drive her home later.

Camille stopped and turned to face Louise. "Will you, please? For me?"

Her voice was so raw that Louise found herself nodding.

"Great," Camille said, regaining her composure. "I'll go down to the farm stand. See if Caroline is there. She can go with you too. I'm sure she'll be thrilled to have the morning off."

Louise watched her grandmother go, as all around her the garden flowers stretched toward the June morning light.

Louise was breathing heavily as they walked the trail up to Sugar Hollow. It was unusually hot for this time of year, but the bright sun was tempered by the thick canopy above them. Every tree and fern and patch of moss was a verdant, oversaturated green, as though they were deep in a tropical rainforest instead of an ancient, fading mountain in Appalachia.

"You okay?" Peter called over his shoulder. His own breathing was easy, and it looked like he had barely broken a sweat. Though it was the first summer since middle school he wasn't training for fall track, he was still in annoyingly good shape compared to Louise, who only exercised when it was mandatory.

Louise rolled her eyes as she wiped the sweat from her brow. "I'll be fine. It's not that bad."

"That's what your grandmother said too. 'Small children do it all the time,' I think were her exact words." He smiled at her in a way that made her heart, already pounding from the incline, beat faster. "You want to quit?"

Louise wasn't going to back down from the challenge. She tried to think of what she'd say to him if this were a week ago, before every exchange felt tougher to navigate. "Of course not. I never quit."

Peter opened his mouth to reply but Louise cut him off.

"I know what you're going to say. And field hockey doesn't count."

He grinned wider and cocked his head to the side. "Horseback riding? Or pretty much every single gym class in middle school."

"Horseback riding was my mom's thing. And I stuck with that for almost a year. Also shut up," Louise said, even though in truth she was grateful for this more familiar version of Peter.

Peter fell back into step beside her as they forged up the path. Caroline was so far up the trail from them they couldn't see her anymore. She had agreed to go with them at Louise's grandmother's insistence, but she had been quiet and reserved for most of the car ride there.

"Is she okay? Caroline?" Peter asked, as though reading her thoughts.

"Not really."

"What's going on?"

"Her mom is sick. Cancer. She doesn't have much time."

"Shit," Peter said. "That's awful."

"Yeah," Louise said. She tried to choose her next words carefully. It felt dangerous to tell Peter about Sarah, to reveal some of the reason she had stayed in Crozet but not the full truth. "I actually went with my grandmother yesterday, to see her."

Louise could feel Peter studying her. "God, that was probably tough, right?"

She nodded. Peter could always read her. "It was hard," Louise admitted in a low voice.

Louise looked up the trail but still saw no sign of Caroline. "But I helped my grandmother too. And I felt like I helped Caroline's mom. And that part was actually really...amazing."

A smile crossed Peter's lips. "Of course it was. Because it's what you do."

Louise swatted a mosquito off her arm as she tried to parse Peter's words. "What I do?"

"Take care of people," he said simply, echoing her grandmother.

"What are you talking about?" Louise asked. "I don't..."

Peter put a hand on her wrist. "Don't do the false-modesty thing. I'm not saying this to start an argument, or get into any of the stuff from before. But you've always taken care of people. Your mom. Me. I mean you must have spent a solid year of your life helping me study or with homework. You help my mom in the garden and say it's for fun. You put everyone else first, always. Ever since the day I met you. It's why I..."

"What?" Louise asked, even though she knew the words that would follow, even though fear coursed through her body. She wanted to hear him say it again.

She held his gaze, each long, brown eyelash making her heart somersault along with the force of his words, the intention in his eyes. He stepped forward, until Louise could feel the electricity surging between them, her body pulled toward him even as her mind struggled against it.

"You guys okay?" Caroline called from somewhere out of sight.

Louise immediately shot back, almost stumbling over a large rock behind her. "We're fine!" she shouted.

Caroline appeared up ahead, taking a swig of water from her bottle.

"So how much farther?" Peter asked.

"Not far. Just follow me."

A few minutes later, they reached a small outcropping of rock. Beneath it, a waterfall flowed down into a large swimming hole. It was a dozen different colors at once, depending on how the light hit it, a shadowy green around the edges, a bright aquamarine in the most direct patches of sun, and almost entirely clear in the shallows, the smooth rocks beneath revealed in vivid detail.

"Wow," Louise said as she moved toward the edge.

"Worth the hike?" Caroline asked.

"Definitely," Peter said behind her.

"So how do we get down to the water?" Louise asked, turning back to face them. She gripped the straps of her backpack, tried to ignore the way her body still tingled. "Through there?" There was no clear path to the bottom, but it seemed possible to pick their way along the rocks.

Caroline set her backpack down on the ground and took off her baseball cap. "There's a path that winds around the rocks. If you'd like to go that way." She began to kick off her shoes.

"Which way are you going?" Louise asked.

"The easy way." She placed her shoes and socks in a neat pile beside her backpack.

Louise followed her line of sight to a long, thick rope tied to a tree directly to her right. "You don't mean...?"

Caroline grabbed the rope and handed it to Peter. "You want to go first?"

A struggle played out across Peter's features. She knew, because she knew Peter better than anyone, that he wanted to jump. But Louise was scared of heights, and he wouldn't leave her alone, the same way he had missed parties and dances she was too introverted and awkward to attend, sat on the bleachers in the back at school events, to be with her.

"He will," Louise said quickly, before Peter could respond. "And so will I."

Peter looked incredulous. "Seriously?"

Louise nodded despite her nerves. Her fear of heights was an endless source of amusement for Peter. He loved to tease her whenever she refused to ride the Ferris wheel at the state fair or on the class trip that spring when she was the one student not to go out onto the deck of the Empire State Building.

Caroline clutched the rope and smiled at Louise. Then she jumped, flinging herself over the edge and splashing into the water below.

Louise peered down over the outcrop and watched her rise to the surface.

For a moment, neither she nor Peter spoke. She felt the magnetic pull from earlier, like he was her center of gravity. But she held her body very still, until she knew she could resist the force, focus on what a colossal mistake it would be to allow herself to give in. She was leaving in three days.

"You really want to jump?" he asked, his voice cutting through her thoughts. "You don't have to."

Louise swallowed her nerves. There was so much she couldn't give to him, but she could give him this one last shared moment. She reached for his hand.

"Together?"

His face cracked into a smile that was so bright Louise felt its reflection on her own skin. He took her hand.

And together, they ran toward the edge.

The air was heavy as they made their way back to the parking lot, a summer storm approaching from the valley. Louise's hair and clothes were soaked, and her shoes squeaked with each step, but she felt lighter, happier than she'd been in days. They had spent nearly two hours swimming, lying in the sun, talking about music and TV shows and books.

But despite the reprieve of the afternoon, reality loomed larger with every step down the trail. She would have to face her mother and grandmother when she got back. Peter and Caroline had grown quieter too, as though they also sensed the realities of life waiting for them. She knew Peter was dreading the fall, staying home in Richmond while all his friends left for college, and Caroline was likely lost in her own, much more serious concerns, navigating the catastrophe of her mother's illness.

A rumble of thunder echoed as they arrived at a steep bend in the trail.

"Not much farther," Caroline said.

The sky was still blue above them, but Louise knew how fast storms could hurtle down from the mountains.

They increased their pace, Caroline in the front and Louise in the back.

Between them, Peter looked down at his phone. "My mom is so pissed. I told her I'd be back by now."

"Sorry, I didn't realize how long this trail is," Louise said as she stumbled slightly over one of the many loose rocks in that stretch. She was about to warn Peter to watch his step when one of his legs rolled to the left and he fell hard onto the ground.

Louise reached him first and knelt beside him.

"You've got to be kidding me," Peter muttered, grabbing his ankle as he pushed himself up to a seated position. "This is a joke. Freaking car accident two days ago and now this? You're bad luck, you know that?" he said, humor in his eyes despite the pain.

"Can you put weight on it?" Caroline asked as the wind picked up out of nowhere, gusting through the tree canopy, swirling leaves through the air.

Peter gritted his teeth and tried to move his ankle. "I think I tore something."

Louise placed her hand on his ankle, and before she realized what she was doing, it was too late. She felt the heat immediately as her skin made contact with his skin, her nerve endings buzzing.

"I don't..." Peter fell silent as more thunder rumbled above them. His eyes traveled from her face to her hand on his ankle.

There was a quiet so distinct that Louise felt it curl around her body, as though the three of them were inside a little pocket of stillness.

She drew away quickly, fingering the strap of her backpack. "We should get back to the car. Before the storm starts. We'll help you, Peter." She stood and hugged her arms to her body.

Slowly, Peter got to his feet. He stepped cautiously at first, then put his full weight on the injured ankle. "I don't think I need help. It doesn't hurt anymore. Not even a little."

"Great," Louise said, her chest tightening, avoiding their eyes.

She took off down the trail, the wind howling violently after her. With one more enormous clap of thunder, the sky cracked open and the forest turned gray with rain.

Rain pounded the windshield. By the time they arrived at Caroline's house the driveway was a river of red clay mud.

"Thanks for...for the afternoon," Caroline said from the back seat. She got out and hurried toward her house.

"The storm should be over soon," Louise said to Peter, hoping to break the tension, so that they could both ignore what had happened on the trail. "The sky is brightening up. Should be fine for your drive home."

Peter only nodded.

Louise wanted nothing more than to spend the next two days

with him in Richmond. And yet she might have ruined any chance at normalcy by being so reckless.

When they passed the farm stand a few minutes later, he turned abruptly into the empty parking lot. The rain had finally stopped.

"I thought you were going to drop me at the house."

Peter put the car in Park and shook his wet curly hair out of his eyes. "What happened out there, Louise?"

Louise felt suddenly claustrophobic, trapped inside the tight space with only Peter and the sound of the car AC. "What do you mean?"

"Please don't act like you don't know what I'm talking about."

"I'm not... I didn't..." Louise searched her mind for excuses, for explanations. She closed her eyes as drops of water ran down her face from her hair. "I can't do this right now."

He shifted in his seat. "Why did you really come to Crozet? Is it because of the accident...because of what you did...how you..."

"I did CPR," Louise said.

"That's not all you did, and we both know it." Peter looked down at his ankle. "I felt it, earlier. Whatever that was."

Her body trembled. "Please, Peter. I want to tell you. I want to tell you everything. But it's complicated...and..."

"You're lying to me," Peter insisted, "about the trail. And about the accident."

Louise shook her head, as though she could force him to take back his questions. She could sense it all unraveling, and she was desperate to put everything back in its place.

"I'm not," she said feebly. "I have no idea what you're talking about. I'm not lying."

"What really happened after the accident, Louise? Why am I alive? Why didn't I have a scratch on me? Why did you leave immediately after, go to your grandma's when your mom hates her? None of this makes any sense, but I was just going to let it go..."

but then after what just happened..." Peter rested his hands on the steering wheel. "Tell me something honest. Something *real*."

She felt like the air around her was constricting her lungs. "I don't... I can't..."

"You can't, or you won't?"

"Please, Peter. Let's just go home. Do all the things we planned. I'm leaving, and...it's... Can we just go back to normal?"

"No," Peter said sadly. "We can't."

Louise reached for her seat belt. She couldn't be in the car with him a second longer.

She took off into the orchard, weaving in and out of the rows of trees so that even if he followed he wouldn't be able to find her. Her feet sloshed in the puddles, spraying her legs with red mud.

At some point, she started to run. She ran to the edge of the orchard and then down the hill that sloped toward the creek. It was only where the grass gave way to the rocky pebble banks, where she knew she was out of sight from the parking lot, that she allowed herself to stop moving.

She bent forward, heart pounding, and watched as the water, flush from the rain, rushed over the rocks. Beyond, the gentle, cloud-shrouded mountain rose in a sleepy incline toward a sky streaked with pink and orange.

It took Louise several moments to process the large black shape on the other side of the creek. It was a bear the size of a boulder, nearly obscured by the tall grass and wildflowers as it lay crumpled in a heap.

She waded into the creek, her mind racing. It must be a different bear, a coincidence. She gasped as the icy mountain water filled her shoes, and she stumbled across the slippery rocks, until she reached the edge of the creek a few feet across, where the grass grew up to her knees.

She sank down on the opposite bank, the bear only inches away. There was no fear this time. The bear was motionless, its eyes vacant. It was the same bear. She knew with a conviction she didn't understand, a dread that sunk into her skin.

Peter's face flashed into her mind. The heat in her hands, the same heat that had brought that bear back to life. Only now that heat was gone as she touched the bear's matted fur.

Louise leaned back onto the wet grass, a phrase echoing back at her across the years. Her great-grandmother, Helene, at the orchard shortly before her death, one of the last times Louise saw her.

Normally, Helene was playful with Louise, in a way she never was with anyone else. She was always ready to offer her a treat or little trinket from a basket she kept for her visits. But that day, her eyes were full of sorrow in a way Louise had never witnessed. Camille told Louise that Helene thought she was back in Rouen, during the war. She kept repeating the same three words in French, over and over, eventually reverting to English. She said the words to Louise, as though willing her to understand them, until Camille took Louise's hand and said it was time to go. They were words without meaning for Louise, until now.

It won't endure.

HONFLEUR, FRANCE
1942

14

HELENE

Helene's mind drifted as she sat through five-o'clock mass in the soaring Église Sainte-Madeleine on the western side of the Hôtel-Dieu. It was obligatory for the nursing students to attend at least one mass a week, and even though Helene would much rather be sleeping, or on the ward with Thomas, she knew she would get reprimanded if she didn't attend.

She let her hand trail over the wooden pew, barely hearing as the priest gave the blessing. All she could think of was Thomas, of the gentleness of his eyes, the firm, certain way he held her hand. It wasn't until the other congregants rose to their feet with a flurry of movement that Helene even realized the mass was over.

She genuflected next to the pew, because she knew the sisters would be watching, and then hurried down the center aisle. The space above her was so cavernous it almost felt like being outside, with wide stone arches and massive columns that stretched seemingly infinitely toward the sky. She passed the wall of flickering candles and exited through the gargantuan wooden door that led out onto the courtyard.

Before her eyes could adjust to the sharp afternoon sun, Elisabeth appeared on the steps in front of her, her face anxious.

Helene stopped abruptly. Elisabeth had no reason to be there. She had attended mass the previous day and was not one to ever voluntarily step foot in the church on her own. "What's wrong?"

Elisabeth climbed the rest of the steps to Helene. "I was trying to sleep, but some of the girls who worked this morning came into the dormitory." She went silent as several civilians filed past them out of the church. She waited until they were gone before she continued. "It's Thomas, Helene."

Helene's stomach jolted. She had seen Thomas just that morning, and he had been in good spirits.

"He came down with a fever," Elisabeth said, her voice low as more people exited. "Right after shift change. The wound was infected. Dr. Weber took him to the operating theater, to clean it out." Elisabeth hesitated. "I thought you should know. I know you've been spending some time with him. I saw you talking the last two nights."

Helene gripped Elisabeth's wrist. "Elisabeth, tell me what happened."

"They were saying he must have already been septic. And… and he started clotting. He threw a clot in his lungs. There was nothing anyone could do."

Helene's body went cold, despite the hot sun.

"His heart stopped, Helene. He didn't make it."

The green grass of the courtyard and blue sky suddenly felt all wrong, nightmarish. The light around her seemed to change, draining all of the color from the day. "Where is he?" she asked calmly.

"Where—"

"Where is he?" Helene repeated, her voice so loud Elisabeth flinched. "Is he still warm?"

"I think you're in shock."

Helene stumbled down one step. "Is he still in the operating theater?"

"I'm not sure. I don't... I don't know."

Helene's legs were leaden, but she pushed herself forward.

"Where are you going?" Elisabeth asked carefully.

Helene ignored her and shuffled down the stairs to the courtyard. She heard Elisabeth's footsteps hurrying to keep up with her on the gravel pathway.

"I'm so sorry, Helene. Please, why don't we go somewhere quiet, somewhere we can talk."

"Don't follow me," Helene snapped. She knew she was being unkind, but she also couldn't have Elisabeth interfere. She ignored everyone and everything in her path as she walked quickly across the courtyard, back past the guard she had seen on her way to church, and into the hospital wing. She concentrated only on the sound of her breathing, on the thud of her heartbeat in her ears as she strode down the first-floor hallway to the operating wing.

The hallway outside the operating theater was empty. It was past the scheduled cases of the day, and no one was inside except for a lone French custodian mopping at the other end. He looked up as Helene entered. He had white hair and a stooped back, likely drawn out of retirement when all the younger men went off to war. He nodded at Helene, then went back to his work.

She opened each door along the hallway, but one after another was vacant. Finally, she reached the last operating theater. Thomas had to be in here.

The walls were covered in square tiles, and there were no windows, only massive circular lights that hung from the ceiling. There was a large sink near the door, and a huge glass-front supply cabinet on the opposite wall.

And in the center of it all, a long table, the form of a body draped beneath a thin white sheet.

Helene felt panic rip through her body. Heat shot down her arms as she pulled the sheet back.

He appeared almost the same as he had earlier that morning in the ward, as though he were only sleeping. His eyes were closed, his lips slightly parted. His skin was pale, but not yet bloodless.

As she reached toward his chest, she could almost sense the last, lingering reverberations of life in his heart.

"You're still there," Helene whispered.

The memory flashed again in her mind, from when she was nine years old. The feral alley cat, its blank, vacant stare, how she had pressed into it until crackles of energy exploded in her hands like fireworks, the way it sprang up from the ground at her touch, nuzzling itself into her palms. And her mother's voice in her ears.

"That's not what we do," Agnes had told Helene as she gripped her so tightly it hurt. "That's not the game we played with roses. That poor creature had died. It was at peace. But you brought it back like it was just a toy. You have to promise me. Never do that again."

But as Helene looked at Thomas's face, at one more thing that had been taken from her, the only beautiful thing left in her life, his vision of the future, her mother's warnings faded away. Maybe just this once. Just this boy.

Helene placed her hands on Thomas's chest. She closed her eyes and waited, but she felt only a few faint traces of electricity, like the last rumbles of a storm.

"Please," Helene heard herself say. "Please."

Then she felt it rush into her, an anger so consuming that it devoured everything, the war that had stolen everything from them, the German soldiers like Vogel who regarded them as kindling, the leaders in her country who let it happen. Herself. For not being able to save her father. For all those years when her gift was dormant, trapped inside of her.

Every second of shame and guilt swirled into her body like a storm.

As Helene exhaled, she felt she would break from the weight of her emotions, and a surge of energy ripped through her body. Her arms shook but she steadied them on Thomas's chest, heat rushing outward down the nerve endings in her arms.

Thomas was there. He was so close she could hear his voice, see his gray eyes on her, as though she mattered to him, more than anyone.

"Please."

Helene's fingers jumped as she sensed a movement so faint she was sure she'd imagined it. She held her breath, and the heat of her palms suddenly receded. A faint but incontrovertible heartbeat pulsed.

The door behind her swung open just as Thomas's chest heaved with a first, perfect breath. Helene didn't turn to see who was there. She didn't care. The only thing that existed in the world was the breath in Thomas's lungs, the contractions of his heart, the proof that he was whole again.

"No, Helene."

Cecelia's voice was sharp as it carried across the operating theater. Helene remained where she was, her hands still on Thomas's chest, as though her touch were the only thing keeping him there.

Footsteps came to a stop directly behind her.

"I found him like this," she said quickly, groping for an explanation. "I only wanted to say goodbye, but when I pulled back the sheet his skin was still warm. I felt a pulse, a weak one, but it's there."

"I'll be taking him now, to the morgue," Cecelia said loudly.

Helene turned to her in shock. Thomas was alive; she had brought him back. There was no need for the morgue.

Cecelia bent her head down until her face was only inches from Helene's, and squeezed her arm. "There is a guard outside," she whispered. "Do not say another word—do you understand me?"

Helene nodded and Cecelia released her.

Cecelia positioned the sheet back over Thomas, whose breathing was shallow but persistent, his eyes still shut.

"I'll be taking him now," she repeated. "Down to the morgue."

"I'll go with you," Helene said. She needed to be there when he woke up, to explain, to reassure him it was going to be okay. "I can help."

Cecelia calmly circled the stretcher to unlock each of the four brakes on the wheels. When she finished, she leaned in toward Helene again. "No, no, you won't," she said. "You'll go back to your dormitory, say nothing to anyone. Pack your belongings. I'll arrange for someone to take you to the train station this evening."

Down the hallway they heard the distant sound of the guard's boots. Helene couldn't believe Cecelia would send her away for saving a man's life. She didn't want to leave, not yet, not before she had a chance to talk to Thomas one more time, to tell him he was going to be okay, that the future would be beautiful. She lifted her chin. "You can't just dismiss me. I didn't do anything wrong."

"There are consequences to your actions," Cecelia hissed. "And you would know that if you had listened to me, if you weren't such a selfish child."

"I was trying to help him."

"No, Helene, you did this for yourself."

Thomas stirred slightly under the sheet. Helene took a step forward involuntarily.

"Goodbye, Helene," Cecelia said, her voice returned to a normal volume.

Just then, the guard peered inside. "Why are you lingering in here?" he asked, surveying them.

"The doctor has requested his body," Cecelia said. "Is there some reason I need to delay the doctor's request?"

"No, Sister," the soldier said after a brief hesitation. "Go on." And with that he turned on his heel and left.

Cecelia followed, wheeling Thomas out of the room, leaving Helene alone in the empty operating theater.

Helene hurried home from the Honfleur train station at nightfall. As she glanced around the once-familiar surroundings, she couldn't shake the feeling that her hometown was a shell of its former self, languishing in the heat.

At her house, Helene slipped through the back door. The cool darkness felt like a relief as she headed up the stairs from the boarded-up shop. Her home was much as she'd left it. The long tables were bare, the register dust covered.

Elisabeth had been in the dormitory when Helene went to pack her things, her eyes wide with shock as Helene told her Cecelia was sending her home.

"Why?" she had asked repeatedly. "You can't just leave. We need you. I need you."

"I'm sorry," Helene told her. And she meant it. As happy as she was to have brought Thomas back, she regretted that it meant leaving Elisabeth there alone. But she couldn't explain why she was leaving. It wasn't safe. If anything, her time in Rouen had reinforced every warning her mother gave her, that at their core, humans could be barbaric. Elisabeth would never betray her, but if she knew about healing, about Helene's abilities, it might put her in danger by association.

And so Helene left Rouen in an anxious haze. Thomas was alive, but she might not ever see him again. Even if she wrote and begged for answers, she knew Cecelia would likely never tell her where he was taken, if she even knew herself.

Despite her mother's letter from earlier that week, a part of her was convinced her grandfather would be at the house. She could almost hear him in the dining room above her, the scratch of his chair against the wood floors, the clink of silverware as he tucked into whatever meager ration he had procured for the day, yet smiling widely as he lied through his teeth and complimented her mother on the meal. Helene had never known the house without him in it, had never spent a day at home without breathing in the smell of his cologne or feeling the bristle of his white beard as he kissed her hello.

But when she opened the door that led to the kitchen, the silence that greeted her was total. He was gone; he had been gone long enough for the house to settle into his absence.

In the kitchen, the stove was dark, the table and counters empty. "Maman," Helene called as she set her suitcase on the floor. "Maman, are you here?"

She walked into the dining room. There was no sign of her mother through the sliding door to the parlor. Helene tried to ignore the fear rising in her throat. For a horrible moment, she imagined black leather boots marching up the stairs, her mother pulled from her bed in the middle of night, pushed along, a pistol at her back.

"Maman," she called again, her voice louder as she trailed her hands along the smooth surface of the mahogany dining table.

It felt impossible that there had ever existed brightness there, but there *had* been good times, the vibration of a dozen voices and the clatter of silverware, the heavy pours of wine, Helene's uncles and father by the piano with glasses of Calvados, her father still tall and broad shouldered. Her grandmother, before her heart failed, serving fish and heaping plates of buttered potatoes, soft golden loaves of bread warm from the oven. Her grandfather in his chair by the radio, a book open on his lap. And Agnes, quiet but reluctantly at home in the loud, affectionate family she had been informally adopted into, far from the solitude and harsh beauty of the mountains where she was raised.

At the window, the last rays of sun were softening into shadows. Helene often wondered why Agnes didn't leave, once her father's drinking took over his life, when he spent his days at the local brasserie instead of at work, or even after his death. She could have taken Helene back to the mountains, to her home and family, to the sisters she so deeply loved and missed. Agnes had insisted that her responsibilities as a healer outweighed her personal desires, that her life was defined by her calling, and she was needed in Honfleur, and now, as she pulled the blackout curtains closed, fastening the stiff fabric tightly, Helene felt a wave of sadness for her mother.

She looked around the unchanged parlor, the tattered fabric of the couches, the worn leather of her grandfather's armchair by the fireplace, and thought of Thomas's promises of the future. Maybe Helene's life could be different. She could walk away from all of it. She had done her part, helped all those men in Dieppe, saved Thomas. Maybe that was enough. Maybe her life didn't need to be defined by sickness and death. She could find Thomas, somehow, beg Cecelia to tell her where he was, create a life with him away from the war.

Upstairs in her room, the floor creaked as Helene made her way to the bed. She lay back, the springs groaning, and fingered the soft patchwork quilt, the loose threads and patches of fabric she knew by heart. She closed her eyes and tried to ignore the hot, sluggish silence around her. Her mother must be with a patient. She would be home soon.

As Helene reached up to adjust the pillow, her palm brushed against a small package tucked underneath. She twisted her body and sat up, pulling out a rectangular envelope. Had her mother or grandfather left her something? She lifted the flap and withdrew a stack of papers. The cream-colored paper was thick, much more formal than any stationary her mother might have kept for personal correspondence.

Helene's hands shook as she unfolded one of the papers. It was stamped in several places, with phrases like "Republique Française" and "Prefecture de Police" emblazoned in red and blue ink. There was a photo of a pretty young woman with wavy brown hair in the top lefthand corner, and a blue thumbprint in the bottom left. It was an identity card issued by the Vichy government after the occupation. Helene knew it well, because she never went anywhere without hers.

The second identity card contained a photo of a middle-aged man with receding hair and thoughtful eyes.

A door opened and closed downstairs, followed by footsteps. Helene vaguely knew her mother would notice her suitcase at the door, heard her name called, but she couldn't look away from the man on the third card. His name was listed as Henri Dubois. He was six feet tall with brown hair and brown eyes. He worked as a pharmacist. Something in his soft eyes and dimpled chin reminded her of her father.

"Helene."

Agnes's voice held a mix of alarm and confusion as she entered the room, the scent of lavender and hand soap and rubbing alcohol carrying through the air. "Helene."

Even in the dark, she could see how much thinner her mother had grown in the last few months. Her hard features were even more pronounced, the bones of her cheeks and jaw rigid little crests. There were new strands of gray in her hair, and her posture was stooped, her shoulders slumped.

She moved quickly across the room, and before Helene could explain herself, her mother wrapped her arms around her, fiercely, squeezing her tight. For a moment, Helene simply let herself be held.

"Why are you here?" Agnes asked when she finally released her. Her eyes were wide and full of worry. "Why aren't you in Rouen?"

Helene was torn between desperate, childish relief at seeing her mother again and shock over the stack of identity cards. She had as many questions for her mother as she knew she did for her. "What are you doing with these?" She held up the cards.

Agnes placed her canvas bag on the ground with a small thud. "I've been on my feet since before dawn. A birth on the outskirts of town. Can we go downstairs where it's cooler, please? You look thin. Let me fix us something to eat."

Helene clutched the envelope tightly as she followed her mother out of the bedroom and down the stairs. In the kitchen, Agnes peered inside a cupboard for a long time, as though hoping something better might appear. She sighed and took out a small tin of canned sardines. "I wasn't able to do the shopping today." She reached for the end of a bread loaf from a bowl on the counter. "There's not much, I'm afraid."

With her grandfather gone, and with the constant demands of her mother's work, Helene wondered how her mother could possibly get on. She felt a stab of guilt, for not coming home as soon as she learned about her grandfather, for not insisting.

"It's fine. You don't have to…"

Agnes set down two plates and motioned for Helene to sit. "I don't have to feed my daughter?"

Helene shook her head as she sat at the table. "You weren't expecting me."

"No, no, I wasn't." Agnes tore the little bit of stale bread into two chunks, placing one on each of their plates. "You weren't supposed to see any of that. If I had known you'd be here—" she used the bread to scoop up some of the sardines "—I would have found somewhere else for it. Although I suppose it's too late now to worry about such things."

Helene put the identity cards on the table in front of her. "So, you help forge papers for people?"

"No, I only help move them. It's easy for me, to move more freely, because of my work. It doesn't arouse much suspicion, or at least it didn't used to."

Helene's heart rate quickened as the silence of the house grew more ominous. She had heard stories of people who had been shot for less than the presence of those papers in their home.

She understood, then, why her grandfather was gone, the truth her mother's letter had been so carefully concealing. "Was Grandpapa a part of this? Was he caught?"

"Not this." Agnes stared down at the blue veins that ran along the backs of her hands. "He was helping move things too, but in a different way, and someone he worked with was careless. That's all it takes, Helene."

Helene knew how hard it was for her grandfather to bite back his resentment, to act with any kind of deference for the Germans. She should have known his complacency was concealing something more. In retrospect, it was surprising for him *not* to try to fight back, to resist in whatever way he could. But it was harder for Helene to believe that her mother, who had spent a lifetime hiding her gift, who never took a chance that might expose their abilities, could be involved in something so risky. She realized, with an ache in her chest, that perhaps she didn't know her mother at all.

"Do you know where Grandpapa is? Is he going to be okay?"

Agnes shook her head. "I don't know. It's impossible to get any real information right now. They searched the house, after they arrested him. But they didn't find anything. We've been careful."

"I found these," Helene said as she raised the papers.

Agnes nodded. "I know. They shouldn't be here. But I can't risk taking them outside. Not now. Not when there's a chance they may be watching me more closely."

"How long have you been doing this?" Helene recalled the weeks before she left for Rouen, whispered conversations between Agnes and her grandfather, furtive looks, nights her mother was gone far longer than would seem necessary. She had been so caught up in her own worries, which now seemed so insignificant, that she had missed all of it.

Agnes seemed to weigh how honest to be. "About a year. Small things, at first. And then more as time went on. Until I knew it was far too dangerous to continue with you here."

Helene had been so angry at her mother for sending her away, when all that time her mother and grandfather had been risking their lives.

"Cecelia sent me home." Helene knew she needed to say it quickly, before she lost her nerve. "She never wanted me there, Maman. I wanted to write to you, but…she told me, right after I got there, that what I can do, what you can do…" Agnes sat up straighter in her chair. "She called it blasphemy, a sin."

"So, you did it anyway then?" Helene nodded. "I'll write to her," Agnes said. "She'll let you return. She has to."

"She won't let me back, Maman," Helene said quietly. "Not after what I did. Not after I brought him back."

Muffled voices drifted up from the alley beneath the kitchen window. Agnes was very still. There was no anger in her eyes, only dismay. "Who?" she asked.

The words lodged in Helene's throat.

"We promised to be honest with each other, didn't we?" Agnes asked.

The events of the last few days clawed at her insides: Thomas—she had no idea where he was—the men who died beneath her hands, Vogel's pistol. Her mother was the only person who would truly understand.

"There was a Canadian," Helene said finally. "In Dieppe. He was a soldier who was injured in the raid. His name was Thomas.

"I helped him. I saved his life. He was going to be okay. Everything was fine." Helene's chest tightened at the memory. "But then it wasn't. For no reason at all. His heart stopped in the operating theater. And he was my age, Maman. He was just a boy. And he had parents and sisters, and a home."

"Helene…"

Helene knew if she didn't finish, if she didn't tell her mother everything now, she never would. She would lose the courage. "He died. For no reason at all. And I couldn't... I couldn't do nothing. I couldn't survive doing nothing."

Agnes closed her eyes.

"I saved his life. I brought him back. I know you always said I shouldn't, that it was wrong. And I couldn't with Papa. But I had to try. And it was different this time. I healed him."

"You didn't heal him, Helene." Agnes sighed.

"I did. You weren't there. You didn't see it. But I did." Helene heard the note of impatience in her tone, but she couldn't help it. She couldn't stand the way her mother was looking at her. It was the same way Cecelia had looked at her, as if she had made some awful mistake when all she had done was save a life.

"No," Agnes said. "You kept him here. For a little while. But, Helene." She seemed to steel herself. "It won't endure. He won't live, not for more than a few days, maybe weeks."

Helene was stunned into silence. It couldn't be true.

"I told you. Time and again. We can't stop death," she said softly. "And we shouldn't. The greatest healing we are capable of is in death, to let a person die with peace, with dignity."

Helene blinked back tears and tried to compose herself. "So, Thomas will..."

Agnes's eyes were full of compassion. "You gave him a little time. A few days, or maybe even weeks. It varies, but my mother always told me that it would endure for at least the length of a single moon phase, but never longer than a full lunar cycle. Any time you gave him is borrowed."

Helene's shoulders shook. A distant part of her admitted she barely knew Thomas, that even if he lived, she would probably never see him again. It shouldn't hurt so deeply. But Thomas's life, his continued existence, felt like the one bright point in a world that had been collapsing into darkness. It felt like her own future was woven into his, that his belief was enough to expand her own life.

"Isn't there any way?" Helene asked when she found her voice again. "For him to stay."

Agnes looked at Helene with a mixture of grief and apprehension. She reached out and rested her hand on her cheek. "We are speaking as adults now?"

Helene nodded, her heart racing at the change in her mother's tone.

"My mother explained it to me this way. That there has to be balance. It's why it won't endure, why it can't hold." Agnes seemed to brace herself. "Unless we restore it."

Helene searched her mother's face. "Restore what?"

"*L'équilibre.* The only way to give your friend more time would be to take it from someone else."

Helene searched her mother's face. For a moment, she forgot about Thomas. All she could think of was her father, the emptiness of the house without him, the missing place in her life for all those years.

"But Papa..." she asked, terrified to even give the question a voice.

Agnes shook her head. "He was too sick, Helene. This boy you mentioned, he died suddenly. But your father." She swallowed. "Your father's life eroded over time. There wasn't enough of him left. And even if I could have... I wouldn't. Not this way."

Helene wiped away her tears. "But there is a way then. If I can trade his life for someone else's." Her mind raced, a tiny spark of hope lighting its way through the darkness. She stood and started pacing. "One of your patients. Or...or at the hospital. There are wards full of people already half-dead. Sick and in pain."

"That won't work." Agnes sighed. "A life in full bloom can't be replaced by one that is already withered. That's not balance. It would have to be someone with time, someone still whole. That's why it can't happen, Helene, why it doesn't even matter. They would resist you. A life such as this cannot be so easily taken. It is entirely different from helping someone die who is already at the end of their life, someone who is suffering."

But Helene's mind was moving again, settling on the carnage in Dieppe, on Vogel's cruel, ratlike face.

"I know where your thoughts are," Agnes said. "The German soldiers at your hospital. The people who arrested your grandfather. Who imprisoned your uncles."

Helene stood at the window overlooking the dark alley. She couldn't face her mother, couldn't bear the judgment in her eyes.

"There's something I've never told you," her mother said slowly. "Something you need to know. Your uncle Matthieu, my youngest brother, died of a fever, when he was little."

Helene turned, confused. "Matthieu is alive, Maman. He's in a prison in Germany."

Agnes raised her hand. "I was ten. And he was three, with the most beautiful smile, and he loved animals, followed my father around for hours in the mud just so he could say hello to the goats and pigs." Her eyes glistened. "He got sick and his heart stopped while he was in my mother's arms. I was right there beside her. But she couldn't let him go. How could she? So she brought him back. And because it was a sudden, quick death she was able to do so. There was enough of him still there."

Helene sat back down at the table. She had never seen her mother so emotional. She was always the solid one, the rock of their family and town. Helene sometimes thought her mother didn't experience emotions the same way as the rest of the world. Only now, she understood she had simply learned how to tuck it all away.

"There was a man, in our village, who lived alone, and was unkind to people. And he…he died, mysteriously, in his sleep, only a few days after my mother brought Matthieu back."

"Did she…?"

"She never told me. But Matthieu lived, when he shouldn't have. My sisters and I suspected why."

Helene put her hand on her mother's. She knew how hard it was for her to talk about her family, how deeply she missed them, especially her four older sisters, with whom she could share the burden and gift of healing. "So that's a blessing then. Isn't it? Your brother lived, as he should have. He was only a child."

Agnes smiled sadly. "It was a blessing. For a time. My mother wouldn't let Matthieu out of her sight. She was so grateful to have him. But over the years, she changed. Slowly at first, little ways she wasn't herself. But it began to carve her out, after a while. She never said anything, but she lost weight, stopped sleeping, stopped working as a healer. When we were all old enough, when she knew we would be okay without her, she took her own life. I was the one to find her."

Helene bit her lip, her eyes burning, until she knew her words would come out steady. "You never told me…"

"No, of course not. Why would I? I wanted her to have peace, at last, to be remembered for all she was and not how her life ended. But you need to know now, with the choice ahead of you."

Helene's vision blurred, but in her mind she focused on Thomas's kind face, her conviction building despite her mother's warnings. What her grandmother had done was different. She took the life of an ordinary man.

Vogel and the men like him were evil.

Helene glanced around the small kitchen, where she had sat beside her mother so many times, clung to her skirt as she made oils and tinctures at the table, squealed with delight as Agnes held shrunken flowers in her hands until they burst back to life in explosions of red and pink and blue. She could feel the room start to shift, fade at the edges as though it were already a memory instead of a real, solid place.

"I brought it back for you," Helene said, searching for words that would anchor her in that moment. "The journal. It's in my suitcase. It's of no use to me there. I'll leave it with you before I go."

Agnes shook her head. "I gave it to you for a reason. Not to borrow, but to keep. Because it's yours. It's been yours since the day you were born. I was only holding it until you were ready."

Helene couldn't comprehend her mother's statement, not in the context of Rouen, of an institution that would so vehemently condemn every word in that book. "But Cecelia… I told you she doesn't approve."

Agnes held up a finger to her lips. "You'll find ways to help people, times that are safe, when the world isn't looking. And you'll learn who you really are, who I have always known you to be."

Helene stood and walked over to her mother's side, wrapping her arm around her shoulders. They leaned their heads together in the darkness.

CROZET, VIRGINIA
2019

15

LOUISE

Louise's wet, muddy legs trembled as she entered the kitchen from the back porch. "Grandma?"

She crossed the space just as her grandmother walked in from the living room. "Oh," she said, her expression changing from surprise to confusion. "You're soaking wet."

"It was raining." The words felt distant in Louise's ears.

Camille made a soft ticking noise. "And covered in mud. Why don't you go up and take a hot shower and get on some dry clothes while I make dinner? Your mom will be here soon. And then we can all chat." She took out a cutting board from one of the cabinets.

Louise couldn't imagine going upstairs to shower, or eating dinner, or doing anything remotely normal.

Camille began to slice a tomato into thick, ruby-red pieces. But when she glanced over at Louise, her knife stopped midair. "What's wrong?"

Louise's throat tightened. "Peter."

Camille set the knife down. "Did he head out?"

"He's not going to be okay, is he?" Louise heard the question come out with a sob.

Camille froze. "How did you…?"

"There was a bear. Yesterday in the orchard. It was hurt."

Camille searched Louise's face. "I don't understand."

"I healed it," Louise said, the words tumbling out. "But it still died." She braced herself. "Is that going to happen to Peter?"

It hurt just to voice the question, as though simply saying the words held the awful power to make them true.

Camille looked down. When she looked back up, her eyes glistened. "No," she said.

Louise wanted so desperately to believe her, but she had already been lied to enough.

Camille leaned across the island. "You have to trust me."

Louise shook her head. "You said you were waiting for Mom, to tell me. Why wait, if he's going to be okay?"

Camille put her hands on Louise's shoulders. "I was. I am. But it's not what you think."

"If you bring someone back, the way I brought Peter back, is it permanent? Does it last?" *It won't endure.* Louise took a deep shuddering breath. "Grandma, if you don't tell me the truth now I will never forgive you. I'm not a child. I don't need Mom here. You have to tell me."

Camille released Louise's shoulders. "No, honey, what you did, on its own, is not… It's not permanent, it won't endure… but, Louise, you have to understand something—"

"How much time?" Louise asked, cutting her grandmother off. All she could think of was Peter, the earnest look in his eyes when he told her he maybe loved her, the hurt in his features in the car, when she had run away from him, from the truth. Soon he could be gone, any second. "How much time?" she repeated.

"I don't know," Camille said, wringing her hands. "I never did what you did. I was taught it was a violation."

The word *violation* landed on Louise with the force of a blow.

"I wanted to," Camille choked out. "Of course there were times. In nursing school especially. Young people…"

"How much time?" Louise demanded a third time. She didn't want to hear her grandmother's stories, listen to her try to relate to Louise. It was irrelevant. All that mattered right now was Peter.

"It's not exact," Camille answered. "My mother said it had to do with the moon cycles. Usually at least a few days. Sometimes longer. For Peter, he's otherwise healthy. But, please, there's something I can do… I can't explain it to you without Bobbie. It's not fair to her, or you."

She had to get back to Peter, to find him before he died. She had to tell him he was right, about everything, that she had been lying when she didn't say it back, that she loved him too.

"Louise, it wasn't supposed to go like this. There are other factors here. Things you have to understand. Peter is going to be okay. I promise. Just give me more time to explain it. Wait until your mom can get here."

Louise grabbed the key to her grandmother's truck and walked out onto the porch, ignoring her grandmother's pleas to come back. She slammed the truck door shut, shoved the key in the ignition, and with a roar of the engine and slosh of mud, she drove off.

As she flew down the driveway, the sky overhead was almost violent with explosions of crimson and purple. The mountains beneath were a dark, glinting gray. The land felt suddenly menacing, all hard edges where before there was softness.

She hit the brakes hard at the farm stand. Peter's car was still there. He hadn't left.

She barely saw the road in front of her, her eyes blurred from tears, but she managed to park on the side of the road and sprint toward Peter's car, mud kicking up from where her feet hit the road.

Peter was out of the car before she could reach it. She threw herself against him as he wrapped his arms around her.

"You didn't leave," she choked out. She clung to his body, the solidity of it. She couldn't believe that he would be gone again, in days, or hours even. It was impossible.

"I couldn't. I just sat there. I'm such an idiot. I should never have said any of that."

Louise's chest heaved with a sob. How could she tell him? How could she ever explain what was about to happen?

"Louise..." Car lights swept over them, and he shielded his eyes from the harsh glare of high beams.

"That must be my mom," Louise said. She felt an illogical relief, like her mother could fix all of it.

But as she squinted into the bright headlights, a man lumbered out of the car and toward them. At first she didn't recognize him, still adjusting to the light. But when he was a few feet away, she saw it was Jake Henley.

"You know why I'm here," Jake said without preamble, his eyes bloodshot.

Every muscle in her body went rigid. She thought of Caroline's face on the trail after she healed Peter's knee, and she knew instantly that she must have told him. Of course, she'd told him. "I don't..."

Peter's eyes moved back and forth between them. "Sorry, who are you?"

"You must be the kid from the trail," Jake mumbled, tripping slightly as he took a step. "Caroline told me what happened. How one minute you couldn't even move your ankle. And the next you were completely fine. Strange, isn't it?"

Peter stepped forward, placing his body between her and Jake.

"I don't know what you're talking about, Mr. Henley," Louise pleaded. She couldn't tell him he was wrong, that she couldn't save Sarah. She couldn't let Peter hear those words, that she was a healer, that a life brought back from death or near death couldn't endure. She couldn't bear for him to find out that way, in a parking lot with a stranger.

Jake held her eyes. And she saw it reflected back at her, the truth about her healing abilities, about her family. "I thought it was crazy too, at first, that Caroline was making it up. But why would she lie about something like that?" He stared past Louise, up toward the orchard. "And then I thought about the stories. About your family. I always thought the people who claimed there was some kind of magic were just old country people with nothing better to do, rambling about your great-grandmother, this French healer…"

Peter looked at Louise, comprehension dawning.

"Sarah always says that nothing makes her feel better than when Camille is there," Jake continued. "That it's the only time she's not in pain. And why, you know? Why would she be any different than the other nurses?"

"We have to go." Louise's mouth was so dry she wasn't sure she even spoke the words. She knew what was coming, what he was going to ask of her. But she couldn't save Sarah. The same way she couldn't save Peter.

"I'm sorry," Jake slurred. "I don't want any trouble. This won't take more than a few minutes. But I have to insist. You need to come with me first."

"I can't," Louise said. "Please know that I can't. I can't do anything." Time was ticking away. She needed to be alone with Peter.

Peter made a noise of protest as Jake went around him and grabbed her arm. She was suddenly aware of how tall he was, his body towering over her, drowning out the sky.

"Let go of her."

"I'm not going to hurt her. I just need her to come with me for a few minutes." Jake loosened his grip. "She's my daughter's friend. I just need her to see my wife. To…to help her." His arm shook slightly as he let go of Louise and he backed away.

Louise glanced toward the house. "My grandmother. She can help. Please. Ask her instead."

Jake shook his head. "She won't. She told me I shouldn't bother getting Sarah seen at Duke like I've been trying. Told me I need to accept this all."

Louise kept her eyes on the front porch, as though willing her grandmother to appear, to guide her, the way she had at Sarah's house.

"She's in so much pain," Jake continued. "Please. Can you at least try?"

Louise looked into his eyes, two bottomless wells of grief. She nodded, before she could stop herself.

"You don't need to go anywhere with him," Peter said into her ear.

"I know." It all raged like a wildfire inside of her, Jake's desperation, her own clawing panic over Peter. She had no idea how to fix any of it. But she could at least give Sarah some shred of peace. It was the only thing in the world she knew with any certainty. "But it's okay. I want to go."

"Then I'm coming with you." He stood taller as he addressed Jake. "I'm coming with her."

"Fine," Jake grunted. "We can take my car."

When they reached his truck, Jake opened the back door and they climbed in.

"What is happening?" Peter muttered but grew quiet when Louise clutched his hand.

At the Henleys' house, Caroline stood on the porch, her face pale. "What did…?" She trailed off as she looked from Louise to Jake to Peter. "Oh," she said. "I'm sorry." A small, little sob escaped her body. "I had to tell him."

"It's okay," Louise said as she held her old friend's eyes. "I understand."

"Let's go inside," Jake said from behind them. "The sooner we do this the sooner you can both go home." There was an apologetic note in his voice as he steered her into the house.

Sarah was sleeping in the bed, her forehead sweaty and eyelids fluttering as Louise approached. Her breaths were irregular, her bony chest rising and falling in labored waves.

"Hi, Sarah," Louise said softly. She placed her hands on Sarah's chest as the slow, familiar heat built inside of her skin. And then she closed her eyes.

The room was silent. Peter stood only inches behind her, hovering protectively.

"Is that...? Is she...?" Jake's voice broke.

Louise kept her hands on Sarah as energy rushed into all the sick places. She pressed deeper into Sarah's skin, and the heat intensified. But Sarah didn't stir or wake.

"Is she better?" Caroline's words cut through the room. She stood beside Jake, her eyes hopeful as she peered down at her mother.

"I made her pain go away." She needed Caroline to hear, to understand. "I can't do more."

Caroline shook her head. "I saw you. I saw you do it." She pointed at Peter. "You fixed him."

Peter's eyes were wide, and she saw the question there, the one he had been asking her for days, what really happened after the accident.

For a moment, they were the only two people in the room, the only two people in the universe. Through her grief, Louise felt gratitude that she had brought him back. She knew now it was selfish, that it ultimately changed nothing for Peter, but at least she had a little more time with him in this world.

She wished she could give that to Jake and Caroline. But even as she eased her pain, she had felt an opposing force, pulling Sarah away.

"I can't," Louise said quietly.

"Mom?" Caroline said quietly as she moved forward.

Sarah's eyes opened, unfocused at first, then blinked into awareness as she looked from Caroline to Louise and Peter and then finally to Jake. "Oh, honey," she said hoarsely. "She shouldn't be here. She can't help me."

At Sarah's words, Jake released an animal-like sound, and he crouched down and put his head in his hands.

"It's okay, Louise," Sarah said as she watched Jake. Her face seemed to drain of color. She placed one hand on top of Louise's. "You can let go, honey."

Louise didn't move. She tried to hold steady.

Sarah's expression was filled with so much love and pain that it was hard to know where one ended and the other began. "It's time for Louise to go home now, Jake."

Jake lifted his head. "She can't. Not yet. I didn't tell you why she's here."

"I know enough," Sarah said. "You think I never heard stories about her great-grandmother? Everyone in town used to talk about Ms. Helene. The beautiful French woman whose orchard never had a bad season, even in drought years, who took care of everyone in town, who some people even called a healer." A cough wracked her body, and Louise's touch sunk deeper until it was gone. Sarah smiled as she turned to Louise. "I knew the second you came back here that you were just like her, just like your grandmother. How could you not be?"

Louise released a ragged breath. It didn't matter that she was like them. She didn't want to just take away Sarah's suffering. She wanted to fix her, and Peter. But she couldn't.

"Can you change it, honey? Make the cancer go away for good?"

Louise could tell Sarah already knew the answer, that she was only asking so her husband and daughter could hear.

Louise shook her head and removed her hands. She felt Peter's arms come around her.

Sarah addressed Peter. "Will you please take Louise back to her grandmother's house? Go on, honey."

Louise's hands continued to pulse with soft little waves of heat. She didn't want to leave Sarah in so much pain.

Sarah reached out to Caroline, who climbed into the bed beside her. "We're okay." She kissed Caroline's forehead. "We're going to be just fine. And I know your grandmother is just down the street, if I need her."

Louise let Peter lead her out of the room, but she stopped in the hallway at the sound of Jake's voice.

"I'm sorry…" he said.

Louise felt no anger, only sadness. She nodded once, the only response she could muster, then followed Peter out into the summer night.

ROUEN, FRANCE
1942

16

HELENE

Helene walked with purpose down the dormitory hallway of the Hôtel-Dieu. None of the fresh-faced guards stationed at the gates outside had questioned her explanation for her return from Honfleur. To them, she was simply another indistinguishable French girl, and so with a perfunctory glance at her identification papers they had waved her inside.

It was mercifully empty at midafternoon, with the sisters and nurses either off on the wards or sleeping, and yet Helene couldn't help but peer over her shoulder as she strode the dimly lit space. She couldn't afford any delays. She didn't have much time.

She tried to focus only on what was directly in front of her. She couldn't dwell on the look on her mother's face as the train pulled away, the way she held her with a tightness that felt so much like a permanent goodbye. She pushed away the forged identity cards hidden beneath her pillow, waiting like an unexploded bomb at the center of her life, and the question of what would be left if it ever detonated.

She crept inside her dormitory. The room was quiet, most of the cots vacant except the dozen or so belonging to the probates and nursing students assigned to night duty. Helene slipped off her shoes until she was only in stockings, her skin sticky from the day's heat. Her bed was already bare, stripped of its linens, the trunk with her uniform open beside it, the contents removed.

Helene carefully set down her suitcase and padded over to Elisabeth's bed, where her friend slept curled in a ball. She knelt beside her trunk. Elisabeth was taller, but Helene could still easily wear her friend's uniform. She undid the clasps, pausing at the click, but Elisabeth didn't stir.

Helene held her breath as the trunk creaked open, and felt for one of the neatly starched and folded squares of gray fabric.

"What are you doing?"

Helene dropped the uniform at the sound of Elisabeth's voice, thick with sleep. She was sitting up in bed, her mouth creased into a frown as her eyes traveled from Helene to the open trunk.

"What are you doing back here?" Elisabeth asked in a hushed voice as she glanced around at the other sleeping girls. There were indentations on her face from where her skin had pressed into the pillow.

Helene looked over at the windows, where the afternoon sun was sinking lower over the city. Every second of passing time represented one less second at her disposal. "I need to borrow one of your uniforms. I'll explain everything later, I promise."

"Thomas's body went missing," Elisabeth said, dropping her voice even lower. "Right before you left. Vanished from the morgue with no explanation. They came and searched the entire hospital for him." Elisabeth watched Helene closely. "But you know that already, don't you?"

Helene tried to keep her composure. "I don't know what you're talking about."

There was an edge of hurt in Elisabeth's expression. "Why are you lying to me?"

Excuses formed in Helene's mind. But she didn't want to hide her true self from the first real friend she'd ever had. Maybe her mother was wrong, that not every part of the world was dangerous to healers, that there were places and people who were safe harbors.

"What if I told you he was dead? Thomas. And that I brought him back." She waited for a reaction from Elisabeth, but her friend's features remained neutral. "You wouldn't believe me, would you?"

The heavy breathing of the girls sleeping was the only sound in the room.

"Is that why Cecelia took you to Dieppe?" Elisabeth asked. There was uncertainty, but not the total disbelief Helene had expected. "I wondered why she'd choose you of all people."

Helene nodded. "Because she's my cousin. This ability is in her blood too. It was different, in Dieppe. I didn't save their lives. I only... I helped them die, with some peace. But I brought Thomas back. And that's why Cecelia sent me away. She thinks it's wrong, evil."

Elisabeth stared at her pensively, then broke into a wry smile. "That's the least of the evil in this world. Cecelia of all people should know that. But I still don't understand why you came back. Why not just stay home? That's what you've always wanted, to go back, isn't it?"

"Because it's not... He won't keep living, Thomas. I gave him time, but it's borrowed. He'll still die. Unless..."

The hinges of the cot creaked as Elisabeth leaned forward. "Unless what?"

"Unless I take that time from someone else." Helene couldn't bring herself to look at Elisabeth, to see the horror or revulsion.

Elisabeth slid off the bed and onto the floor beside her. "You mean you have to kill someone? For him to live."

Helene flinched at the casual way Elisabeth had said it. She seemed calm, curious.

"I know it's awful. I know what you must think of me."

Elisabeth didn't speak for a long time. Finally, she faced Helene.

"My name isn't Elisabeth," she said softly. "My name is Irene. Your cousin knows that. And Mother Elise. A few of the other sisters. They're why I'm here. Why I'm Elisabeth Laurent from Calais. And not Irene Berkowicz from Caen." She clenched her hands together.

Helene remembered the yellow stars worn by some of the families in Honfleur, Jewish families, the shops with signs in their windows, the foreign neighbors who had vanished over the last year, their French families left with nothing but vague explanations about deportations.

"Last summer my father got a letter in the mail, a green ticket, for a..." Irene's lip curled. "They called it a status review. He wasn't a citizen, but my mother is. She was born here. So even though we had heard stories, he thought—we thought it was just a formality. We thought he would come home. He died from the flu, a few months later, or that's what they told us." Her eyes glazed over. "In June, my mother was the one to get the letter."

Horror washed over her. As awful as the occupation had been for her family, she couldn't fathom the experience of Irene's family. Helene's mother and grandfather chose to put themselves at risk, but Irene was at risk simply for being herself.

"She knew she didn't have much time. There was a priest in our town who knew about the sisters, who knew they had been able to help people like me... I couldn't tell you. I'm sorry."

Helene's chest ached for her friend, and she pulled her into her arms. "You have no reason to be sorry, *Irene*," she whispered into her ear.

"I only told you that so that you would know it's okay," Irene said as they drew apart.

"What is?"

"What you have to do. My father was a watchmaker. He was

kind. He followed every rule, because he thought people were better than they are. Even when they wanted him to turn himself in to the police station, he went believing the best. He kissed me, and my mother, when he left the house that morning, and he told us he'd be back soon."

The more Irene spoke, the more Helene's purpose for being there took hold.

"They don't think we're real people," Irene said, loud enough that Helene had to check around to make sure no one awoke. "They've taken everything. And they won't stop. They'll keep taking until there's nothing left of any of us. Vogel is in the medical ward. Pneumonia. He was admitted last night with a fever."

Helene's pulse quickened. She hadn't fully formulated her plan when she left Honfleur. She had to get to the German ward, find Cecelia after, convince her to disclose where Thomas had been taken, but she hadn't thought of exactly how to go unnoticed.

"The guards will stop me. I'm not assigned."

"Then be someone else." Irene extended her uniform to Helene. "Anne is assigned to that ward. Since the landing, no one pays much attention to shift times, so you can go now." Helene followed Irene's gaze to where Anne slept soundly. "She'll be asleep for at least a few more hours. She won't even know."

"What about the other sisters? The other nurses? They'll know Cecelia sent me home."

"Tell them she asked you back. They won't question it until it's too late."

After supper, as the shadows lengthened on the walls of the convent and the chimes of Église Sainte-Madeleine rang out to signal nine o'clock, Helene left the refuge of the lavatory. As Elisabeth instructed, she emerged as someone else entirely, no longer Helene Paré but Anne Corbin.

When she entered the medical ward, Marie, the ward sister, approached her immediately, arms laden with a tray of pill cups.

"What are you doing here?" she asked. She was one of the older sisters there, white haired and wrinkled, but she was softspoken, often singing as she worked the gardens on her days off. "Where is Anne?"

Helene lifted her chin and tried to maintain her composure. "Anne is sick. Sister Cecelia told me to cover her assignment."

Marie pursed her lips. "Sister Cecelia said nothing to me about this."

"It only just happened." Her heart raced as the eyes of the men and the other nurses on the ward seemed to turn their way. "Anne came down with a fever this morning."

Marie shifted the tray as a female voice called out. "Sister, I need your help."

Another cry for help rang out, a doctor this time. "We're full tonight. There's a fever going around. Help where you can. I'll speak with Sister Cecelia in the morning."

Moments later, Aimee, a middle-aged lay nurse, thrusted a tray of thermometers at Helene. "Are you here to help or not? Start at the back. Work your way forward. Record each one on their chart."

Helene nodded absently and reached for the metal tray.

Take something from them.

Helene clung to Irene's words like a guidepost as she moved among the rows, stopping to examine the patient in each bed, a blur of strange, unfamiliar faces, men brought in from other parts of France to fight during the failed landing. Many of them were asleep, their skin flushed with fevers.

She found Vogel at the back of the ward, in a quiet corner with no other patients immediately nearby. He sat partially upright, his eyes trained on the ceiling, a book propped open against his chest. With a small movement of his head, he caught her eyes.

He seemed unsurprised to see her, as if he had been waiting for her, as if he knew all along that their paths would cross again. And she felt it too, that it had always been inevitable, that whatever had started between them on the rocky beach of Dieppe, as Helene pleaded for Thomas's life, was unfinished. There always had to be a conclusion. But as Helene stood there, she understood that, for the first time in weeks, for the first time in years, her fate was not in the hands of a man in a uniform.

This time, she was in control.

Vogel covered his mouth as he let out several deep, barking coughs. When it stopped, he leaned back against the pillow, his eyes glassy.

"You went home," he said in a congested voice as she approached his bed. "I watched you go, yesterday, from my post."

Helene tried to steady herself as she set the tray of thermometers on a small table by Vogel's bed. "I came back."

Vogel cocked his head, his small eyes watchful, the muscles in his jaw taut. But he only nodded. His features were as sharp and unpleasant as ever, but he looked different out of uniform, as though it had never really fit him.

"I heard the boy died," he said. "The one from the beach."

Helene balled her hands into fists but released them before Vogel could notice. She picked up one of the thermometers. "He did," she said carefully, shaking the thermometer back and forth to distribute the mercury.

"I also heard his body went missing," he said quietly, emphasizing each word.

Helene placed the thermometer under Vogel's tongue. His eyes probed hers, but she refused to look away.

"How strange." She let the image of Thomas's survival, the hope for his future life, glow inside of her like a flame.

"Yes, a strange accident, I suppose," Vogel said once Helene had removed the thermometer. "Unfortunate for his family, who may never get his body. Maybe it would have been for the best then, if you hadn't stopped me on the beach."

"Yes, sir," Helene said, a calm washing over her. She didn't have to be afraid of him, and that knowledge expanded inside of her, until she could feel her power over him in every cell. "Maybe it would have been."

Vogel opened his mouth to speak again but coughed instead, grimacing with the movement. "You don't have to be polite to me, you know. You can say how you really feel."

Helene set the thermometer back down and picked up the chart attached to the end of his bed. "We both know that's not true," she said as she recorded the numbers into a little black box.

When she glanced back up at Vogel, he was smiling. "See, that wasn't so hard, was it? I think that's the first honest thing you've ever said to me."

His face contorted again, his body wracked with another coughing fit. In one swift motion, before she could change her mind, she knelt by his bed and put her hands on his chest. She closed her eyes so that she didn't have to look at him, so that she could focus only on what Agnes had taught her, a tide receding, a pull instead of a push. She felt his heart beneath her hands, heard his breaths change instantly, from rough and labored to smooth and peaceful.

In that fraction of time, Helene could see the future unfold exactly as it should, Vogel cold and lifeless as he always should have been, Thomas alive, his gray eyes holding hers. There would be an after for both of them, and nothing in the before would matter, not the guns or the soldiers or the bodies on the beach. All that was taken would be restored. Irene's mother and her grandfather and uncles, a million souls returned intact. All that was broken could be healed. And Helene knew it, for one gorgeous moment, she knew a world that was better.

Her arms began to shake uncontrollably, great currents of electricity running through them. She opened her eyes as Vogel's mouth widened, hungrily searching for oxygen. She could feel the shape of his life, the basic elements of his existence, the weight of his soul. His memories, one after the other, raced through her consciousness. For one endless, shuddering breath, Helene held that extraordinary force, and the power to erase it.

Helene saw a fear in his eyes that felt like victory, like she was taking back all that was theirs, but suddenly, she could sense an opposing tide fight against her. He wasn't like the boys on the beach, who weren't going to make it and surrendered to the peace she gave them. He was sick with pneumonia, but he was otherwise healthy, and he began to fight. She knew this act was necessary, but the pain in her own body was becoming nearly unbearable. She had to bite her lip to keep herself from crying out, and she pleaded with herself to not let go, to not fail.

"Helene!"

At first she was sure the voice was in her head. It sounded like her mother.

But then she felt a hand on her shoulder.

"Helene!" The voice was in her ear now, a harsh whisper.

"No," Helene managed to say. "Please."

But even as she heard herself beg, the tide in her hands rushed back out to an invisible sea. She felt Vogel's heart accelerate, the rhythm frantic and urgent.

Thomas's face flashed in her mind. Irene's voice when she talked about her family. She shook the hand off her shoulder. She had to try again.

"Come with me now, Helene," Cecelia said firmly. "It's over."

"What did you do?" Vogel asked, his chest heaving as he looked up at Cecelia. "What did she do?"

Helene reached her hands back toward his chest, but when Cecelia pulled her back again, she had no energy left to resist.

"She's not well. I'll take her off the wards now."

"Tell me, what you were doing...what that...that was?"

"You're feverish, sir," Cecelia said to Vogel. "I'll make sure to send a nurse over."

Vogel pushed himself up in bed. "Send her away from here. She's not to set foot in this hospital again. Or I'll have her arrested. That's an order, Sister."

Cecelia narrowed her eyes, then leaned over Vogel's bed until her mouth was only inches from his ear. "You are only alive right now by God's will and my grace. And if you try to tell your superiors, no one will believe you. They will see you as weak, and poisoned in the mind. So, you will say nothing of this."

Vogel's jaw twitched at this challenge to his authority.

"And you will not harm her," Cecelia continued, any trace of subservience gone. "Or you will wonder, every time you go to sleep, for as long as you're inside these walls, if you will see the morning."

Cecelia straightened as Vogel's face became pale.

"Good night."

Cecelia guided Helene out of the ward. "Don't say a word."

Helene let her cousin lead her down the long hospital hallways until they reached the empty chapel. "I have to go back there," she said immediately. If Cecelia hadn't stopped her, it would have worked.

Cecelia placed her body directly in front of the chapel door. "No," she said. She held her head high, in a way that echoed her posture in Dieppe, when she had stood in front of Vogel's gun to save Thomas.

Helene had to make her understand. "Thomas will die. If I don't…if I can't finish what I started back there, what you stopped."

Cecelia didn't move. "I know."

"You have to let me go back there, Cecelia."

"I can't do that."

Helene tried to push past her cousin but she grasped her by the shoulders, towering over her. "It's over."

Panic clawed inside her. She couldn't let Thomas die. Not when she had been so close. "But I can save him."

Helene struggled against Cecelia's grasp, but she was surprisingly strong.

"You'd let a man like that live, instead of someone who is good and kind? You'd choose a Nazi over Thomas? Are you that much of a coward?"

Helene struggled harder. She wanted to scream until her throat was raw. She was furious at Cecelia for stopping her, but even more furious at herself for her failure.

Cecelia released Helene's shoulders and caught her wrists. She placed Helene's hands on her own chest. "If you have to take a life, take mine. I won't fight you, Helene. My soul won't resist. It will be easy."

Despite her calm demeanor, Cecelia's heart fluttered like a hummingbird.

"Go on," Cecelia said, pressing Helene's hands tighter to her chest. "Save him. Take my life. I'm giving it to you."

Helene felt horror rise in her throat. "You would really give your life for Vogel's?"

"Not for his life. No. For yours."

Helene's arms shook as Cecelia released her hands. She moved them quickly away from Cecelia's chest, from her rapidly beating heart.

"I can't do that."

"But you could take his life so easily?"

"I wanted to. I tried."

Cecelia's eyes shone with a compassion Helene knew she didn't deserve. She felt the fight leave her body and collapsed into the nearest pew.

"I know what you're feeling," Cecelia said as she sat across the narrow aisle.

"How could you?" Helene asked, her voice hollow as Cecelia folded her arms on the bench in front of her.

"I did what you did. Once. I brought someone back. I brought so many of them back." She fingered the rosary around her neck. "When I was your age, even a little younger. Working as a nurse in a field hospital in Belgium. I was sixteen. They sent me to Étaples, a field hospital called St. John's. I had been there only a few weeks when the battle of the Somme began."

Cecelia stopped for so long Helene wasn't sure if she would continue.

"There were so many of them," she said with a deep breath. "Thousands of them. They never stopped arriving. And so many of them were… There was nothing we could do for them. I couldn't even… I couldn't even help them, because there were so many other men who needed us, the ones who might actually survive it, and so they were alone, usually, when they died, calling out for us, or for their mothers, or home.

"I helped who I could. I prayed for it to end. I believed it would end. But they kept coming. Boys, most of them. Not much older than me. By winter everyone was sick, even the other nurses. I would go days without sleeping, or eating, because there weren't enough of us, and there wasn't enough time."

Cecelia cleared her throat. "And then, one morning, when there was snow on the ground, we received a transport of men from the front. I just couldn't watch any more of them die. And so, I brought them back. One after the next. I didn't care if it wasn't permanent. I mended tissue and bone, repaired organs and arteries. I felt such a fire inside of me, all those months of fear and grief the fuel." She paused. "I always wondered. Where they were. When they did die. Sent back to the front most likely. Cold and muddy and afraid, bombs exploding over their heads, alone. You see, I didn't do what I did to help those men, Helene. I didn't even know them. I did it because I was afraid to watch more people die. I did it for myself."

Helene didn't want to absorb the truth of Cecelia's words, but she couldn't help think of Thomas, of how much she had done for him had been selfish. What if he had been at peace, and she'd wrenched him back to a world set afire?

"Is that why you think this is wrong? Because of what you did in the last war?"

Cecelia exhaled deeply. "I was so lost in shock after that war. I didn't know who I was, or what to believe. But I knew my mother was waiting for me, that she would find a way to help me understand, as she always had." She hesitated. "I had written to her, about what happened. My...my father found the letters." Her features hardened.

"He claimed to be a religious man," Cecelia said in a low voice, her eyes distant, as though remembering what had happened all those years ago. "He was also a controlling one. My mother was terrified he would find out about the healing. She would never speak of it unless he was out of the house. He wouldn't let her work, help people in town. After they married, he forbade her from even using herbs at home. I suppose he had loved her once. But all I ever saw was his cruelty toward her. And he was furious, and horrified, when he found out what I had done."

Louise thought of her own father, his kindness. He had never known about healing, but he was such a gentle soul, always ready to dance with Louise balancing on his toes, or twirl her in the air. She knew he would have accepted her.

"He disowned me. Told me I wasn't welcome in his house. Told my mother he would kill her if she tried to help me. And I was completely alone."

"Why didn't you come back to Cordon?"

Cecelia fingered her rosary again. "I was penniless. And even if I could have found a way back there, I also... My father was right. That there was something evil in me. I wanted to be forgiven, because I couldn't forgive myself, for bringing all those boys back from the comfort of eternity only to die again in the mud. I needed... I needed absolution. And this place—" she motioned around the chapel "—offered that to me. They took me in, gave me shelter, and a purpose."

"They know about healing?"

Cecelia shook her head. "Only the mother superior who was here at the time. I confessed to her, and was ready to confess to the priests, seek absolution for my sins. But she told me not to." She smiled weakly. "She was so full of grace, and compassion. She told me I was a child of God, and that I could live a righteous life. But she also wanted to keep me safe, and she knew enough of the world, and the men in it, to know that a confession could be dangerous. She told me God knew my confession. And that was enough."

Helene felt like she was seeing her cousin for the first time, not the strict, unyielding force, but the terrified girl, cast out of her family, desperate to find a new home.

"I'm sorry," she said. "I'm sorry that happened to you. But your father was wrong. You have to know that now."

"Perhaps," Cecelia said into the quiet. "After Dieppe. After I helped so many boys die with peace, it's harder to accept that it's not of His making. Honestly, Helene, I'm certain of so little these days. But I am certain that life is sacred. But so is death. As nurses, we protect both, hold both within us. To betray one is to betray the other. We help a soul live, if it's their time to live, and we help a soul die, if it's their time to die."

Her cousin's words echoed her mother's, but Helene had never seen death as sacred. She had only ever seen it as an enemy. She was still the same scared little girl she was all those years ago. Resistant to her mother's teachings that there could be beauty at the end of a life. It was why Agnes brought Helene with her to all of those quiet houses, showed her how to bathe a body, place flowers on their chest, close their eyes so it would appear like they were simply sleeping. "It's not the end you think it is," she always told Helene. "There's peace here. They're safe. Their pain is gone. And the living are the ones who carry it now. As healers, we must carry it, Helene. Always."

She had been so sure, after Dieppe, that she was now the healer her mother was. But when it came time for her to face the death of someone she cared for, once again she hadn't been able to accept it.

Helene looked up at Cecelia. "Do you know where he is?"

Outside the chapel, the hospital was still caught in the swirl of activity from the aftermath of battle, footsteps and voices sounding deep in the night.

"Yes," Cecelia said as she turned to face Helene head on.

"You helped get him out." Agnes's face flashed in her mind, all that she had risked, so much danger that was yet to come. "It's not the first time you've done something like that."

Cecelia didn't answer, but Helene saw the confirmation in her eyes.

"Can I...would I be able to see him?"

Cecelia pursed her lips. "Would it change anything?"

Helene shook her head. She knew that she couldn't save Thomas's life, and in so many ways, it would be simpler to never see him again, not to have to say goodbye.

"Then why? If I take you to him, you will be putting yourself at enormous risk."

Helene held Cecelia's stare as resolve settled into her chest. She thought of her mother and grandfather, who'd chosen resistance, Cecelia and the nuns who risked their lives to hide Irene. And Thomas, who fought for the world even when it would have been so easy to stay safe an ocean away. So much of her own life had been about hiding behind her mother. But it had always been an illusion that she could hide. Even Thomas's dream for her had never been a real choice. For Helene, for the women like her, she would always carry the weight of duty, the infinite, fragile beauty of humanity. All she could do now was move forward, the way she had on the beach in Dieppe, find ways to be useful, even in the darkest night, and trust that the sun would rise again.

"I'd like to help," she said, careful to keep her voice steady. "I want to fight back in whatever way I can, like you."

"What would your mother say, if she knew you were risking your life?"

Helene followed Cecelia's gaze to the stained glass above, the beatific smile on the face of the Virgin Mary, and felt an unexpected swell of grief. The time in her life where her mother could keep her safe, act as a bulwark between Helene and the true horrors of the world, was over. She would never be that girl again.

"I think she'd say she was proud of me."

Cecelia studied Helene's face and nodded slightly. "Tonight," she said. "Once a week the sisters provide alms to the sick and elderly, the homebound people in the countryside. Or at least that's what the German guards think. You'll come with me, to assist." Cecelia stood. "There will be more like him, Helene, more people you will want to save. More monsters inside these walls. And far more outside. I can't lock you away. Or be your warden. So I need to know. Is it over? Will you respect the rules as long as you are under our care? Because if you can't, I won't allow you to stay."

Helene knew that to follow Cecelia's request, she would have to live with the hatred she felt toward Vogel, and the other men like him. She knew how hard it would continue to be, for however long the war lasted, to live and work alongside them.

"I can't respect someone like Vogel."

"Of course not. You think I have respect for these men? When I know the evil in their souls, the destruction they have caused?"

"Then why...?"

"I respect life, Helene. *All* life. I don't treat human souls like numbers to be added and subtracted. Violence does not solve violence. Vengeance is not justice."

Helene thought of Irene, about all she had endured, the fact that she was only alive because she was pretending to be someone else. Cecelia made it sound so simple. But it wasn't.

"I can't respect all life, not theirs."

Cecelia clasped her hands. "Because you're human. As am I. Which is why I put my faith in God. I follow God's will, and mercy, even if I find it near impossible at times to understand. Can you trust in God, Helene?"

Helene hadn't believed in God since she was a little girl, when her mother used to take her to church on Sundays, before her father died, before the war and occupation, before the world revealed itself, again and again, to be a ruthless place. God felt like a fairy tale, a tattered, lost remnant of childhood. Helene shook her head.

Cecelia stepped across the aisle. "Then trust in me. The sisters who would risk their lives to keep you safe. The nurses you work beside. These are just walls. Stone and brick and mortar. None of that is God. God is these women. So if you can't believe in God, believe in them. Stay here, for them. And for the people who need you."

CROZET, VIRGINIA
2019

17

LOUISE

The house shone with light as Peter and Louise walked up the creaky porch steps. Louise found it difficult to even put one foot in front of the other, to keep moving toward what she knew was ahead. She had barely spoken to Peter on the short ride back from the Henleys'. She didn't know what to say, or how to say it, how to possibly explain to him that he was living on borrowed time.

But she had to tell him; he deserved to know, to have the chance to say goodbye to his family, to use his remaining time in the way he wanted. She tried to picture how it would happen. She would find somewhere peaceful, the guest cottage, maybe, or the bench in the garden, near the magnolia tree. She would hold his hand and put aside her own grief, be there for him.

Before they could get to the door Camille came out of the house, hair askew and face full of worry. "I found your car at the market. Both of your cars. I didn't know where you'd gone."

"Is Mom here yet?" Louise asked. Sarah was dying, and she couldn't save Peter. It was all over. She needed her mother there, more than ever. She had always told herself she was her mother's tether, that she kept her anchored to the world. But now she felt as though *she* would lose her grip if her mother wasn't there beside her.

"She got held up with appointments. But I called her as soon as you left. She's on her way."

Louise stumbled past Camille into the house, Peter following close behind.

"Where were you?" Camille asked.

Louise collapsed onto the old, worn couch in the living room. "The Henleys'. Jake came to get me. He wanted me to heal her."

Camille looked from Louise to Peter.

"He knows," Louise said. Camille sat down heavily in the armchair across from her. "He knows I brought him back."

Camille folded her hands on her lap. Louise could see her try to compose herself, gain some handle on what was happening.

As Peter joined Louise on the couch, Camille's expression formed a question only Louise knew was there, whether Peter knew *everything*. Louise shook her head no.

"Good," Camille finally said. She addressed Peter. "Can you give us all a little time, to discuss things as a family? You're exhausted and it's been a long day. I'll pack you up some food and you can take it down to the guest cottage. It's a little dusty but there are clean linens, and soap in the shower. It'll be hot in there but the window unit still works fine."

Peter nodded blankly.

Even through the haze of her own exhaustion, Louise knew how overwhelmed he must feel, after learning about her abilities, how she'd used them to save his life. She didn't want to be away from him. Time was moving horrendously fast. She could feel it slipping through her grasp with each passing second.

"Grandma, I don't..."

"Louise, we need to talk. Me, you, your mother. Just us. I promise you'll be able to explain everything to Peter. But first..."

Louise was surprised when her grandmother's voice caught. "But first just us, just family, okay?"

Peter's eyes met Louise's, searching for confirmation that everything would be okay, that life would right itself. But she didn't know how to give it to him. She didn't have the words.

All she could do was lean her head on his shoulder, feel the solid presence of his body. He rested his head on top of hers and they relaxed into each other. They were in this together.

"Okay," he said. "That's fine. I think I need to lie down for a minute. I haven't really slept in a few nights."

Camille got up and strode to the kitchen, and when she returned she held out a key and a paper bag of food. "Louise will come get you, once we've settled everything here." She set a hand on his shoulder. "It will all be fine. I promise."

He rose from the couch, and with one last intense look at Louise, he left.

"You should rest too, for a little while," Camille said as she stood at the front window watching the driveway. "We can talk about what's next once your mom gets here."

"What is there left to talk about?" Louise closed her eyes, defeat enveloping her. "It's all over, isn't it?"

"No, Louise," Camille said softly. "It's not over. Not just yet."

Louise's eyes snapped open at the slam of the door. In one quick motion, Bobbie dropped her purse, ran to the couch, and took Louise in her arms. She squeezed her eyes shut again as the full weight of the night, of the past few days, pressed into her.

"I'm so sorry," Bobbie said, her voice muffled as she buried her face in Louise's hair. "I didn't know. I promise I would never have left you if I did."

Louise let out a sob as she and her mother tightened their grips on each other.

When Bobbie finally released her, her makeup was smeared.

She straightened and addressed Camille. "How could you have not told me sooner, not told her sooner? After everything that happened, and you still kept this from us."

Camille stepped forward from where she stood near the staircase. "I didn't tell you because he's not going to die. You're not going to lose him, Louise." A tiny strand of hope threaded through the grief and fear inside of her. "Sit," Camille said quietly to Bobbie. "Please sit."

Camille herself sat in the armchair, but Bobbie didn't move. "You told me on the phone that it was temporary, that we had to tell Louise together."

"I wanted to tell her together how Peter could *live*. The way she can save him.

"You gave Peter time," Camille said to Louise. "You saved his life, but only temporarily. But you can keep him here, living, if you replace his life with another, if you end a life."

Louise's hope frayed. "What do you mean replace his life with another? You can't mean…"

Camille nodded as a terrible clarity settled into Louise's mind.

"I can…we can…kill people?"

"Only if it's their time," Camille said quickly. "If they need help letting go. But yes, we have the ability to still a beating heart." She paused, her eyes distant. "My mother tried once, she told me, to save a good man's life. She tried to take the life of an evil man. But he wasn't dying, and he resisted, violently. But it's not like that, if a soul wants to leave. If someone is ready."

If the only way to save Peter was by taking someone else's life, then it wasn't really a way at all, unless… "So then…someone sick, someone about to die. A hospice patient. Someone in pain. If they were suffering then it wouldn't be…it would be compassionate, wouldn't it?"

"It doesn't work like that. I thought the same. But my mother told me it can't be someone who is already dying."

For a few moments, no one spoke.

"You see," Camille said shakily. "I can save Peter. I'm old, but I'm healthy. There's nothing wrong with me, not physically."

Camille came and knelt in front of Louise, who felt a creeping sense of dread. She couldn't fathom a world in which she could do what her grandmother was suggesting, not even for Peter.

Camille's blue eyes, when they met Louise's, were full of tenderness. "You think I just made this decision? I made it the minute you told me what happened, when you both were here, sitting on the porch. And I think you know why, Louise. I think you've seen it. That I haven't been quite myself."

"What are you talking about?" Bobbie joined Camille, sliding onto the floor next to Louise's legs.

"Even before all of this, I was going to tell you both, soon," Camille said as she leaned back against the couch. "Your father has known for a few months. My brother. And Jim. I had to tell them both, to plan ahead."

"Plan ahead for what?" Bobbie asked, anxiety rippling in her voice.

Camille looked at Louise, who felt herself struggle against the truth, even as tiny connections began to fall into place: her grandmother's unexpected retirement, Jim's words about a sale. And there were other signs, trivial ones, things she had brushed off for months, slips in her grandmother's phrasing, or mixed-up names, plans that were forgotten, food left on the stove, all moments she had chalked up to her simply getting older.

Louise didn't want to put it together, didn't want it to be true, but she could feel reality rush toward her.

"I went to your grandfather soon after I was given the probable diagnosis in December, the next day actually. To make him my power of attorney, to finalize my will and advanced directives. I had made all these decisions before the doctor told me what I already knew, of course. I made them all when I watched Mama go through it." She placed her hands in her lap and took a long moment before continuing. "I was always very clear about what I wanted the end of my life to look like, should it come to this."

A slow realization dawned on Bobbie's face. "Dementia?"

Camille nodded. "Same as Mama, more than likely."

"How long has this been going on?" Bobbie asked.

"It started more than a year ago," Camille said. "For a long time, I tried to convince myself it was just getting older. It was only little lapses, now and again, some clumsiness, feeling off, emotionally. But then…" She paused and looked down at her hands. "I saw things in myself that reminded me of her."

Bobbie's face crumpled. "Why didn't you tell me sooner?"

"What difference would it have made?"

"I could have been here helping you. Making sure you were okay."

"You have your own life. I would never have let you be my caretaker."

"Why didn't you tell me, when I got here?" Louise struggled to formulate her thoughts. She knew there was some right question to ask, some way to sort it all out, prevent what was careening toward them.

"I knew you'd argue with me," Camille replied. "You're as stubborn as your mother. But guess what? I'm even more stubborn."

"Mom, you can't possibly mean this. You're not acting rational."

Camille let out a small laugh. "Barbara, what would a rational response be to this situation exactly?"

"I don't know." Bobbie stood and began to pace the room. "There must be something else that can be done. Something in one of Agnes's old books or…or someone we can talk to. That midwife healer friend of yours who lives in the valley, Naomi or Natalie?"

"Naomi." She sighed. "Naomi is the first person I called after you guys came here. She knows more about healing than I do, more than even Mama ever did. I told her what I was thinking. She told me it should work."

Louise's thoughts were muted as her mother and grandmother talked. When she was little, their combined voices were so soothing, conversations about politics or nursing techniques, gossip over people in town. But right now, the sound only brought her grief.

"There has to be some other way."

"Barbara."

"You're sure that there isn't a loophole, or someone else, or…"

"Barbara, that's enough!" Camille's voice rang out.

Louise looked up, shocked. She had never heard her grandmother raise her voice like that.

"I know what's ahead of me," she said. "I watched it with Mama. And I have known it every day since, that I would never want to live the way she lived at the end." Her chin trembled. "She…she begged me, for months, to let her go. But I was so scared of losing her. It took me so long, too long." She gazed out the window at the inky blue sky. "I'm not scared, not of death. I'm so much more scared of losing who I am. Of putting you in that position, to have to ask you…of making you shoulder that burden."

"Mom, please, you wouldn't be—"

"It's not your decision, Barbara. It's mine. And how beautiful it is, to be able to end my life on my terms and save the life of someone Louise loves."

Louise tried to focus her thoughts as the full weight of her grandmother's words landed on her. "Could I even do it…?" she asked, trying to voice the unbearable question. "How would I even…? I mean, killing someone, is it something I could…?"

Louise's mother stopped pacing, as though she could no longer outrun what was coming. She stood very still as she turned to face Louise. "You could," she said softly. "Because I did."

Louise watched her mom, uncomprehending. She didn't understand. How could she have done what her grandmother was asking: end a life?

Bobbie crossed the room and sat beside Louise again. She took her hands, glancing once at Camille before she spoke.

"I couldn't tell you, Louise. Not this. Not when you…" She cleared her throat. "Not when you looked at me the way you used to look at me, when I was still a nurse, like I was your hero. You used to dress up in my scrubs, use my stethoscope to listen to everyone's heart and lungs. You looked at me like I hung the moon."

She glanced again at Camille, and Louise saw a decade's worth of anger and regret in her mother's eyes.

"I was working a night shift. Assigned to a patient in the ICU." She hesitated, and Louise squeezed her mother's hands, willing her to continue, to finally give her the answers she had wanted for so long. "Her name was Teresa. She was very old, almost ninety, with advanced dementia. Heart failure. COPD." She closed her eyes as though forcing herself to remember despite the pain of it. "She was so sick, and she was with us for months. Her family wouldn't talk about end of life, or agree to hospice. They wanted everything done, and I watched this poor woman get a feeding tube placed, and a tracheotomy in her neck. She had pressure ulcers everywhere, no matter how careful we were with her skin. It was awful, Louise. It broke my heart. More than anything I'd experienced as a nurse."

Louise thought of Sarah, the focus of all her care on comfort instead of curative measures. She was at home, surrounded by her family, with a team of hospice doctors and nurses managing her pain. She couldn't imagine someone she loved being kept alive to suffer the way her mother described.

"I was giving her a bath, cleaning up her bed, the little things I could offer her, that felt so insignificant, but at least were something." Her grip tightened even more. "And I just felt this need to put my hands on her, to stay longer than I normally would, so she wouldn't feel alone."

Louise was only vaguely aware of her grandmother coming to sit on the other side of her on the couch. She couldn't tear her eyes from her mother as she spoke.

"I can hardly describe it," Bobbie continued hoarsely. "Only that I felt...surrender, like she had been waiting all that time for someone to simply let her go. And I saw her...flashes of her life, pieces of her. Felt this warmth, like nothing I had ever known." Her features softened. "I thought I was delirious. Too many night shifts. But her heart stopped. Almost as soon as I let go of her."

"Mom..." Louise began to speak, to tell her mother that it was okay, that she had given her peace, and no one would blame her.

"It happened a second time," Bobbie said quickly, as though she needed to get all the words out at once. "A few weeks later with a similar patient. I didn't understand it. It was a coincidence, right? But because they both died unexpectedly of cardiac arrest, with no identifiable cause, at night while I was alone with them, there was an investigation by the hospital."

Louise's heart plummeted. She couldn't imagine the shame her mother must have felt, to be implicated in the deaths of her patients. She felt the pieces of her childhood fall into place, why her mother quit nursing, why she had been so shattered after they moved, the long stretches of depression.

"I was cleared," Bobbie said tersely after a few moments. "They couldn't find any evidence of wrongdoing. But of course, something like that stays with you. Follows you around. I never could work as a nurse after that, even in a new hospital, new city. I couldn't let it go, the horror of what I'd done. Even if it helped them, even if it was the choice I would make for myself, I never would have..." Her eyes glistened. "Consent still matters. What a family wants matters. They weren't on hospice. They were in an ICU."

"You didn't know," Louise managed to ask, "about healing?"

Bobbie shook her head. "Not then. Not until it was too late."

"I told her," Camille said in a strained voice from beside Louise. "When she told me what happened after the second patient. I told her immediately. About all of it."

Louise thought of the journal, the last entry, her grandmother's plea for forgiveness.

"You had no choice then, did you?" Bobbie asked, the anguish clear in her tone.

"I've never forgiven myself, Bobbie. You have to know that. And I promise if I had known that there was any possibility something like that could happen... My mother always taught me intention mattered, and awareness... She never thought either... She would have insisted I tell you. She loved you so much, was so proud of you."

Bobbie released Louise and placed her hands on her mother's. It was the first time Louise had seen the two women touch in more than a decade.

"You're not still angry?" Camille's voice was almost pleading.

Bobbie wiped her eyes. "I know you were doing your best. And I failed too. In almost the exact same way, by thinking I was protecting Louise, withholding this all from her. I was so mad at you, Mama. But then I acted so much like you." She tried to smile. "Which made me even more mad at you. But I love you. And I'm so sorry I couldn't find a way to tell you that sooner. I thought we had so much more time."

She looked at Louise. "I'm so sorry, honey. For not telling you. I just couldn't separate it, how I found out, what had happened, with the healing itself. To me it was more like a curse, this horrible moment in my life that I couldn't ever leave behind. I felt like I lost everything, my career, my friends from work, my relationship with my mother. And I was so consumed by guilt. I could barely remember how to breathe after I found out. You were the only..." Her voice was hoarse. "You were the only reason I was able to keep going. This bright, beautiful reprieve. And every time I thought of telling you, it just felt like..."

"It would make her life harder," Camille whispered.

Bobbie nodded as she wiped her eyes again. "I hated keeping it from you. Taking you away from our life here. All I ever wanted was for you to be happy, and safe. I thought I could pretend for both of us, convince myself it never happened. Move on."

Louise knew that her mother's trauma didn't erase the years of lies. But mostly she felt a deep, overwhelming sense of grief, that her mother had been so alone, that she hadn't been able to share that pain with anyone. Even if she wished she had told her, she also understood why she hadn't. She thought of Peter, how terrified she had been to be honest with him about her feelings, how she had chosen the stability of their friendship over the danger of an unknown future. She and her mother had both convinced themselves that the safety of a lie was preferable, that honesty was a dangerous, reckless proposition. But they were both wrong, to believe life could be so easily partitioned, that love could flourish without risk, that joy could exist without sorrow.

For a while the three of them were quiet.

"If Peter did live, it wouldn't be much time then, would it?" she asked her grandmother when she was finally brave enough. "Because you're..."

Camille smiled. "Because I'm old and decrepit. And he's not."

"I didn't mean..."

Camille patted Louise's knee. "Don't worry, I'm not offended, honey. And it's not an exact trade. You're not giving Peter a specific, concrete number of years and days. You're giving him the catalyst, a spark. After that, it's his life, his time."

"So, when then?" Bobbie asked. "When does this have to happen?"

Camille surveyed the living room, the threadbare cushions and flickering lamps. "Soon. The kind of healing you did, after death, won't last long. I already told you the old healers kept track of time through moon cycles. The shortest time between someone being brought back and dying again was a single phase of the moon."

"How long is that?" Louise asked as panic rose in her throat. "It's been more than three days."

"About a week, give or take," Camille said. "So, it should be soon, a day or two at most, to be safe. I would like…" She recovered herself. "I'd like a day, to work in my garden and walk the orchard, paint a little, finish some letters I've started. To my brother, Daniel. And Sam. Some of my friends and the families of patients." She looked at Bobbie. "I need some time with Jim. I told you he already knows about the dementia. I had to tell him to put plans in place for the orchard. But he'll take this hard. And I'd like to explain it to him. Finalize some business things. And of course, I'd like to spend time with you both. Say whatever is left for us to say."

Bobbie's face was ashen, but she nodded.

Camille addressed Louise. "Tell Peter he needs to stay a few more days. Tell him it's important. He'll need to be here. After it's done."

"Okay," Louise said, as though any of this were comprehensible.

"But Louise, you can't tell him."

"He knows, about the healing. About the accident. It's okay."

"He doesn't know he's on borrowed time, what's about to happen, how it will happen. Would you want to think you were alive only because someone else traded their life?"

Her grandmother was right. She couldn't put that burden on Peter, even if she herself would carry it the rest of her life. She would find a way to live with it, because she knew it was her grandmother's choice.

Louise opened her mouth to argue but Camille cut her off. "He trusts you, Louise. And you won't give him a reason to doubt it. Enough talking now." She looked at Bobbie. "Everything will seem easier in the morning."

Neither Bobbie nor Louise moved. They only watched as Camille rose, unwilling to propel the night forward, to make time continue onward.

"It's going to be okay, girls," Camille said. "This is no great tragedy."

"It doesn't feel that way," Bobbie said as she stood too.

Camille took Bobbie's face in her hands. "It will all be fine. There is still some time, for all of the things we need to say. And what a gift to be able to say goodbye now, when we still can."

Gently, she kissed Bobbie's forehead. It was easy to forget that before their falling out, before the years of anger and resentment, they were mother and daughter; that there had been an entire lifetime that existed before her, a world in which they were each other's centers.

"Mama?" Bobbie asked her. "I'd like to take a walk with you, if that's okay?"

Camille smiled. "I'd like that very much."

ROUEN, FRANCE
1942

18

HELENE

The back door of the truck slid open, filling the dark, cramped space with salt air and the glow of moonlight. Across from her, perched between apple crates, Cecelia nodded in the shadows.

"We're here."

Helene's knees and back ached from the tight quarters as she climbed out of the delivery truck. Their driver, an elderly man with a long, gray beard, reached out a hand to help her down.

"Careful," he said quietly.

Helene's legs shook as she stepped forward. They were parked along a narrow dirt road, miles from the nearest town. Vast limestone cliffs lined the shore below, and the channel churned endlessly to the horizon.

"How much time do you need, Sister?" the driver asked as he assisted Cecelia out of the truck. His eyes moved constantly, peering up and down the isolated road.

"Not much." Cecelia lifted a large canvas bag out of the truck. "Dropping off supplies. Be back in an hour."

He got back into the truck and it took off with a low rumble, its headlights off as it jostled its way back down the road.

"We need to move quickly, Helene," Cecelia said, straightening the veil of her habit. "Follow me closely. Watch your steps."

"Where are we? What is this place?" Helene asked as she gazed out at the wide expanse of sea. She had forgotten what it felt like to not be surrounded by walls and people and voices, to be somewhere so free.

"A way out. For men who need to escape," Cecelia said simply and began to stride toward a small rocky path that led down the cliffside, clutching her bag closely to her side.

Helene followed behind, grateful for the round moon that shone above them, giving them light as the path veered sharply downward. Cecelia moved confidently, her head bowed. This place was clearly familiar to her.

As they descended, the chalky white stone of the cliffs grew rougher and more weathered, and Helene had to reach out to balance herself.

"Are we near Dieppe?" she asked, her voice low, as Cecelia quickened her pace. It was hard to get her bearings in the dark.

"We could be near Dieppe but I'm not sure," Cecelia said. "I only know we're somewhere along the coast. They don't tell us the exact location, and we don't ask. It's safer that way, for everyone." Cecelia glanced back at Helene. "Follow me now. It's not much farther."

Cecelia stepped onto a narrow ledge that ran along the cliffside, barely wide enough to hold one person and with a steep drop below it. She made slow, careful movements up the ledge, her veil swirling as gusts of warm sea air blew up from the channel.

Helene's foot wobbled, tiny rocks scattering off at least twenty meters beneath. She took a breath and forced herself to keep going.

After a few minutes of climbing, Cecelia finally stopped at a wide, circular opening in the limestone. "We only have a few minutes. Before we need to start back. The longer we stay the greater danger we put them in. We can't be certain our movements aren't being watched."

Helene nodded, but she felt her heart accelerate. She had thought only of getting to Thomas, of seeing him, of holding his hand. Everything else, what she would say, how she would say it, had felt too precarious to think about.

Inside, it took Helene a moment to adjust to the darkness. The cave was much larger than she expected, nearly the size of her family's shop. The walls were smooth, dripping with water from above, and it was cooler than it had been out in the August night.

Several faces stared at them from the back of the cave, a dozen men, the air heavy with the smell of sweat and urine.

Cecelia took a step forward and the air seemed to shift with an audible relief.

"Thank God it's you, Sister," came a voice in English.

"Watch it," came another.

"Sorry," called the first voice, the tone slightly sheepish. "Didn't mean any disrespect."

"It's the Lord's name you took in vain. Not mine."

Many of the men pulled themselves up to stand. A few remained on the ground, their legs stretched out in front of them. As she followed Cecelia deeper into the cave, Helene noticed that one had his arm in a makeshift sling, and that another's head was propped up on a different man's lap.

Cecelia handed a bag to one of the soldiers on the ground. "Sulfa. Morphine. Some bandages and tourniquets. Everything you requested."

"Thank you, Sister." He was older, close to middle age, with wrinkles around his eyes.

"Helene?"

Helene hadn't allowed herself to think about what it would

be like to hear his voice again, the miracle of its very existence, when she had felt the complete stillness of his heart only days earlier.

"You're here." Thomas made his way to her. The lightness of his features was subdued, as though he had aged several years.

"I am," Helene said. It was physically painful, to know in a matter of days or weeks he would die again, that she had brought him back only to be in hiding in this cold, wet cave. Remorse flooded her for failing to take Vogel's life. She could have been here right now to give Thomas his life back. And instead she was here to say goodbye. She looked down at his leg, at the ease with which he stood, all traces of his wound gone.

He followed her gaze. "Bizarre, isn't it? Hurt like hell the last time I saw you. They told me it was infected, that I had bacteremia. That's the last thing I remember..." He trailed off. "I don't really understand it, to be honest. I woke up in the back of a garbage truck covered with a sheet," he said as a little bit of the old light flickered back. "How did you get here?"

Helene tried to smile. "Nothing as exciting as that."

Thomas glanced at Cecelia, who knelt beside a wounded soldier at the back. "Here I thought I was living a life filled with danger. And you were some innocent girl. All along you were the brave one."

"I'm not." Nearly every decision she had made in the last week, bringing Thomas back, failing to kill Vogel, had been out of panic and fear, not bravery.

"They would shoot you for this," Thomas said, serious. "Don't be modest. It doesn't suit you. You're remarkable, Helene."

From the back of the cave, Cecelia addressed Helene. "We'll need to be going."

Helene looked at Thomas as the night slipped away from her, as she felt him begin to blur at the edges, as though already only a memory. She fought to hold on to the present, onto Thomas, and for a moment, she could almost pretend they were back on the beach, not as it was in Dieppe, but a beach a thousand miles and years from the war, just the two of them together with the rocks and the waves, and he was only a boy asking her to talk to him in the glittering sun.

"Can't you stay a little longer?" he asked, as though reading her mind. She saw it in his eyes too, the reverberation of their first meeting, the acknowledgment of the strangers they were that day, of how in the chaos and brutality of war that one conversation, all of their conversations, were precious.

"It's not safe."

"Then come back."

"But you'll be gone." She couldn't meet his eyes when she lied to him, even if it was for his own peace of mind. Outside, the sea slammed against the rocks below, violent and restless. "They'll get you out by then."

"Come with us then. You can get out too."

If things were different, if Thomas had a full life ahead of him, she could almost envision a world where she said yes, where she left everyone and everything behind, created a new life in Canada, or America, away from the ugliness of the war. But a part of her knew that even then, even if such a future existed, she couldn't abandon Irene, or her mother and grandfather, even Cecelia, who despite everything had trusted her enough to bring her to see Thomas. "I can't leave. This is my home."

Thomas made a soft noise. "Not right now it's not. They took it away from you. We'll get you out and then you and I can go anywhere you'd like. Anywhere in the world."

Helene smiled. Thomas was a little more weary than he had been in Rouen, but he was also the same, so trusting that the world was malleable, that he could mold it into whatever form he chose. "It's still my home," she said. She bit her lip until she could taste the slight metallic tang of blood, punishment for the loss of the boy in front of her, and her part in it.

Cecelia made the sign of the cross on the forehead of one of the men and stood up. "It's time," she said, her voice loud and carrying in the confined space.

Helene suddenly felt the weight of Thomas's hand in her own. It rooted her to the spot, as though she were a part of her surroundings, part of the vast white cliffs, and the sea itself. She looked up at him, and she remembered why she was here. She wanted to spend however long was left of the war fighting back. She wanted to be brave. And even though it broke her heart, she couldn't waste one more second while Thomas was still in this world.

In one swift motion, she reached up and kissed him. At first he was too stunned to react, but then he wrapped his arms around her as though he had done it before. Helene didn't care that the others were watching. All she could do was hold him there, the beat of his heart next to her own, imprint every last detail into her soul.

Thomas gazed at their hands, still intertwined, wonder softening his features. "I'll come back then. And I'll win this whole godforsaken thing for you."

Helene smiled, desperate to keep the night from swirling forward. All they had was this small moment.

"This will end, Helene. There will be an after. And you'll have a big, beautiful life. That I know for certain. More than anything."

Helene nodded as her throat tightened and eyes burned. "Be safe, Thomas."

Thomas squeezed her hand. "And you."

Helene heard Cecelia's footsteps behind her, but she couldn't bring herself to let go of Thomas's hand.

"I have to go."

Thomas held her eyes, as though he too were trying to memorize her face.

"You said that already."

"We can't be late, Helene. Our driver will be waiting."

She took a deep breath. "Goodbye then."

Thomas shook his head. "Not goodbye. We've found each other too many times already. I know we'll find one another again. Say good night instead."

He kissed her again, once on each cheek. She closed her eyes to try to slow everything down, to keep him there a second longer.

"Good night, Thomas."

She followed Cecelia out of the cave, the night sweeping back over them, the sky impossibly bright compared to the darkness of the cave. Helene focused on her breaths as she walked down the narrow ledge, each one bringing more salt air into her lungs. She filled herself up with it.

When they reached the path and climbed back up to the top of the cliff, the smell of the sea reminded her of a home that felt farther away than ever.

The road was empty. Helene swayed as the exhaustion of the last few days began to hit her. She felt dizzy, disoriented, the black sky, yellow moon, and gray sea blurring together into one infinite void.

But just as the world began to spin around her, she felt a hand in hers. Cecelia. Heat flowed into her skin, up her arms and down her back and chest, until the raw, jagged edge of pain inside of her melted.

From down the road, there was the rumble of the truck engine. But Cecelia didn't let go. The sea seemed calmer now, moving in gentle, rhythmic waves beneath the moon.

The truck was only a few meters away when it cut out abruptly, the driver peering over at them from behind the wheel.

"Are you ready, Helene?" Cecelia asked quietly. "To come back with me to Rouen. Is that your choice?"

Helene released Cecelia's hand. She knew the darkness would only deepen, that if there was an end to the occupation, to the war, it would only be achieved through more bombs and battles and devastation. But as she stood on that cliffside, she knew she had to try to fix what she could of this broken world, do what she had spent her life watching her mother do for the people who needed her.

Helene looked back over the channel, her eyes lingering on the horizon, where the edge of the world she knew met the vast, unfathomable future gleaming just beyond it. Cecelia's words from earlier that week echoed in her mind. Only now, for the first time, she understood their meaning.

"I didn't choose this," Helene said now. "I didn't choose any of it. But I'm here. And I'm ready."

CROZET, VIRGINIA
2019

19

LOUISE

Peter was sitting on the garden bench when Louise walked into the backyard. The dense, ancient limbs of the huge magnolia tree were a canopy above him, the branches dotted with sweet perfumed white flowers the size of cantaloupes.

"You were supposed to go to the guest house," Louise said as she approached him. Each footstep took effort as she crossed the yard. Her entire body felt heavy, weighted down by the events of the evening. Her mind held an overwhelming swirl of emotions. It made the night take on a surreal, hazy quality, as though she were meeting Peter in a dream.

"Funny thing," Peter said when she sat beside him, his expression slightly dazed. "I don't really remember sitting down. Your grandmother told me to leave. And I left. But I guess this is as far as I got."

For a few minutes, neither of them spoke. Louise heard the distant crunch of gravel, the murmur of female voices, her mother and grandmother setting off down the road on their walk. She was acutely aware of the proximity of Peter's body, the rise and fall of his chest with his breathing, of how impossible it all was, that they were there together on that summer night, that out of the infinite, spinning parts of the universe, their paths had collided.

"You were right, you know," Louise finally said as a small bird took off from a branch of the magnolia, briefly silhouetted against the velvet blue sky. "I was lying. About your knee. About the accident. About how I brought you back."

"I know," Peter said quietly. "I don't understand it, but I know."

"And I think you were right about New York too," she said, her voice amplified in the stillness of the night. She felt like she was back at the swimming hole, about to step off a ledge. She plunged forward. She didn't want to waste any more time, not after that night, not when she suddenly saw life for exactly how brief and fragile it was. She didn't want to spend four years studying a subject because it was easy, because the answers were always simple, far removed from the messiness of real life.

"I don't want to go," she said quickly, before she could stop herself. "Not to the summer program. Not to NYU in the fall. I want to stay here, for now, figure out what I really want. But I know it's not New York. Getting buried in student debt to live in a city I don't even really love."

"What changed your mind?"

Louise motioned toward the orchard, the horizon painted by the mountains. "All of this." She hesitated. "Helping Sarah. Saving you."

She shivered despite the heat of the evening, felt a little ripple move across her body, a pull away from the solitude and secrecy of generations, toward one person she knew would handle the truth with care.

"Do you want me to show you how?"

Peter nodded, his mouth half-open. Louise stood up from the bench.

"Follow me."

She led him toward one of the magnolia tree's lowest branches, a long, knotted limb that ran parallel to the ground. It was massive, sturdy enough to hold both their weight. As a little girl she used to balance on it, pretend she was a gymnast while her grandmother and great-grandmother played the part of judges from their lawn chairs.

The flowers spread among the huge, glossy green leaves were faded at that part of the tree, their white petals wrinkled and drooping toward the ground.

Louise traced the tree limb, her fingers shaking as she reached the first flower.

She rested her palm on a delicate blossom, inhaled the scent, notes of lemon and vanilla and earth. The warmth in her skin surged as the petals curled up, forming a perfect ivory saucer that stood out against the verdant leaves.

Cautiously, she raised her gaze to Peter's face, but his eyes showed only trust, belief in what he was seeing.

"Wow," he said softly.

Louise felt her cheeks relax into a small smile. The pit inside of her stomach, the dread of the next few days, loosened ever so slightly.

With Peter watching on, she moved on to the branches that surrounded them, until all around their heads, the sky was full of bright, white blooms.

CROZET, VIRGINIA
1950

20

HELENE

Helene didn't bother to look up from her desk as the door flew open, carrying with it a gust of warm spring air, even as all around the Virginia mountains remained in their brown winter dormancy.

"We're closed," she said in her halting English, not waiting to see who was at the door. The women's center in downtown Crozet was a tiny building, with only two rooms and a rudimentary kitchen. But it worked well enough as a clinic for the Augustinian sisters when they trekked over from their convent in the valley. "Hours are nine to two."

Helene felt a flicker of annoyance at the interruption, especially when the hours were clearly posted on the door. The sisters had already left for home, waving goodbye as they walked out in their white habits to their van. Helene would take the truck back over the mountain when she was finished. But first, she had to finish the paperwork, carefully fill out and file each patient chart.

Since she was the sole lay member of the convent, she felt a sense of obligation to help with the more menial tasks, though she was by far the most skilled and experienced nurse there, particularly since she was able to supplement her scientific knowledge with her inherited abilities. Cecelia had given Helene her reluctant blessing, shortly after their trip to the cave, to use her gift as long as she didn't try to halt the natural progression of life or death.

"I think God has greater battles right now," she told Helene, as she explained her change of heart. "I had forgotten what healing could look like, the beauty of it. I think we all have to adapt, do what we can to take care of each other."

And so Helene had spent the last years of the war learning how to be both a nurse and a healer at the same time, finding little moments of mercy and grace even as the world around her rocked and shattered.

When the order sent a mission to Virginia a few years later, Helene begged Cecelia to go. There was nothing left for her in Honfleur, only her uncles, who were so lost and adrift in their own pain that they could scarcely take on the burden of Helene's. Irene had moved to Canada, to live with her mother's cousin. And so, Helene had jumped on the opportunity to leave Europe, to put an ocean between her and the ruin of her home.

In Virginia, Helene found satisfaction in the minutiae. It was a distraction, a way to keep her mind busy, to avoid thinking of her family or Thomas, everything she had seen over the past decade.

"I apologize, ma'am," came a soft, lilting voice from the door. Helene recognized the accent. All the people in the mountains spoke like him, halting and quiet, barely moving their lips. Helene had been in Virginia for nearly two years, and she was only now starting to fully understand their dialect.

The man was younger than she expected. She was twenty-five and he couldn't have been much older, thirty at most. He was clean-shaven, which was unusual for these parts, with neatly trimmed hair and pressed clothes, as though he had dressed for church instead of a trip to the clinic. She hadn't seen him here before. He wasn't one of their regulars, most of whom were either elderly people with heart and lung problems, or GIs with chronic injuries.

He was tall, and broad shouldered, and his cheeks weren't ruddy from alcohol like those of so many of the young men back from the war. But he leaned on a cane for support.

"Did you need to be seen for something?" she asked him.

He hovered in the doorway, half inside and half outside. "I..." He took a step and the door closed behind him, shutting out the breeze. "I actually came here to see you."

Helene tensed. When men learned she wasn't a nun, they either pursued her relentlessly, inappropriate and flirtatious, or worse, they grew angry when they discovered she was French, muttered about collaboration. She never bothered to defend herself, explain to them that she'd spent the last years of the war risking her life aiding the resistance in whatever small ways she could, delivering medical supplies to underground hospitals, helping wounded soldiers trapped behind enemy lines. She didn't tell them that her mother and grandfather had sacrificed their lives to share the fight against evil, that her uncles came home broken men from their time as prisoners in German camps.

She didn't owe them an explanation for who they thought she was.

"I was here," the man continued, "a while back. For bronchitis."

Helene watched him closely, her body alert, every nerve ending awake. Years could go by, years of peace, years of not living as a captive in her own home, of waiting every day for them to find her out, line her up in the courtyard and execute her like all the rest, and yet the fear remained as a muscle memory, embedded in every fiber of her being.

"You didn't take care of me," he said, and this time his voice was soft. "But I saw you. I... I always planned to come back. My name is John. John Winston."

His eyes were kind, and his tone was gentle, but she had known enough men like him, the ones who could take their humanity off like a winter coat, slip in and out of it whenever it suited.

"I'm sorry. I'm scaring you, aren't I?" He moved back toward the door. "I can leave. I shouldn't have come."

Some of the fear inside of Helene released at his acknowledgment. It was unusual for a man to be willing to make himself small, to take up less space so that she could have more of it. "No, it's okay," she said. She kept her tone professional. If he needed her help, it was her duty to provide it. "Please, what do you need?"

He let one hand rest on the doorknob, and he glanced back toward the parking lot, as though he were imagining a future where he simply left, where the possibility of what could be died on the vine. Helene saw it too, for an instant, a window closing. She had accepted, years earlier, that her life would be quiet, full of purpose. She didn't deserve joy, or love, or beauty. She had survived. Her family had not. Neither had Thomas nor so many boys like him. Or Irene's mother, who had been murdered in the same camp as her father, along with millions of Jewish people. It didn't matter that Irene had forgiven her failure, that they'd found a way to build a new friendship in the last dark, catastrophic months of occupation, when countless bombs fell on Rouen and set the world on fire, the hospital now filled with injured civilians.

It felt selfish to want more than to merely live. But in that moment, as this man looked at her, Helene remembered what it felt like to believe in more. "Can I help you?" she asked again.

She stood and smoothed her gray, starched uniform, tucked a piece of brown hair behind her ear. She was aware of how plain she must look. She followed the sisters' leads, never bothered with makeup or the little jewelry of her mother's she had taken from home. In the two years she had been in Virginia, she hadn't felt the need to try to make herself pretty. Everything here was so rough, so hard, and it was a relief, to be somewhere there was no sea, no soaring cathedrals, only fading mountains and squat houses and red clay earth. She could be how she felt here.

He removed his hat, and when he looked at her, his eyes were filled with hope, hope that was scarred and weathered, blunted by war, but persistent.

"It's taken me a while, miss. But when I saw you, I knew I'd like to come back here and ask you this. But I... My family has an orchard near here. It's beautiful this time of year when the peach blossoms are just starting to bloom." When he smiled, he appeared ten years younger. "The whole horizon is pink."

He took a step toward the desk. She felt a sun slowly rising in her body, a gentle thaw of what she'd assumed would always be frozen.

"Would you like to take a walk with me?"

Helene felt the corners of her mouth twitch, the muscles out of practice. She knew what her mother would say if she were there, that even in a life of duty there was space for love, or her father, who'd prized books and music and found beauty everywhere, her grandfather who'd been a romantic at heart, or Thomas especially, who believed so much in the future. She knew they would tell her to say yes, to run recklessly toward a life of joy and love, to give everything she had for even one minute of hope in a world where it was never a sure thing. She felt a small stirring inside of her, like a tulip fighting its way out of the earth, drawn toward the promise of spring.

"I'd like that," she told him. "I'd like that very much."

CROZET, VIRGINIA
2019

21

LOUISE

Louise would always remember the sky on her grandmother's last day, pale blue and strewed with clouds and a gentle sun. She would remember Jim's face, etched with grief, when he brought her grandmother back to the house. They had met at dawn, and Louise knew that her grandmother had used a few of her last, precious hours to say goodbye.

She would remember the smell of coffee in the kitchen, her grandmother's slippers shuffling on the floor as she made them eggs and toast, the sunlight as it gleamed through the window above the sink.

When Bobbie sat down at the breakfast table, she looked up at Louise with panic in her eyes. "You're leaving tomorrow," she said. She was pale and her eyes were bloodshot. Louise wondered if she had slept at all. "We're supposed to catch a train to New York at seven in the morning." She reached for her phone. "I'm going to have to reschedule, something next week maybe. And email the program director."

Louise reached across the table and placed her hand on top of her mother's. She felt oddly at peace, relieved that for the first time in her life she had made a decision completely for herself. "I'm not going to New York, Mom."

Bobbie was momentarily taken aback, but then she nodded. "Of course, there's so much going on right now. And your grandmother... Of course you don't want to leave home right now... I'm sure they'll understand. I'll call them, and then you can have the summer to get ready."

Louise took a deep breath. She heard Peter's voice in her ear. *Tell her.*

"I'm not going to NYU in the fall either."

At that, Bobbie fell silent. Louise could hear Camille's footsteps come to a stop behind them.

Louise felt a small trace of the old fear: that the world might stop entirely if she didn't do everything possible to make her mom happy. But she wasn't a little girl. And she couldn't waste another day of her one brief, fragile life. She thought she could be safe, smart enough to never experience pain, but all she had really done was hide from life, too afraid of the hurt to open herself up to joy.

"I'm so sorry, Mom. I know how much you wanted this for me. But it's not what I want."

Bobbie gripped Louise's hand. "You were going to go to NYU for me, because I wanted it?"

"I thought I wanted it too."

Guilt washed over Bobbie's features. "I'm so sorry, for making you feel that way, Louise."

"It's okay," Louise said quickly, tightening her grasp on her mother, willing her to understand. "I loved sharing that dream with you. I loved that it made you happy."

"But it's not what's going to make you happy," Bobbie said, not a question but a statement.

"I don't think so. I'd like to take some time, to think about it. But I think..." It felt like one last hurdle, and the hardest one, to admit to her mother what she had realized about herself, about the kind of life she wanted. Because it was the life her mother once had.

"You think maybe you'd like to go into a career where you can use it?" Bobbie said, holding up her hands. "This."

"How did you...?"

"Louise, I know you better than I know myself." She glanced at Camille, who had joined them at the table.

"You know there are options. She could be a massage therapist," Camille said thoughtfully. "On my hardest days as a nurse, I sometimes fantasized about that, how lovely it would be to just give people the world's most incredible massages. You'd get the best tips."

Louise tried to smile at her grandmother's attempts to lighten the situation. Even ahead of her own death, she was still trying to take care of them.

"Or a doctor," Camille continued. "Go to med school." She rolled her eyes. "Although let's be honest. That's a lot of debt. And you'll be so busy charting and fighting with insurance companies you won't have time to actually put your hands on a patient."

"Or a nurse," Bobbie said firmly. "She could be a nurse, if she wants to."

Louise felt a stirring inside of her at her mother's words. "But you—"

"I know what I've said," Bobbie interrupted. "I just thought... I thought maybe I could protect you from it." She squeezed Louise's hand tighter. "Because it will hurt you, honey. I loved it. Before everything happened. But it was so hard. Every day it was hard."

"I know," Louise said as the image of Sarah flashed in her mind. She knew what her life would be like as a nurse, as a healer. But she also couldn't imagine it any other way. "You don't have to protect me, Mom."

Bobbie took a shaky breath. "No, but see, I'm your mom. I have to try."

"You could go back," Louise said, even though she knew it was a childish hope, that life wasn't so easily fixed. "Be a nurse again. Be a healer."

Bobbie's eyes shone. "Maybe," she said, in a way that told Louise she didn't really believe her own words. "Maybe one day."

Camille draped an arm around Louise. "You should have seen her with Sarah, Bobbie. She's a natural."

Louise turned her face up toward her grandmother. "You really think that?"

"You didn't look away, Louise. And that's all it really means. To be a nurse. To be a healer. It's standing in a room with someone in pain, and not looking away."

Camille reached for the small leather notebook, which was still on the table from where Louise had returned it. She picked it up and fingered the cover before handing it to Louise.

"I asked your mother if she wanted it." She turned to Bobbie, who gave a small shake of her head. "But she wanted you to have it. It's yours now, honey. All of the things you won't learn in nursing school, if you do go one day."

Louise didn't want the notebook. She only wanted her grandmother.

Camille placed it into her hands. "It's going to be okay. Life goes on. The same way it went on for them, through wars and great hardship. It must have seemed impossible, at times, but my mother and grandmother kept going. And so will you. Keep it safe."

They were all quiet after that, holding onto one another at the table, until the sound of a screen door broke them apart.

"That's Peter," Louise said as she wiped her eyes with the back of her hand. "I told him I'd meet him after breakfast." Louise thought of their conversation under the magnolia tree, the words that had spilled out of her, about healing, about college, about everything but the one truth that scared her the most. She was still so terrified to lose him.

But as she looked at her grandmother, she realized it was useless to pretend that she had any control at all. Life was messy. She could lose him no matter what she did. She almost had. And if she hadn't brought him back, she would never have had the chance to fix it, to go back to the moment he told her he loved her, and say what was terrifying but also deeply, profoundly true.

Bobbie pushed back from her chair and walked toward the coffeepot. "I think that boy has spent his whole life waiting for you."

CROZET, VIRGINIA
1959

22

HELENE

Helene stopped walking abruptly. It was midnight, and pitch-black, the summer sky moonless and heavy with an approaching storm. Her flashlight cast a small light on the dirt road in front of her, but otherwise the entire world seemed to exist only in darkness.

Despite the chorus of cicadas and frogs and crickets, Helene could hear the soft footsteps behind her. It wasn't the first time that summer those little footsteps had followed her down the porch and the driveway, but it was the first time she'd decided to acknowledge their presence.

"You don't have to hide," Helene said as she turned quickly, shining the flashlight on the road behind her, on her daughter.

"How did you know?" Camille asked, squinting into the bright glare.

She wore only a thin cotton nightgown, her skinny legs visible above her dirt-caked rain boots. Her long curly brown hair was matted and tangled. No matter how carefully Helene brushed it each night after her bath, Camille's hair always found its way back to its naturally wild state. Everything about Camille was slightly wild, and Helene loved that about her daughter, loved that she fit in the hills and hollows of Virginia. She was so much like John, happiest barefoot and muddy, splashing through the creek that ran behind the orchard, or making dirt pies after it rained.

"You are not a very good spy." Helene raised a finger to her lips. "You let the screen door slam."

Camille flushed, her features crestfallen. "I'm sorry, Mama."

Helene walked over to Camille. "You're not supposed to get out of bed and leave the house at night. We have talked about this, have we not? You could have woken your baby brother up too, with the noise."

Camille hung her head. "Yes, Mama. He didn't wake. I stayed on the porch for a minute to make sure."

"Then why are you here?"

Camille looked up. Her green eyes were enormous, full of apprehension. Helene knew Camille was expecting a scolding. For seven years, it had been Helene's job to dole out the punishments and enforce the rules, because John could never bring himself to discipline his only daughter.

Sometimes, Helene caught herself staring at Camille as she played with her dolls, chattering away. She wondered if she could simply keep her there, in her sweet little world, keep away all the grief and loss and pain, barricade the doors and never let her leave. But of course, Helene knew it wouldn't matter. She could lock every door and life would still find its way in. It wasn't her job to keep the world from her daughter. It was her job to prepare her for it.

"I wanted to follow you, Mama," Camille said. "I'll go home, though, right away. I promise."

Helene still couldn't believe her daughter even existed, that such a miracle of a creature was truly hers. After the war, after all the pain and evil and heartache, Helene had been ready for a life of solitude.

But John had an answer for every one of Helene's excuses from the moment he took her hand in the orchard on that warm spring day after he came to the clinic. And when Camille was born, Helene no longer had any defenses at all. Her daughter was the sunrise after an endless night, and the light Camille emitted reached every dark corner inside of Helene, until she was forced to see herself the way her daughter saw her, as someone worthy of love.

"Do you know where I'm going tonight?" Helene asked as she knelt to be at eye level.

Camille shook her head.

"I'm going to visit the home of one of your friends. Alberta."

Camille's eyes widened in excitement. "Can I come play with her, Mama? Please?"

Helene felt a tiny flicker of regret but pressed forward. "I'm afraid you can't play with Alberta tonight. She's sleeping." Helene stopped as she struggled for the right words in English. It would be so much easier to explain in her native language. She felt a stab of longing for her own mother. She wished so desperately she could go home, just once, sit at the kitchen table in the old house in Honfleur, smell the salt air and speak her own language and witness her mother meet her granddaughter. She missed Agnes, but she hadn't realized how much she would want her mother when she became a mother herself, that the loss would only expand with time, not lessen.

"I'm going to see Alberta's little brother, Robert."

Camille looked at her, confused. "Why? Is he sick?"

Helene nodded. "Yes, my love, he's very sick." She took Camille's little hands in her own. "You know how he hasn't been at school for a little while? It's because he hasn't been well. And they finally discovered why. He has something called cancer. Leukemia. In his blood. He is going to die, Camille. I'm helping his parents take care of him. You can come with me, if you'd like. And I'll show you how I help him, how you...how you can help him too. But it will be very sad, and very hard to see him. I want you to be sure."

Helene watched as her daughter struggled, a range of emotions dancing across Camille's delicate features. She knew it was her daughter's birthright, the same way it was hers, that healing could be a tremendous gift, ensure a life of intention and service. But after having a son, holding him in her arms and knowing that his life could be anything he wanted, she also wondered if maybe it would be okay to let the gift remain hidden.

"It's okay. Why don't I take you home?" Helene said. She had no specific memory of when her mother had first told her about healing, exposed her to it. It had simply been a part of her life for as long as she could remember.

But as Helene took Camille's hand and began to lead her back to the house, Camille tugged away from her.

"No, Mama, I... I want to come." Her lip quivered as she looked defiantly up at her, feet planted firmly. "I want to help Robert. I won't cry. I promise."

Helene felt a piece of her heart break at her daughter's promise to be brave. But it had also been years since she had someone beside her while she worked, another set of hands in the darkness. More than anything, she missed her own mother. And she didn't want to be alone anymore.

As if sensing her mother's emotions, Camille reached out her hand again. Behind her the night sky lit up with a thousand fireflies.

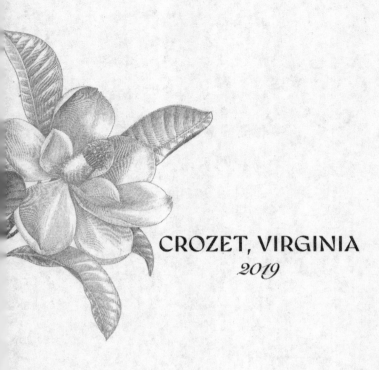

CROZET, VIRGINIA
2019

23

LOUISE

Peter was sitting on the guest house's porch.

"Will you take a walk with me?" Louise asked.

She offered her hand, and he accepted it, and it didn't feel new or remarkable. It felt right.

When they were surrounded by the deepest, oldest part of the orchard, where the trees grew thick and gnarled and wild, Louise stopped. Peter's expression was questioning but also patient. He hadn't asked for an explanation once, not since they sat together under the magnolia tree and she'd asked him to stay in Crozet a little longer.

Louise took a deep breath as the tangled branches above them crowded out the sky. Peter watched her, his entire body still in a way it rarely was, as though he had always known that every moment of their lives would lead to this morning in the shadows of the orchard.

"I was so scared to tell you the truth, about the accident, about how I really saved you." Louise paused. "But that wasn't all of it."

"What else were you scared to tell me?" His voice was cautious, but also hopeful.

He stepped closer to her, until he was only inches away, and her heart skipped inside of her chest.

Louise had brought Peter there to say the words, but standing here she understood that some emotion could only be expressed by touch.

Peter let out a soft note of surprise as she kissed him once. She pulled back, a shy smile playing on her lips, until he grabbed her face and tugged her back toward him. Everything faded around them. The wind quieted. The birds went silent. Louise felt bathed in a light unlike any she had ever known.

When they finally drew back, Peter's palm still on her neck, his face cracked open in a grin and the trees rustled in the breeze again. "You could have led with that."

Energy radiated up and down her body. She allowed herself to fill up on the possibility of what was next, of long summer days that spilled into each other, and fall together in Richmond. Peter could take community college classes and Louise could apply to nursing school for the second semester. They could even travel together, use Peter's generous graduation money from his grandparents, visit the towns mentioned in her grandmother's journal, Honfleur and Cordon, the sea and the mountains, all the places where the book of healing had been written. The future shimmered with new possibility.

"I want to spend the summer with you. Just us."

"You mean it?"

Louise nodded. "I mean it."

That grin grew impossibly wider, and he kissed her again.

After, Peter looked over her shoulder toward her grandmother's house. "Why did you need me to stay here? What's going on?" he murmured, his hand on her waist.

Some of the brightness inside of her dimmed as she thought of her grandmother, of what came next, the reason Peter could live. "I actually need to get back." She worked to keep her voice steady. "Can you wait? A little longer." She tried to hold on to the hope she felt when she kissed him, with the promise of tomorrow, even as she felt storm clouds looming, a grief she would have to weather, the same way the women before her had weathered their own squalls and tempests. "Will you wait here, at the guest house?"

Peter looked down at her hand, woven inside of his own. "Of course."

Louise began to walk back to her grandmother's house, but she paused after a few feet and turned back. Peter hadn't moved from where they'd stood under the apple trees.

"I should have said it at Kyle's party. After you said it to me," she told him.

She took a small breath. She felt the ground shift beneath her, as though she were back in the mountains, jumping off the ledge into the blue depths beneath.

"That maybe I've always loved you too."

CROZET, VIRGINIA
2008

24

HELENE

Helene sat on the bench in the garden and blinked into the sunlight. She felt her mind clear, as though coming out of a heavy fog.

"You're here," she said, noticing her daughter beside her. She couldn't remember why they were sitting in the garden, how they had gotten there. It felt like it had been both years and seconds since she last saw her.

She looked around the yard, as a recollection surfaced. She remembered sitting on this very bench, right after her granddaughter came home from the hospital with baby Louise. Barbara had been exhausted, just a child herself, overwhelmed and struggling to nurse the constantly hungry baby.

Helene had insisted that Barbara take a nap. It was late evening, the witching hour as she called it, and the baby was inconsolable, red faced and screaming. Helene walked with her, singing French lullabies, swaying her in her arms.

The memory flickered, like an old movie, and Helene fought to hold on to it. Camille had been there too, standing beside her as she walked up and down the garden path, bouncing the baby on her shoulder, until she finally quieted, her little body heavy with sleep. They sat together, watching her with deep love, because she was theirs, would always be theirs.

Helene had told Camille something important that day. She knew that. But what had it been? She searched the memory, until finally, the words rustled up like a breeze.

"It's okay, Cami, if you don't tell Barbara. If she never knows. Never passes the knowledge or responsibility to this little soul. And it's okay if you do tell her. I know you've struggled with this since she was young. But there's no one right answer. There never is when it comes to our children."

"Will it lessen her life?" Camille had asked, her expression serious. "Because it has been the gift of mine, Mama. No matter how hard it has been. It's also been a tremendous privilege."

Helene had felt overwhelmed at her daughter's words, the confirmation she had always needed, that healing added to her life instead of subtracted from it.

"She's a nurse, Cami. She found her way to a life she loves on her own, a career where she helps people," Helene had said. "And she'll continue to find her way, with or without the magic."

She had buried her nose in Louise's head, inhaling the scent of baby powder, the unbearably sweet newborn smell. She understood why her daughter had kept their ability a secret from Barbara all these years. Camille believed, the way all young mothers must believe, that she could always protect her child from pain, that by the sheer force of her love, she could create a world without suffering for her. Only of course, she was wrong. The world would always find its way in. All you could do as a mother was try to prepare them for it.

Helene's vision blurred as the scene disintegrated, until all she felt was the memory of the weight of Louise in her arms, the miracle of her existence, that a part of Helene resided in her tiny, perfect body.

Beside her, Camille looked much older than Helene remembered, her brown hair streaked with gray.

"I'm here, Mama."

"Are you sad?"

Tears streamed down Camille's face as Helene took her hand. She hated to see her daughter cry. It always had been that way, from the days of skinned knees and goose egg bruises.

"Yes, Mama. I'm very sad."

Helene studied Camille's hand. She felt like she was in a deep lake, rising slowly to the surface, and with every inch the world grew lighter and clearer. There was sunlight ahead, and she fought her way toward it.

"It's time?" Helene said, and it came out as a question even though she saw the answer in Camille's eyes.

Helene glanced around the garden, at the flowers and weeds, at the fat bumblebees and delicate butterflies that flew in small circles. In the distance the mountains, her mountains, fringed the horizon. She knew the land, every inch of it, as though from an old dream.

She closed her eyes as she tried to recall a different dream, a narrow wooden house with an attic bedroom, the smell of salt and fish, her father's strong arms, her grandfather's white beard, her mother's scent, the kind face of a boy on a beach, a white habit in a stone church.

"Are you sure you're ready?" Camille asked.

Helene opened her eyes. She felt herself sinking again, dragged toward the murky depths, but she struggled against it.

"I am ready," Helene said. She squeezed her hands into fists as the current pulled at her. She needed to tell her, to say it out loud. "Thank you."

Her daughter's face grew distant in Helene's vision, as though in any moment it would be gone, swept far out to sea. "For what?" Camille said.

A warm breeze stirred the hair on the back of her neck. In

the distance, she heard gravel on tires, voices from the orchard. She tried to hold on to it.

"For loving me enough to let me go."

Camille leaned her head on Helene's shoulder. The world, her brief sense of clarity, slipped away, but for once, she wasn't afraid.

CROZET, VIRGINIA
2019

25

LOUISE

After hours of talking and walking and crying together, Louise sat with her mother and grandmother on the front porch, the sky fiery shades of red and orange. They sat in silence, Louise in the middle, until the moon rose over the mountains.

Louise couldn't speak. It didn't matter how many times her grandmother assured her that it was her decision, that she wanted to die on her own terms; losing her was shattering. And it was made all the more painful because Louise would have to be the one to end her life if they wanted to save Peter's.

As if reading her mind, Camille looked over. "You don't get to torment yourself over this. That is my one request. And if you do, I will come back to haunt you."

Louise tried to smile but couldn't.

"I mean it, kid," Camille said, her expression now solemn. "I would have made this choice, with or without you. And soon. But doing it this way, doing it now, means I get to save his life. I told you before. I don't want time. It doesn't mean anything to me unless I'm still fully myself."

Louise leaned back on the porch swing and for a while they were quiet again. She was wracked with grief, but she also knew that as a hospice nurse, her grandmother had likely formed her beliefs about the way she wanted to die a long time ago.

"One thing I forgot to ask," Camille said finally. "I was going to put it up for sale, you know? The orchard."

Louise wasn't surprised Jim had known before she and her mother did. He was Camille's best friend.

"We don't need to pretend there's another way. My brother certainly doesn't want it. Even Jim, because of course I asked. But he's too old to take on something like this himself. And that's fine. I'm at peace with it. But will you make sure whoever buys it promises to keep it as an orchard? I can't bear the thought of it being torn down and turned into a neighborhood of identical modern farmhouses." She gazed out at the hills, deep green in the twilight, the trees lush and heavy with fruit. "It's silly. Mama should have probably sold it after Daddy died. She was never really meant to be a farmer. Or me. But it was his home. And so it was hers too. And then mine, of course."

"I'm not selling it," Bobbie said quietly.

Louise turned to her mom in surprise. She had never expressed any interest in the orchard.

"It's where I brought Louise home from the hospital, where I became a mother. It's my home too."

"Still?" Camille asked.

The moon gleamed above the mountains, and a whip-poor-will cried in the distance.

"Always."

Camille reached across Louise and took Bobbie's hand. "Thank you."

"Besides," Bobbie said, her voice thick. "If Louise goes to nursing school at UVA, it would be nice to have a place to stay. And someone needs to take care of Jim, right? He's going to be lost without you, Mama."

Camille sighed. "He'll be okay."

"He will be," Bobbie said firmly. "I'll make sure of it."

"It's getting late," Camille said, her chest rising and falling in slow, even breaths.

Louise's own breaths grew shallow, more rapid with each moment that passed. She wanted to run, to fly down the porch steps on bare feet and race down the hill to the creek like she had as a little girl, to look for tadpoles and minnows, to dig in the dirt for worms. She wanted to be four years old again, when time was gorgeously infinite, when everything and everyone in her life was fixed.

Camille put an arm around Louise's shoulder. "You don't need to be scared," she said.

Louise had never felt more scared in her life. She didn't know if she could ever do what her grandmother was doing, trade her own life to save someone else's. She knew, even if her grandmother said it was what she wanted, had planned for, that it was also, unmistakably, a gift that went beyond any love Louise had ever known.

"Aren't you?"

Camille squeezed gently. "I'm scared of missing you two. But not of death."

"Will it hurt you?" she asked when she found her voice again.

Camille shook her head. "No, honey."

Louise looked over at Bobbie. She nodded, her eyes full of tears.

"Go on, Louise," Camille said. "Waiting will only make it harder."

Louise felt the night sky expand around her, the million immeasurable pieces of the world dwarfing her existence. She felt inadequate, too small and insignificant for the weight of what was asked of her, to hold something as precious as a life in her hands.

"I don't want to say goodbye to you," Louise said, desperation in her voice.

"I know," Camille said softly. "I don't either." She took a deep breath, a tremor of grief cracking her calm exterior. "So, we'll say good night then. And trust that there will be a dawn."

Louise closed her eyes. For a while, they simply sat together, their limbs entangled, their heads bowed.

Finally, Camille gently opened Louise's hand and placed it over her heart. Louise kept her eyes on the sky, where the stars glowed impossibly bright. She felt her grandmother's heart beneath her touch, each beat an echo of the one before it.

Louise rested her head on her grandmother's shoulder as heat blossomed like one of her moonflowers.

Camille released a quiet breath through her nose, and Louise's hand was pulled deeper into her grandmother's chest. She felt no pain there, only a tender, spreading release.

Camille's heart slowed, and the entirety of her grandmother's life exploded inside of her, like a new universe being born.

Each exquisite image soared into her consciousness, until she was surrounded by a constellation of not only Camille's memories, but also Helene's, and Agnes's, each holding the lives and recollections of the women before them inside their own souls.

She saw Agnes, on her bicycle in a town by the sea. The sky above her thundered with distant bombs. But there were still births, and deaths, people who needed her. As the world around her ripped in half, the last image that crossed Agnes's mind had been her daughter, the feel of her head on her chest while she slept, and she knew only peace.

Louise saw Helene, not as she had known her, white haired and delicate, but young and strong, serious and capable in a gray uniform as she moved up and down the aisles of a hospital ward. She saw her at the end of the war, framed in a window overlooking a courtyard as Allied soldiers streamed through the gates. She was searching each face for the one she knew would never come back.

Louise saw the orchard, all its beautiful variations. She saw it in April when the hills were covered with peach blossoms, and the ground was soft and newly green. When John took Helene's hand, and she felt the first tiny shift, a new life beginning. And in winter, when the land was cold and gray and streaked with freezing rain, when Helene squeezed her eyes shut in labor until a new world revealed itself.

Louise saw a striking, dark-haired woman named Irene, visiting Helene from her home in Canada with her daughter, named for her own mother, Esther. The way the two women laughed and wept as they clung to each other, as their two little girls waved shyly between their legs, the living, breathing proof that despite all they had witnessed and endured, the ruined world had found a way to move forward.

And there was Helene again, older this time, in her midseventies. She lay at night in the bed with her husband as Camille slept in the recliner next to them. John's breathing was labored, his mouth open. Helene stood and walked to the window. There was snow on the ground, a white stillness that covered the orchard, but still, she opened the window, letting in a blast of icy air. It was an old habit, learned from her time with the sisters. She had kept it, through all her years working as a hospice nurse, a healer, every time a soul was ready.

She walked back to the bed and climbed in beside John. His body was warm, but his hands were cold as she took them in her own. For a long moment, she stared at his wrinkled face, blessed with the lines of old age. Another face rose in her vision, another goodbye, a lifetime ago, a boy she barely knew, and yet who she had carried, through all those long years, as she built a new life in a new world, with a man who had strong arms and a gentle heart, who loved her the way the boy might have loved her if given the chance.

She squeezed John's hand as his breathing slowed, as she felt him drift away from her, as she let him go.

Time rushed by in a cascade of images and Louise saw Camille now, in nursing school, where she was always the smartest and most dedicated student in clinicals. And in countless homes during her years as a hospice nurse, where her hands were a steady presence at the end of life, a guidepost for the families who relied on her to help their loved ones depart.

In a simple cotton wedding dress, walking down the aisle underneath a canopy of pink blossoms. A few years later, pregnant with Bobbie, her belly enormous, straining the seams of her scrubs. Then she was under the magnolia tree, sitting in a rocking chair, an infant sleeping on her chest, her face tired but radiating joy.

A soft wind rustled across the hills of the orchard. The porch steps creaked, and Louise opened her eyes.

She saw her grandmother not as she was now, but who she had been then, the memory Camille returned to most often, where she had been most at home. A little girl in a cotton nightgown and mud-caked rain boots. Freckles on her nose and long hair that ran in tangles down her back. Camille searched until she found her, a tall woman down in the orchard, her hands trailing over withered leaves until they were green again. And then Camille was gone, down the porch stairs and among the fireflies that danced in the moonlight, following her mother toward the gentle hillside.

★ ★ ★ ★ ★

BEHIND THE BOOK

It started in a hospital room. Two night shifts over the course of twenty-four hours. I had been an inpatient pediatric nurse for a year, but it was the first time I was assigned to the care of an actively dying child.

I was terrified, of being so close to death, of the raw proximity of it, of failing miserably as a nurse. But my patient's family had created a space that felt like home, full of voices and warmth and a vast, unyielding love. And from the moment my shift began, I understood that I had never in my career been a part of something more important, that for as long as she was my patient, I would carry the weight of her soul.

Those two nights changed me as a nurse, and as a person. *The Moonlight Healers* is a reflection of those changes, when I came to understand that death, even the death of a child, can contain multitudes—grief and darkness of course, but also beauty and true healing.

I wanted to write a story where the characters grapple with the same issues I did working as a nurse in a hospital, particularly in terms of end-of-life care. The idea of a magical healing touch was twofold. One, touch is absolutely a real tool nurses use. Therapeutic touch is something we learned in nursing school, a real evidence-based intervention that can alleviate pain. Two, it was an easy, and enticing, next step to imagine a world where that touch could be amplified, where it becomes a superpower that can take away any amount of suffering.

I always knew that nurses were going to be at the core of this story, and I chose the setting of World War II France for Helene because of the richness of nursing history during wartime, the struggle she would face as a healer surrounded by the carnage of war. The Hôtel-Dieu (translated quite poetically to hotel of God) was a real hospital run by the Catholic Church in Rouen, and while my characters are fictional, Cecelia is very loosely based on a real-life Augustinian nun and hero of the French resistance, Agnès-Marie Valois, also known as the "Angel of Dieppe," who did put herself between a Canadian soldier and a German luger. Her real life is even more remarkable than fiction and worth delving into.

As for the present-day setting, the orchard outside Crozet was inspired by two orchards near where I live, where bears roam and the trees explode with pink every April. There is a natural magic to the Blue Ridge, where the mountains are ancient and the sky glitters with fireflies, where life still feels a little bit wild. I knew that the magic abilities of these characters would be both grounded and enhanced by such a setting.

This book may have started in a hospital room, based off my own experiences as a scared nurse, but it ultimately became a love letter to all nurses, to the ones I learned from and worked beside, to the real-life healers. I hope you've enjoyed this story. I hope it has sparked tough questions, but most of all I hope it has left you with the same hope and light my characters find, even in the darkest nights.

ACKNOWLEDGMENTS

The journey to write this book was long, winding, and full of self-doubt. But I was lucky enough to have so many wonderful people in my corner who made it possible and who were there to guide me every step of the way.

To my incredible agent, Jessica Felleman, who was there from the beginning and helped guide and shape not only what this story would become, but who I am as a writer, thank you. This book would not exist without you, in any shape or form. I am so lucky to have you in my corner.

To my fabulous editor, Melanie Fried, who took a leap of faith on a former nurse and stay-at-home mom, and molded my story into an actual book, your keen insight and judgment were invaluable. Thank you for pushing me outside my comfort zone and shepherding this book to where it needed to go.

Thank you to the entire team at Jennifer Lyons Literary Agency.

Thank you to the team at Graydon House and HarperCollins: Susan Swinwood, Loriana Sacilotto, Margaret Marbury, Amy

Jones, Ana Luxton, Diana Lavoie, Ambur Hostyn, and Stephanie Conlon. And to everyone else on the sales, production, and subrights teams who worked behind the scenes, a huge thank-you. It has been such a privilege to benefit from this gold standard team of professionals.

To the friends in my life who are also family, especially the Gertie Girls: Mary Catherine, Chrissy, Liz, Laura, Liz, Ellen, and Ally. You were all along for the ride of this book from idea to publication, and your cheerleading and positivity (especially on the group text) kept me going even when I felt like a failure.

To my late grandmother, Patsy Jewett, who found such joy in writing throughout her life and was generous enough to share that joy, and her memoirs, with me. And to my parents, Jon and Betsy, thank you for always reading my stories.

Thank you to my husband and best friend, Rob, who has believed in me from day one, and who is the entire reason I was able to write a book with four small children. I love you and I am so grateful for you.

And to Ryland, Bobby, Rosie, and Millie. Mama loves you, always.

DISCUSSION QUESTIONS

1. Healing is the primary theme of the novel. What does healing mean to you? Did the story challenge your own views of what healing means?

2. Helene lives during the occupation of France in World War II, but in many ways, she begins the novel sheltered from the more dangerous realities of the war (her family's involvement in the resistance, the secret identity of her Jewish friend, Elisabeth). How does Helene change as a character as she loses that naivete?

3. Louise learns, quite suddenly, that she has a magical healing ability. What would you do in such a situation? If you could have any magical ability, what would it be? For what purpose would you most want to use it?

4 Mother and daughter relationships are at the core of *The Moonlight Healers*. Discuss the similarities and differences between Helene's relationship with Agnes and Louise's relationship with Bobbie. How do both relationships ultimately evolve over the course of the story?

5 Death with dignity is an important theme of the story. Camille, who reveals she has been diagnosed with dementia, makes the decision to offer up her own life for Peter's. Discuss the factors that went into this choice. How did you feel about it as a reader? How did the novel impact your views on the larger societal conversation surrounding assisted death and the right to die with dignity?

6 What do you think Louise's life will look like now that she knows the full truth of her healing abilities? Will she go to nursing school? What will her relationship with Bobbie be like?

7 Discuss the two settings in the novel—an orchard in contemporary Crozet, Virginia, and a hospital in war-torn France. How did the settings impact your understanding of the characters who inhabited them?

8 Helene alludes to the fact that her ancestors were persecuted for their healing abilities, a reference to the European witch trials where some of the women accused of witchcraft were in healing professions such as midwifery. Why do you think that, historically, healers, particularly women, might have been criticized or condemned by societal institutions? Why would establishments such as churches or hospitals have been fearful or judgmental toward alternative or folk healers? Does any of that legacy remain today?

9 Discuss the love stories in the novel. Does the relationship between Helene and Thomas have any similarities with Louise and Peter's relationship? Did Helene truly love Thomas even though she knew him for only a few days? Does the fact that Louise and Peter's relationship is rooted in friendship make their love more "real"?